Author photo © www.mattchristie.com

Vina Jackson is the pseudonym for two established writers working together for the first time. One a successful author, the other a published writer who is also a city professional working in the Square Mile.

*Also by Vina Jackson*

Eighty Days Yellow

# Eighty Days Blue

Vina Jackson

An Orion paperback

First published in Great Britain in 2012
by Orion Books Ltd,
Orion House, 5 Upper St Martin's Lane,
London WC2H 9EA

An Hachette UK company



All the characters in this book are fictitious, and any resemblance to actual persons, living or dead, is purely coincidental.

A CIP catalogue record for this book is available from the British Library.

Typeset at The Spartan Press Ltd,
Lymington, Hants

Printed in Great Britain by Clays Ltd, St Ives plc

The Orion Publishing Group's policy is to use papers that are natural, renewable and recyclable products and made from wood grown in sustainable forests. The logging and manufacturing processes are expected to conform to the environmental regulations of the country of origin.

www.orionbooks.co.uk

# Eighty Days Blue

# 1

## *A Meal of Oysters*

In the middle of Grand Central Station, he kissed me.

It was a lover's kiss – brief, soft and affectionate, full of the lingering memories of a day spent in blissful denial and a reminder that this would be our last night together in New York. We hadn't spoken about the future yet, or the past. Hadn't dared. It was as if these few days and nights were a window between those two looming spectres, best forgotten until the inevitable passing of time forced us to face them head on.

For the next twenty-four hours, we would be lovers, just an ordinary couple, like any other.

One more night and one more day in New York. The future would keep.

It seemed fitting to spend a few of our last minutes together in Grand Central, one of my favourite spots in the city. It's a place where the past and the future meet, where all the disparate fragments of New York mingle – the wealthy, the poor, the punks and the Wall Street girls and boys, tourists and commuters – each passing on their way to separate lives, united only by a hurried few moments of scurrying, all briefly sharing the same experience, racing for a train.

We were on the main concourse, next to the famous four-sided clock. After the kiss, I looked up and around, as

I always did when I was standing there. I liked to gaze up at the marble pillars and vaulted arches holding an upside-down Mediterranean sky, the zodiac view that ancient cartographers imagined angels or alien life forms might have when looking down on the Earth from the heavens.

The building reminded me of a church, but having always been ambivalent about religion, I had more respect for the power of the railroad, proof of man's never-ending desire to go somewhere. Chris, my best friend in London, always said that you never really know a city until you've sampled its public transport, and if that was true of anywhere, it was true of New York. Grand Central Station summed up all the things I liked about Manhattan: it was full of promise and alive with the energy of people rushing to and fro, a veritable melting pot of bodies in motion; the opulence and grandeur of the gold chandeliers hanging from the ceiling were a promise to everyone who passed through with nothing but a dime in their pocket that somewhere overhead, opportunity waited.

Good things happen in New York; that was the message of Grand Central Station. If you worked hard enough, if you threw your dream in the ring, then one day you'd get lucky and the city would throw a chance right back at you.

Dominik took my hand and pulled me along through the crowd to the ramp leading down to the Whispering Gallery at the lower level. I'd never been to the Whispering Gallery in St Paul's Cathedral in London either; both were things on my never-ending to-do list of places to visit and things to see.

He stood me in the corner, facing one of the pillars that joined the low arches and then ran to the other side.

'Summer,' he said, his soft voice coming through the

pillar as clear as a bell, as if the wall were talking to me. I knew it was an architectural phenomenon – sound waves apparently travelling from one pillar to its opposite across the domed ceiling, nothing more than a bit of acoustic magic – but it was eerie nonetheless. He was a dozen feet away, with his back to me, yet could have been whispering straight into my ear.

'Yes?' I murmured to the wall.

'I'm going to make love to you again later.'

I laughed and turned to look at him. He grinned at me wickedly from across the space.

He walked back and took my hand again, pulling me into another embrace. His torso was pleasantly firm, and he was nearly a foot taller than me, so even in heels I could rest my head on his shoulder. Dominik wasn't bulky – he didn't work out at the gym, or at least not that he had ever mentioned – but he had a lean, athletic physique and the fluid movements of someone who enjoys being inside their body. Today had been hot, coming to the end of a New York summer, the sun during the day so harsh and scorching you could fry an egg on the pavement. It was still muggy, and though we'd both showered before we left Dominik's hotel, I could feel the heat of his skin through his shirt. His hug was like being enveloped in a warm cloud.

'But for now,' he whispered, into my ear this time, 'let's eat.'

We were standing right outside the Oyster Bar. I didn't recall having mentioned to Dominik my love of raw fish – another of my idiosyncrasies that he had guessed correctly. I had half a mind to tell him that oysters made me squeamish, just to make the point that he might not always be right, but I had been wanting to go to the Oyster Bar since I arrived in New York and wasn't going to turn the chance down now. Besides, I'm suspicious of anyone who doesn't like oysters, and he might feel the same way. I didn't want to tell him a lie that might backfire.

It's a popular place and I was surprised that he'd been able to get a reservation at this late notice, though knowing Dominik, he'd probably booked in advance and never mentioned the fact to me. We still had to wait for twenty minutes to be seated, but the waiter brought the menus immediately and waited to take our drinks order.

'Champagne?' Dominik asked, ordering a Pepsi for himself.

'A bottle of Asahi for me, please,' I said to the waiter, watching a hint of a smile pass across Dominik's lips as I ignored his suggestion.

'The menu is rather overwhelming here,' Dominik said. 'Shall we share some oysters to start?'

'Are you trying to fill me with aphrodisiacs?'

'If ever there was a woman who didn't need an aphrodisiac, Summer, it's you.'

'I'll take that as a compliment.'

'Good. I meant it as one. Is there any particular variety of oyster that you prefer?'

The waiter had reappeared with our drinks. I waved away his offer of a glass: beer is meant to be drunk from a bottle. I took a cool sip and glanced at the menu.

They even had oysters from New Zealand here, grown in the Hauraki Gulf, not far at all from my home town. I felt a fleeting ache, a passing pang of homesickness, the curse of the weary traveller. No matter how much I liked whatever new city I happened to be in, I was still at least occasionally plagued by memories of New Zealand. Seafood was one of those things that reminds me of home, of warm days and cool evenings spent in the sea, digging my heels into the soft, wet sand at half-tide to pick out tuatua and pipi, the shellfish that live in shallow waters on sandy beaches, or of Friday nights at the local fish and chip shop, ordering half a dozen deep-fried oysters served in a white paper bag, covered in salt and served with a big slice of lemon.

I asked for half a dozen of something local, whatever the waiter thought was good, and Dominik asked for another half-dozen of the same. Homesickness or no homesickness, I hadn't come all the way to New York to eat seafood from the Hauraki Gulf.

The waiter disappeared to the kitchen, and Dominik stretched his arm across the table and laid his hand over mine. His touch was colder than I expected, considering the heat of his body, and I shivered involuntarily in surprise. He'd been holding his glass with that hand, I realised, and it must be cold, though he always ordered his Pepsi easy on the ice.

'Do you miss it? New Zealand?'

'Yes. Not all the time, but when something reminds me of home, a word or a smell or a sight of something, then I do. Not my friends or my family so much, because I talk to them on the phone and by email, but I miss the land, the ocean. I found living in London hard because it's so flat. Not as flat as the parts of Australia I've lived in, but still flat. New Zealand has a lot of hills.'

'It's like reading a book, watching your face. You give away more than you think. It doesn't all come out in your music, you know.'

He'd been disappointed that I had left my violin in my flat before returning to his hotel room just a couple of streets down from me. I promised that I would fetch it and play for him again before he left. He'd booked an overnight flight and would be taking a cab to the airport tomorrow at around 4 p.m., returning to London, to his duties at the university and his home full of books near Hampstead Heath. My fortuitous week off was coming to a close and I would be back with the orchestra, rehearsing for our new show, on Monday.

We hadn't discussed what would come next. In London, just before I left for New York, we'd had a loose sort of arrangement, a relationship of sorts but an unstructured one. He'd told me that I was free to explore, so long as I told him the details afterwards, a requirement that I had enjoyed. I got a kick out of telling him what I'd been up to, and sometimes I did things or avoided them just for the sake of the following confession. I hadn't mentioned that point to Dominik. He was like the priest I'd never had. He'd seemed either amused or aroused by my adventures until the night that he saw me together with Jasper, when everything had gone so badly wrong.

I hadn't told him about Victor either, the man that I had fallen in with in New York. I wasn't quite sure how to broach that. The games that Victor had played had been so much more perverse than Dominik's tastes. Victor had even sold me, had given me to his acquaintances to use as they wished. I'd gone along with it all, enjoyed most of it. Would I tell Dominik about that? I wasn't sure. It was only forty-eight hours since I left Victor's party, because he had wanted to mark me permanently as his slave, his property, and I had refused. The suggestion of a permanent mark had been just one step too far. Already it felt like a lifetime ago. Being with Dominik had washed the sting of Victor away, at least for the moment. I was also sure that Dominik had known Victor in London and that added a whole layer of awkwardness to the situation.

'How's London?' I asked, changing the subject.

The entrée arrived quickly, despite the reviews I had read suggesting the service was slow here. A dozen oysters were fanned out like jewels on a large white platter with a lemon in the middle, cut into halves, each half covered with white muslin, tied tightly at the top, trapping the seeds inside as if one miscreant pip escaping from the flesh of the fruit might ruin the whole dish.

Dominik shrugged. 'You haven't missed much. I've been working – lecturing, working on some papers in my spare time, doing a lot of writing.' He glanced up at me, caught my eye, hesitated for a moment and then continued. 'I've missed you. Some things have happened that we should talk about, in due course, but for now, let's enjoy tonight. Eat your oysters.'

Dominik brought an oyster to his mouth, resting the shell on one palm as he flicked the fleshy meat into his mouth with the delicate silver fork the waiter had provided. There was something savage about the way that he had extracted the juice from the lemon, so firmly you might say he crushed the fruit, rather than squeezed it. Then, almost as the next step in a well-practised ritual, he sprayed black pepper across the dish with two fierce twists of the grinder. He speared the fish neatly, deftly, not allowing a spare morsel or a drip of juice to stray from its trajectory to his tongue.

I preferred to ignore the fork and just suck the oyster straight from the shell, enjoying the slippery feel of it, the slap of flesh wet against my tongue, untampered by utensils, the salty juice coating my lips.

I looked up to see Dominik watching me.

'You eat like a wild creature.'

'It's not the only thing I do like a wild creature,' I said with an attempt at a sly smile.

'I can't deny that. It's one of the things I like about you. You abandon yourself to your appetites, whatever they might be.'

'In New Zealand, they'd think this a refined way to eat seafood. Back home, I've seen people bite the tongues off pipi, the shellfish we have in the shallow water near the shoreline. They flick their tongues out of their shells when you pick them out of the water and the real enthusiasts bite them straight off, eat them alive.'

Dominik smiled. 'Were you one of those, eating sea creatures alive?'

'No, never had the heart to do it. I thought it cruel.'

'You admired it in other people, I bet, though?'

'Yes. Yes, I did.'

I suppose it's just part of being naturally contrary and something of a rebel, but the more likely a food is to split a room into lovers and haters, the more likely it is that I will enjoy it, or at least admire people who do.

'Fancy a stroll?' Dominik asked, thanking the staff on our way out.

They responded with a warm goodnight. Dominik was a generous tipper. I had read somewhere that you should always pay attention to the way a man treats animals, his mother and waiters, so I filed this bit of information away in his running positive column.

I looked down at my shoes. Black patent stilettos, and as I had only brought my smallest, most glamorous purse, I hadn't had room for a spare pair of flats.

'We can get a taxi if your feet hurt,' he continued.

'Yes, these heels weren't made for walking.'

I thought he would head to the road to hail a cab, but instead he grabbed my wrist and pulled me forcibly to the side. He pressed me up against the wall outside the restaurant by the stairs leading to the East 43rd Street exit and ran his hands down the sides of my body and round to my backside. I could feel the bulge in his trousers against my thigh. I thought he was getting hard, but I couldn't be sure, so I reached a hand down to check. He batted my probing fingers away. Damn him. His habit of getting me all fired up and then leaving me hanging drove me crazy. The quicker we got home, the better.

'I'll have you off them soon enough,' he said as he set me down again, not bothering to whisper.

A middle-aged woman standing in the now long queue outside the Oyster Bar, dressed in cream trousers, faux-snakeskin court shoes and, despite the heat, a pink cardigan, tutted at us.

Dominik linked his arm through mine, and we walked west up 42nd Street to Park Avenue, jostled by the Saturday-night crowd, a sea of partygoers, tourists, showgirls and spectators, all jazzed up and on the lookout for a sniff of the action. The fun part of the weekend was just beginning for most; their energy was gaining an almost manic edge, feeding off the bright lights and flashing billboards, the traffic whizzing by and Times Square Tower soaring into the sky above us like a gaudy middle finger flipping the bird to the more respectable parts of town.

'Did you still want to see a show?' I asked, hoping the answer would be no. We'd floated the idea earlier of behaving like tourists and catching a play on Broadway. True, we'd spent most of the day in bed together, but I for one wasn't worn out and I didn't want to waste our last night.

'I'd rather watch you,' he replied, his eyes glittering, and my heart raced in response as I remembered how much Dominik liked to watch, how aroused he had been after each of the private concerts he'd arranged where I'd played my violin for him in various states of dress and undress. I thought of the precious Bailly that he had bought for me after my own instrument was damaged, on the grounds that in return I would play Vivaldi for him – nude. How after the first solo concert in the crypt in London, he had fucked me against the wall, right there and then, before taking me home to his house in Hampstead and asking me to bring myself to orgasm while he sat in his office chair and watched.

We stood at the intersection while the rest of the world rushed past, and I imagined that if that moment were caught on film, the picture would be of just Dominik and me, our bodies clearly delineated in a whirl of colour, as if we were the only two people who existed, whole, on the streets of New York, while the rest of the population was indistinct, people blending together in a blur, each individual as featureless as the next.

We took a lengthy walk down Broadway, past Union Square, and then veered off towards University Place, avoiding the faded glitz and glamour of Fifth Avenue. By the time we reached my place, my feet were killing me, though the sensation was numbed by the couple of beers I'd had with dinner and the light-hearted feeling I had walking alongside Dominik, with his arm threaded through mine, as if all my troubles had been swept away, at least for one more night and one more day.

Dominik didn't know it, but we were standing outside the apartment that I shared with a Croatian couple, Marija and Baldo, who played in the brass section of the orchestra and spent most of their evenings out. When they were in, they filled the flat with the sound of their lovemaking, heavy breathing and head-board thumping, Marija so loud that I was envious, though of course she may have been faking it. I wasn't sure of the status of their relationship, whether they were married, cohabiting or perhaps living in sin, each on the run from their own respective partners, which would explain why the fire of their lust never seemed to dim.

'My violin,' I said, 'it's inside, and I promised to play for you one last time.'

He took a step closer to me so that I could feel his firm body pressing against my back, then brushed his hand gently up the inside of my thigh.

'Of course. I'll wait here if you like,' he whispered softly into my ear.

The tone of his voice was utterly casual, and a little amused. He seemed to be enjoying the effect that his presence was having on me as I desperately fiddled with the fob that opened the main entryway to the apartment block with fingers so shaky that I might have been trying to solve a Rubik's cube.

'No,' I said, 'come in. It's Saturday night, so my flatmates are probably out, and if not, I'll introduce you – they're friendly and won't mind a visitor.'

I couldn't remember the last time I had invited a man

home. Neither Dominik nor Darren, the man I'd dated for six months in London before Dominik and I met, had ever visited me at my flat. I'd picked up the odd one-night stand during my single months, but even then I always insisted on going back to theirs.

There was no real reason for my reticence; I'm just cagey about my personal space. I'm also messy, and I hate commuting, so I tend to end up living in cheaper, small rooms in more expensive parts of town, rather than taking somewhere larger in a less expensive suburb and needing to take the subway every day. My room in the East Village apartment was tiny; if I wanted anything larger, I'd have to move to Brooklyn. Marija and Baldo occupied most of the space and consequently paid two-thirds of the rent between them. I had a small room with just a single bed, a hanging rail with all of my clothes and shoes on display, a couple of photographs from home and a few books scattered here and there. I didn't have a desk, not a single piece of furniture other than the bed and the rail. Ever since I left New Zealand, I'd made a point of travelling light, so wherever I ended up I could pack up and ship off again with the minimum of fuss. I begin to feel edgy when I own more than I can fit into a single suitcase.

I pushed open the front door to the apartment and felt around on the wall for the light switch, sliding my purse onto the kitchen counter.

'Hello?' I called out, taking Dominik by the hand and leading him inside.

He stood in the kitchen and looked around, while I knocked lightly on the Croatians' bedroom door to check if they were in. There was no response.

'They're out.'

'Good,' he said, striding over to me and picking up a handful of my hair, then tugging it gently.

He suddenly swivelled me round so I stood facing the bay window in the living room, looking out into the small communal courtyard shared by the residents in our block. It was dark outside now, and with the lights on and the blinds open, anyone who happened to be sitting in the pocket-sized garden smoking a cigarette or standing at their own window and looking over at ours would likely have been able to see if not everything, at least our silhouettes, me in my short black dress and Dominik in his collared shirt and tie. We'd both dressed for a night out, in case we ended up falling into one of New York's classier bars. He looked good in a suit, never so formal that he might have been on his way to work, but not uncomfortable, like the sort of man who had owned the same outfit for ten years and resurrected it from the wardrobe once or twice a year for weddings and funerals. There was always something of a casual air about Dominik; he had the confidence of a person who knows they're in the right skin, so no matter what he wore, he looked good. He had an easy style.

Underneath that unwavering polite veneer, though, lurked a very dirty mind, and it was that dark edge beneath all the social niceties that stopped me from getting bored and moving on, as I usually did with men after a few months of dating.

I wonder what Dominik is going to do next, I thought, staring into the minuscule garden, watching the fairy lights that a neighbour had erected to cheer the place up flickering like fireflies. Push me against the window? Make me lift my dress up round my waist and then stand back and stare at my arse? Fuck me in full view of the neighbours? He hadn't snaked his hand under my dress yet, so unless he had noticed the absence of a pantyline when we had been kissing, him stroking my body through my clothes, he would be unaware that I had elected to leave my knickers at home and had spent all night enjoying the occasional flurry of cool air between my legs.

'Take your hold-ups off,' he said, 'but without bending your knees. And don't look back at me.'

I could hear the smile in his voice; he was enjoying this, coming up with a new game that he knew would turn me on. It was the change, the surprise, that filled me with a rush of arousal. So long as I didn't know what was coming next, then it was exciting. My mind would just stop thinking and relax, all my powers intent on following his next instruction. It stopped me from thinking about the laundry that I needed to do, rehearsals next week, when my next pay cheque was coming and what bill I needed to pay first. The sound of Dominik's voice washed every other thought from my head, and when I wasn't thinking, I made up for it by feeling, all my physical senses now on hyper alert, so that even the lightest touch, the softest breath of air on my skin, sent me half mad with desire.

It's more difficult than it sounds, removing a pair of hold-ups without your knees bending. I rolled up my dress, offering Dominik a glimpse of flesh, and hooked a thumb under the sticky band at the top, the lacy border that separated the stocking part from the top of my thigh, and pulled downwards, spreading my legs wide apart so that I could bend over at the waist to touch my toes while keeping my legs perfectly straight. Then I balanced all of my weight on my other foot and gently removed my stiletto, just for a second, so I could hook the stocking over my heel and toes and then slip the shoe back on again. Then the same on the other side.

'Hand them to me.'

I held my hand out behind me, still staring straight ahead through the glass. I wasn't sure what he was going to do next.

'Give me your hands.'

He hadn't specifically said that I should hold my hands behind my back, but that's what I did, because Dominik always meant exactly what he said, and if he had wanted me to turn round, he would have either told me so or spun me to face him. So I stood with my legs spread, facing the window, my shoulders twisted back in my sockets, chest forward and arms straight and stiff, my hands clasped in the prayer position with my thumbs facing my butt.

The hold-ups made a surprisingly efficient pair of hand-cuffs despite the stretch in the light fabric. He used both, tying my hands with two elaborate loops, joined snugly at the wrists so my circulation wasn't hindered, but even if I wriggled, I couldn't engineer my way free. I suppose I could have got out of it if I really tried, but escaping didn't appeal to me. I liked the idea of being subject to Dominik's will, a prisoner of my own choosing, to do what he wanted with.

He put his hands on my shoulders and turned me to face him. The ache in my feet following the endless high-heeled walk to downtown was becoming pleasant now, a sharp, exhilarating reminder that I had given my body to Dominik to use and therefore any sensation that I had was because he wanted it.

It had occurred to me before that if I could apply this mindset to other parts of my life, there'd be nothing I couldn't achieve. Once started, I was like a train on its tracks, headed straight for whatever outcome awaited me with total disregard to any discomfort of the journey. Submission wasn't something that I could apply wherever and whenever I willed it, however. I needed a trigger. When I was growing up, I had my violin teacher, Mr van der Vliet, who had never laid a finger on me in any way other than as a teacher to a student, but for some inexplicable reason I had felt so bound to please him that I practised far beyond the norm. Now it was Dominik who commanded the same power over me, albeit because I had granted that power to him.

He bent down, his eyes locked on mine, ran his hand up the now bare skin of first one leg and then the other, from my ankle to my thigh, stopping just before where my pantyline would have been if I had been wearing any. His eyes were like granite; he had that look that he got when he was drifting into the path of his own desires, a place beyond conscious thought, where the body is the driver, if you just allow it to take over.

My breathing was beginning to grow ragged. I loved it when he did this, I really did, but God, every time his touch got close I just wished that he would slide his finger inside me. Patience has never been a strong point of mine.

He straightened and walked round behind me, grabbing me by my wrist restraint as if the stockings were a convenient handle. I struggled to keep up with him, walking backwards, my heels clattering on the polished wooden floor.

He pushed me face first onto the bed, my arms still tied tightly behind my back. I turned my face to the side so I could breathe and watched him, out of the corner of one eye, as he kneeled down by the foot of my pillow and fumbled under the bed, his expression turning into a satisfied grin as he found the bottle of lubricant and box of condoms that I kept there. Not such a secret hiding place after all, I mused. Perhaps I wasn't so different from other women. Or perhaps he always dated the same type.

Dominik pulled my dress further up so the fabric bunched round my waist, my bare arse now on clear display. He drew a breath, now realising for sure that I had spent the evening with him in my short black dress without any knickers on.

I flinched as I heard the sound of his belt unbuckling, uncertain whether he meant to slap my arse with the leather strap or merely undo his trousers so he could fuck me. Either outcome I would have enjoyed, providing I got the latter eventually. I held my body perfectly still, waiting for his next move, hoping that it would come soon, otherwise I feared that I might explode.

I didn't want to give him the satisfaction of seeing me beg for it, but I wanted him inside me so badly that it felt as though time had slowed down. Every second that he stood near me but didn't touch me filled an hour.

It was like being on a knife's edge, perpetually trapped in that narrow place between desire and fulfilment. I enjoyed it and hated it at once. Every time he stepped away from me my desire for him multiplied, but each time he touched me he brought me closer to satisfaction and closer to it all being over.

He knew it too. As much as I tried to temper my responses out of pride, he had obviously paid attention during the course of our encounters and he knew how to play me as if I were an instrument. He didn't own all of me, and he never would, but for as long as we were in bed together, he owned my body, whether I wanted it that way or not.

I was entirely at Dominik's mercy.

I jumped as I heard the sound of a wrapper tearing, and the snapping sound of the bottle of lube flipping open.

Then I felt his finger inside me at last, probing, exploring, just one at first, then another, and another, and another, until I was sure that he wouldn't be able to fit any more inside. I tried to shuffle back against him, to bend my knees and gain some purchase on the bedding so that I could drive myself backwards into his hand, but with my wrists tied and my body flat on the bed, all I could do was wriggle helplessly like a caterpillar on an entomologist's table, or a butterfly pinned to a dissection board.

He was surprisingly still behind me, likely taking pleasure in watching me try to worm out of my plight. I felt more exposed being half, rather than completely, naked. Somehow there was something more pornographic about having my top half covered and my bottom half nude, as though my naked arse and genitals were more shocking without my bare breasts to offset them. Half-nakedness was the pose of perverts, of old men at bus-stops with their shirts on, trousers down and coats open. At the wish of another, half-nakedness had an edge of humiliation, a feeling of ownership to it.

'Spread your legs apart,' he said.

I did.

'Further.'

My thigh muscles were beginning to ache, as he had me almost doing the splits. I was still on my knees with my chest pressed into the bed and my hands behind my back, only barely able to keep my balance. He dropped down into a crouch and then ran his tongue lightly all the way from my knee to the top of my inner thigh, on one side, then the other. He stopped just short of licking my pussy, but he held his mouth right against me so that I could feel his hot breath against my lips.

I pushed back slightly, hoping to feel the touch of his tongue.

'Oh, no, you don't. Stay still.'

Despite my best efforts to play it cool, I began to moan, and rock back and forth slightly.

'Want me, do you?' he teased.

His tone was mocking. At any other moment, I might have wanted to slap him, but right now I felt as though my body was on fire and I would have done anything to get him to touch me, even if that meant I had to crawl across the floor on my hands and knees, begging for it.

'Yes.'

'Yes? You don't sound very sure. Perhaps I'll leave the room until you are certain.' He stood up and stepped away.

'No, please, please don't go. I want you more than anything.'

'More than anything – that's better. And if I give you what you want, what will you do for me?'

'Anything you want. I'll do anything you want. Just please, please fuck me. I can't stand it any longer.'

'Anything I want, huh? You should be careful what you promise. I might hold you to that.'

'I don't care. Please touch me,' I whimpered, my pride forgotten under the strength of my lust.

He stepped closer and pushed the head of his cock inside me, but only a few inches. Then he waited.

I clawed the bedspread in frustration.

'Beg,' he said softly. 'Tell me what you want.'

'Fuck me, please. For God's sake, fuck me.'

Finally, he pushed all the way, filling me to the brim. The heat of his cock inside me just about sent me through the roof at the first thrust.

He gripped my wrists tightly and drew in and out as I pushed back against him.

He filled me until I began to ache, and he was spent.

We both paused, panting. He bent down and gently untied my hands. I stretched my arms out cautiously, the blood rushing back to my wrists.

'Stay there,' he said, as if I could go anywhere with him still inside me.

He pushed himself off and lay down beside me, stroking my hair with one hand as he ran the other between my legs until he found my sweet spot and I began to moan again. I thought it was unlikely that I would come in this position, on my front, but I was willing to let him try.

'Turn over,' he whispered, maybe seeing the look of uncertainty on my face. I flipped over onto my back.

He continued with his one-handed rhythm, raising himself up so he could see what he was doing. I watched him watching me, his gaze intent on the path of his fingertip. He looked down at me looking at him and smiled. One voyeur recognising another. Then he ran his free hand up my torso and between my breasts, tracing a line round each nipple on the way. He placed his hand very lightly over my throat.

'Close your eyes.'

He was a quick learner, Dominik, and with my eyes shut, blocking out any remaining distractions, and his other hand busily pleasuring me, I was caught in the throes of my own orgasm before long, an almost painful wave of pleasure that started at my groin and travelled all the way up to my brain before it floated away into nothing a few seconds later.

I opened my eyes to see Dominik looking down at me, his self-satisfaction evident. I don't orgasm easily and, besides Dominik, have had only one or two lovers who've managed it without my assistance.

'Good girl,' he said. Corny though it might be, it was a phrase that never failed to give me another hot flush.

We decided to relocate to Dominik's hotel room for what was left of the night. The hotel's double bed was infinitely more comfortable than my single one, and he had a view over Washington Square Park.

We made love again in the morning, both still half asleep and spooning. I nestled back against him to find his erection pressed into the cleft in my arse and, soon after that, inside me. We lay side by side, his arm round me protectively and a hand resting on one of my breasts as I pushed gently into him. There was something tender and nostalgic in our lovemaking. The bitter reality of our parting had quelled the fire of the previous night and left only desire and longing in its wake.

I stood by the window, nude, and played for him one last time, 'Message to My Girl', my favourite of the New Zealand Symphony Orchestra and Split Enz collaboration, though of course not the same without the rest of the orchestra, the flute and the piano, and the voice of Neil Finn. It was the first time that I had played anything for him outside of the classical canon.

He didn't know the lyrics, didn't have the same sense of

home that I did when I played that song, couldn't see the vision I had of Aotearoa stretching out in my mind's eye. Nevertheless, I hoped that at least a bit of the magic and my longing for it came out through the strings.

I put the Bailly away and sat down on the bed beside him.

'Shall we get breakfast?' I asked.

It was brunch by the time we arrived. I took him to Caffe Vivaldi on Jones Street, just a few blocks west of the hotel. It was one of the reasons I moved to the Village. I've always been a little sentimental, and the name of the café felt like a good sign, especially once I heard they had an open-mic night and were receptive to musicians of all sorts. I hadn't spoken to the owners about playing there, but I liked to sit and soak up the atmosphere. The area wasn't what it used to be by all accounts – the bohemians had moved to cheaper parts and been replaced by the wealthier middle-classes, who liked the community feel, boutique coffee shops and nearby parks, which explained why my rent was expensive despite the small room – but some of the magic lingered, and I couldn't help but think I might soak up a little of the energy left behind by all the musicians who had sat in those seats before me.

They also had great food and served Bloody Marys with just the right amount of spice. I ordered one, becoming more accustomed to having an alcoholic celebration for one, while Dominik always sipped an espresso or a Pepsi.

Maybe it was the booze that made me bold. I'm not usually one to disclose my feelings, especially to lovers, but each minute that passed drew us closer to the time that Dominik would have to leave, and the speed of the hands flying round the clock on the nearby wall made me throw caution to the wind.

'I'll miss you, Dominik.'

He put down his fork and looked at me. 'I'll miss you too.'

I paused, gathered my thoughts. 'Thank you for coming. It really meant a lot for me having you here, even for a short time. Things will pick up for me, I'm sure, but I can't leave New York. My music . . . I've had some trouble settling in, but it's going well now, with the orchestra.'

'I'm glad. And you shouldn't leave – stay and make the most of it. I can't leave London now either. I'm working on a few projects independently, but I'm contracted at least to the end of term at the university.'

I nodded.

'It's not so far, though,' he mused. 'A seven-hour flight at worst. There's weekends, it will be half-term before long, and to be honest . . .'

'I'm not sure it would work between us full time,' I finished.

'No. There's still a lot we haven't talked about. I know you haven't spent all of your nights alone in New York, and neither have I in London. I don't think that should change now. We're not . . .'

'Dating?'

He laughed. 'No, not dating. I don't think it's as simple as that.'

'But I don't feel the same way with anyone else. Like I'm giving myself up. You're the only person I feel like that with.'

I still hadn't told Dominik about Victor. That was different, though. I'd allowed Victor to do the things he did to me, but I didn't want him to do those things in the same way I wanted Dominik.

There was a time, not so long ago, when I would have thought that Dominik's expression was inscrutable, but now I knew him better, I could follow that look in his eyes. Lust. Heat. Agreement.

'Good,' he said. 'The same is true for me. I don't do this sort of thing with everyone, you know.'

My turn to laugh. It sounded like the sort of phrase that a woman would say in a sitcom, the morning after a one-night stand.

'I mean it,' he continued, taking my hand across the table. 'I don't understand it entirely myself, but I know this feeling. You make me want to . . . do things to you.'

'You make me want you to do things to me.'

'Well,' he smiled, 'at least we're in agreement.'

'So it's settled, then?'

'You mean, it's settled that nothing is settled?'

'Yes.'

'I'll come and visit again, enjoy the orchestra, make the most of New York. I mean that – make the most of it, in any way that you want to. But you must keep me informed, as we agreed.'

He ordered another espresso, and I asked for another Bloody Mary. I didn't plan to get drunk in front of him, but the spice and the vodka took the edge off the wave of misery that I felt rushing closer with each minute that drew us closer to the time he had to go.

We spent the rest of the afternoon in Caffe Vivaldi, drinking coffee, talking and laughing, listening to the pianist playing Billy Joel in the background. Dominik had already checked out of the hotel, and he only had a carry-on overnight bag with him. He travelled light, like I did.

When the time came for him to go, I walked with him back to the steps of the hotel on Waverly Place where the limo he had hired for the airport run was already waiting.

His kiss goodbye was brief, soft, affectionate.

A lover's kiss.

# 2

## *After Summer, Autumn*

The cab dropped Dominik off at the porch of his North London house. He hadn't managed to get much sleep during the overnight flight from New York: too many thoughts clouding his brain, memories swirling like a personal tsunami of emotion.

It was still early morning. A slight drizzle was carried by the wind and peppered the swaying trees of the heath nearby.

He unlocked the door, walked into the hall and, following the customary beeps, cancelled the alarm system.

Dropping his carry-on bag and his laptop case to the floor, he kicked off his shoes and was awed by the silence now surrounding him. With the door closed, outside sound was banished – bird cries, the rustling of leaves in the trees welcoming the rain, the sparse traffic on the hill and all evidence of day-to-day life.

It felt like a terrible weight was falling on his shoulders.

Dominik realised it was the awful pressure of loneliness. Now that he was alone, in his own house, sheltered among the bookshelves and familiar sights, he felt bereft. From the moment they had parted in Manhattan, when the limo had come to pick him up, all the way to JFK and the bustle of check-in, security and airport queues, the presence of others had steered his mind away from the fact that he had left

Summer on her own. In another city. Not helpless, but abandoned. With her demons, her contradictions, those wondrous appetites he both craved and feared.

Would he have been so attracted to her, felt the flutter of romantic intentions had she not been so different, imperfect, dangerous to know?

Could he have fallen for her if she'd been meek and responsible, like so many other women he had been with?

No, if this was love, it was the sort of love that is unconditional. He had to accept her waywardness. In fact, he wanted her to be a free spirit, a sexual adventuress.

For the first time in five days, Dominik had time to reflect.

And it didn't make him feel any better about the situation and its paradoxes.

He checked his diary. His next lecture was the following day. He had only missed a couple of tutorials by dashing so impulsively to New York. He knew there would be no problem rescheduling them, with all the time still left before the students' finals.

He needed a shower. Shedding the clothes he had travelled in as he walked up the stairs to the bathroom at the end of the long corridor, Dominik tried to order his mind.

He stood still under the water rivulets, watching the sweat invisibly pearl down his body all the way to his feet. He washed away his exertions and unknown sins, purposefully blanking out the world. He focused on the way the hold-ups had left a pink band across Summer's pale flesh when he had finally released her from their bind just thirty-six hours ago in New York. As they'd trekked back from Grand Central, he had had thoughts of tying her up, but the revelation of her hold-ups and the beautiful way their shade of pale beige had contrasted with the milky landscape of her upper thighs even after he had unveiled her bottomless state, with both appreciation and a mild element of surprise.

He tried to recall the way she sometimes held her breath when he fucked her, as if trying to conjugate the rhythm of his thrusts with the rise of her desire. He had noticed it before, those first times in London, but now realised it was an integral part of her sexual make-up, an unconscious inner mechanism to assist her in settling on the same wavelength as her partner. No doubt she did so with other men, had done many times.

He looked down at his body under the flow of the warm water from the showerhead. His cock was at half mast, in homage to Summer and the sweet memories she evoked. The circular ridge beneath his glans was redder than usual, a witness to the frenzy of their recent dalliance.

He had been telling the truth when he said she made him want to do things to her. Things bad and sweet, things daring and dirty, revealing and tender, things that many women would resist. But Summer was not many women. His cock hardened, breaking the flow of the shower's cascade.

The day before yesterday, as they walked arm in arm along 42nd Street, they had passed a sex shop on Broadway going south, one of the few left in the city since the recent clean-up. Summer hadn't noticed, but Dominik had for a brief moment experienced the urge to walk in and buy something he could use on her – handcuffs, some form of restraints. It was just an impulse, but there was something seedy about the shop's unwashed window and its dubious contents, and something proletarian about using handcuffs on a woman. He had resisted the impulse and refrained from taking a detour into the shop, but the idea of tying her up had taken seed in his mind, and the revelation of her hold-up stockings later had been all too perfect, as if she'd read his mind and presented herself to him in full readiness for whatever the darkness of his imagination demanded.

It had been the same with Kathryn, the young married woman so many years ago now, who during their brief affair had helped Dominik realise his attraction to dominance.

Like Kathryn, Summer had this power to evoke his secret ghosts, draw them out, whisper disgraceful things to him and assure him she wouldn't mind, would not be shocked or disgusted. She awoke the dominant side of his personality, invited the worst of Dominik in the secure knowledge she could handle it. To the point of making him wonder who was actually in charge.

His mind rushed forward and a mass of thoughts raced to the surface.

He certainly wanted more than just dating – that curious euphemism – or fucking Summer. He wanted her fully, her body and her mind, but not in a possessive manner, this despite those surprising pangs of sexual jealousy he had experienced when seeing her with Jasper or imagining her with others. It was not a question of ownership. Something powerful inside him just wished to see how far he could take her, take himself, whatever the pain and mixed emotions it would unearth. She craved his domination; that much was obvious.

So that was the way he should continue to act with her. He would be someone who could control her, lead her on that journey. And why should feelings be excluded in the process?

Yes, in his way he already knew he loved her, but it was an all-encompassing love, a terrible love. It said to him that one day he might wish to see her with another man again, but this time specifically instructed by him, not just a whim or an accident.

The thought made him uncomfortable.

All of a sudden, he had an urge to jump out of the shower and make a beeline for the nearest phone and call her. He wanted to scream at her down the line, tell her all the bad things he yearned to do with her, to her, and be soothed by the balm of her acceptance. It would still be the middle of the night back in Manhattan, though, and she was probably blissfully sleeping like an innocent following the inevitable strain of their few days together. Besides, Dominik had never been a fan of phone sex. As a man who lived by words, it carried no emotional charge; it was just too easy!

He extended his hand to reach for the soap and began washing.

Days went by in a daze.

Life unfolded on automatic pilot through lectures, tutorials, marking, research, drafting lectures and papers. Dominik didn't see the time go as he busied himself with mundane matters, the business of his civilian life.

His communications with Summer were sparse. Like him, she was uncomfortable with the politics of lengthy telephone conversations, so much of their contact was through emails and text messages. Impersonal, almost businesslike, to the point.

It was a cruel game. When she expected him to be tender, he was remote or demanding. When she begged for his instructions, he was vague. Dominik wanted to keep her on edge. He wanted to be always in charge. Dominant. A role he was growing into.

A handful of days later, Dominik was walking out of the university on his way to the Tube, lost in a daydream full of inconsequential digressions, when he heard his name being called.

'Dominik?'

It was Lauralynn, the blonde cellist he had hired to perform with Summer in the crypt all those months ago. He'd entirely forgotten about her since the brief telephone conversation that had put him on the road to New York.

It seemed she had been waiting for him to complete his lecture. She was standing in the street outside the grey-bricked building, wearing a black pencil skirt cinched at the waist, which highlighted her voluptuous curves, towering heels and a white blouse through which her red bra was all too much in evidence as it strained against the outer material in an almost aggressive fashion. A calculated portrait of sin if ever there was one. Her yellow locks fell to her shoulders, carefully bisecting the oval of her face à la Veronica Lake.

Dominik was annoyed by this interruption to his routine, his mind already absorbed by an article he had been planning to tackle as soon as he had reached his desk at home.

'Back from New York, I see,' Lauralynn said.

'Yes,' he answered. He couldn't quite remember if he had told her he was going, but who cared?

'You hung up on me last time. That wasn't nice.'

He looked her in the eyes and detected a strong sense of

predatory mischief. He decided to play this by ear, see where it might lead.

'You saw her in New York, didn't you?'

'Who?'

'Our violinist friend, of course,' Lauralynn said. 'Still your little plaything?'

'I wouldn't put it that way,' Dominik responded, slightly taken aback.

'I'd be fascinated to hear how you do put it, Dominik,' Lauralynn remarked.

Dominik was about to walk away, irritated by both her uninvited familiarity with him and her mistaken assumptions. How could she know anything of what existed between Summer and him? Then he remembered how she had been connected to Victor, and her too-eager involvement with the scene he had directed in the crypt, an involvement he now knew was orchestrated by Victor. Although he had not raised the subject with Summer in Manhattan, he had strongly suspected she had held certain things back from him. The fact that Victor had also been in New York could not have been coincidental. The man was duplicitous and cunning. Surely Summer would not have succumbed to him.

He held back his impatience and asked her, 'What is it you want?'

'Just a chat, nothing more.' She smiled impishly. 'Don't worry, I'm not into guys.'

Dominik agreed and they made their way to a nearby wine bar with an upstairs room where, at this particular time of day, one could still enjoy a quiet conversation without too many eavesdroppers hanging around to interrupt the flow.

'So what's this all about, Lauralynn?'

'I liked your style, at the crypt.'

'You saw it all?'

'Not quite. The material of my blindfold was loose enough.'

'I see.'

'I know Victor. He had a good inkling of your plans for Summer and engineered it with me that myself and the two other remaining members of my quartet would make ourselves available for your scene.'

'So you all knew?'

'No. Just me, and Victor . . . I had to report back to him,' Lauralynn revealed, an awkward smile stretching her lips.

'The bastard,' Dominik said.

'Not really,' Lauralynn remarked. 'He's just a player. Like you. Like me.'

'I'm flattered you're willing to accept me into your circle.'

Lauralynn took a sip from her glass of Beaujolais. The wetness of the red wine shone across her full lips.

'Oh, but you are, Dominik – you're one of us. More than you know. To some it comes naturally, to others accidentally. It's just that you don't always realise at first. Doms, subs, it happens gradually, almost without your being aware of it. Until the day comes when you assume it fully, accept it, banish the personal doubts. It's nature, not nurture, you see.'

'An interesting perspective on things,' Dominik admitted, still curious about her intentions. 'So is Victor behind you now getting in touch with me, by any chance?'

'No, not at all,' Lauralynn replied. 'This is just me

putting out feelers. We haven't been in contact for ages, in fact. I'm on a solo mission, so to speak.'

'Tell me more,' Dominik said.

Lauralynn shuffled in her seat and sat back against the brown leather of the alcove armchair, facing him with a flirtatious look spreading across her attractive features as she brushed away a strand of blonde hair from her eyes with an imperious gesture.

'No, you tell me, Dominik. How do you feel when you're commanding a woman, getting her to do things that common mortals would disapprove of? Does it give you a kick, provide you with pleasure, or do you feel detached, like a spectator? I'm interested in finding out, in determining exactly what you are. Or could be.'

'That's a lot to consider,' he replied, standing to fetch another round of drinks from the downstairs bar.

'I like to use people,' Lauralynn had said, later that day, as they had continued their conversation over a meal in Chinatown. 'It brings me alive.'

She hadn't been trying to justify herself; it had just been a matter-of-fact statement in which she took no pride or vicarious enjoyment. An explanation.

Dominik's initial reaction had been one of denial. Surely this didn't apply to him too. He loved women. He wasn't cruel to them, was he? In the act of seduction, there was not only sexual enjoyment at play, the naked pursuit of pleasure, but also a deep desire for closeness, empathy, a determination to understand what made a particular woman tick. Even down to wanting to know how she felt.

Later, tossing and turning in bed that night, equally aroused and fascinated by the can of worms Lauralynn had opened, he couldn't help thinking back to Kathryn and the new cravings she had triggered inside him.

And, he reflected, also within herself, which had shocked her to the extent that after their break-up, Dominik knew, she had not only remained with her husband but in reaction to the affair embarked on a complete new life, leaving the area and giving birth a couple of years later to twins, following IVF treatment. She who, in his presence, had always professed a profound disdain for the idea of ever having children. Could the discovery of her own submissive streak and the perception that it made her a new woman, the dangers it unveiled, have caused her to flee from him? From his clutches?

Maybe, he decided, and sighed.

It couldn't have been his fault, though, surely. The kernels of dominance and submission had already been there, buried deep inside both Dominik and Kathryn long before they had met each other. Like embers waiting for the soft breath of an unknown deity to come back to life and burn afresh.

Had they not come across each other, their lives would in all probability have continued their untroubled flow along more . . . normal roads. Vanilla ones, he realised.

Once the cat had been let out of the bag, however, there was no closing the lid on those feelings, Dominik knew. At least as far as he was concerned. He just didn't know what self-discipline and heartbreak it had taken Kathryn to reject the siren call and turn away from him so decisively and return to the straight and narrow. The abnegation.

He couldn't find sleep. Stray sounds of birds in the garden outside his bedroom window reached him, amplified, deafening in their quietness. In retrospect now, he admired

Kathryn's resolve, the way she had sacrificed herself. Sadly, Dominik knew he didn't possess such fortitude. He had been bitten, for ever contaminated like some sexual form of vampirism, and had abandoned himself willingly to the embrace of the ghosts of lust without a second thought. He had found them set ablaze again when he had first encountered Summer.

This time, Dominik was determined to get it right. If Summer genuinely craved to submit to him, that is what he would give her.

He would learn the art of loving domination, take her on a journey from which both of them would emerge as new people. Hardened but tender, walking the tightrope, wondrously alive.

He thought back to those years between Kathryn and Summer, the times of indulgence and cruelty. The knot in his stomach tightened as he evoked the memories of the madness.

Exploring the dark, murky streets of the Internet, he had cruised chatrooms and forums and met scores of women whose desires matched his. He'd learned a whole new vocabulary and repertoire of clandestine encounters, a curious etiquette of alternative sexuality. Some encounters had proven liberating, others awkward and less successful, some even comic for Dominik with his developed sense of irony.

As a voracious reader, he was already aware of some of BDSM's practices and avenues, but was surprised by how prevalent it was, behind the everyday masks of respectability. The whole world seemed involved in it, a complete parallel world of which he had hitherto been so innocently unaware. Fiction was one thing, but real life was another altogether, and it had proven full of untold surprises.

His wilderness years. Dominik closed his eyes.

The man he had met at the Groucho Club was a friend of a friend of a friend. Dominik had been vouched for, somehow.

'You'll still have to be vetted by a couple of the others,' the other man said.

'I quite understand,' Dominik had answered.

The stranger had made a phone call, and an hour later they were joined by two others. Well-dressed businessmen, suited and tied. A few drinks later, he was formally approved.

'How do you find them?' Dominik asked.

'Chatrooms, ads, by personal recommendation . . .'

'Recommendation?'

'You'd be surprised.'

'Jesus . . .'

'All quite normal women. No money changes hands, ever.'

The spokesman for the group was in his early fifties. Earlier in the conversation, he'd mentioned he'd returned just a few weeks back from his holidays, sailing his boat along the coast of Turkey. Another was a surgeon, an imposing black man originally from Ghana, and the third had some unspecified high-powered job in the City.

It was agreed Dominik would be invited to join their next session.

They met in the cellar bar of a large, impersonal hotel right by Victoria Station. Two of the other men in the group were already there, nursing beers, when Dominik arrived. No introductions were made.

The young woman walked into the bar ten minutes later, accompanied by the group's leader. She seemed barely out of her teens, although when you looked at her closer in the calculated semi-darkness of the bar, there were dark circles under her pale grey eyes and thin lines across her neck. She appeared at first hesitant, even shy, but after a few drinks, she relaxed and loosened up. She was a student nurse, she revealed. On subsequent occasions there was a much older assistant bank manager who'd travelled up from the south coast, and on another occasion a single mother who wanted to be a writer and who, having uncovered some of his non-academic publications, later mailed him a few stories she was working on; they were actually surprisingly good. Sometimes the group booked the hotel in Victoria, but on other occasions they would use a hotel near Old Street or, one time, the basement of an empty shop on Old Compton Street, which one of the guys had access to through his job. The hotels were principally chosen for their busy nature and the fact that five or six men entering the lift to the upper floors together with a single woman would not attract undue attention.

'Your first time?' he asked the student nurse, that first night. This was still at the bar. Two of the other men had walked over to the counter to pick up another round of drinks.

'Yes,' she said.

'Me too.' He attempted a smile.

'That's nice,' she replied.

'Why are you doing it?' It wasn't quite what Dominik

wanted to ask, but somehow the right words couldn't form on the edge of his lips. She looked so young, if worn out.

'You know, a fantasy. I think all women have them. Just want to know what it would feel like. Silly, no?'

'No, not at all.' The others returned and their one-to-one conversation came to an abrupt end.

Once they were all in the hotel room, the young nurse was summarily stripped. She had lovely, round breasts. High and firm. She had been ordered to shave herself below and had followed her instructions to the letter. She wore no knickers, just hold-up black stockings.

The leader of the group unzipped his trousers and presented his cock to her, forcing her down to her knees. She took him into her mouth. This was a signal for the other men to undress. Dominik looked around at the ocean of male flesh now crowding him. They came in all shapes and sizes, and he was glad to see his was not the smallest, or the fattest. Some feelings never changed in the company of others, despite his usual self-assurance and ease with his own body.

While she hungrily sucked on her first cock of the evening, others began to touch her, greedily exploring her, forcing her, feeling her up like a prime cut of meat. Cocks hardened, jutted. His eyes took in the room, the scene of the crime. The window looked out on a dull panorama of city roofs. On the bedside table was a small pile of condoms and various tubes of cream and lube. On a desk near the fridge, someone had placed a couple of bottles of wine, both red, plus three glasses and a mug. A few sex toys were scattered around, including a monstrous two-headed dildo that surely wouldn't fit into any woman's apertures without tearing her apart, he thought.

It turned out it did fit. An hour or so later, after she had been used by every man in the room in succession and on some occasions together, two men busied themselves stuffing the dual-purpose black dildo deep into her vagina while the other extremity was, inch by inch, forcibly buried into her anus. The young nurse breathed heavily as the operation took place, on all fours on the bed, her mouth impaled onto the thick cock of a heavy-set red-haired man.

'Good girl,' someone said.

By then, Dominik was already spent. He had fucked her in every way he could wish to, had once even felt her gag on his hard cock when it hit the back of her throat as the black medic thrust into her from behind and the motion threw her involuntarily forward more than she had expected.

The others kept busy. Between fucks, they would hand her a glass of wine, later water, which she requested, and some would gently mop her brow when the sweat began to drip from her fevered forehead. She never complained or asked for a break. He looked at the scene, trying to place himself in the skin of a dispassionate observer. One of her hold-up stockings was badly torn, and the one on her other leg was bunched up round her ankle. She was ravaged, but still rather beautiful as the men in the group circled the bed, moving along to play with her in turn.

He gazed at the men surrounding their conquest. He wondered what it must feel like to have a penis in one's mouth, what it would taste like, how it would fill his insides. What it would feel like to be a woman. His mind was entranced by the sheer beauty of submission and the undercurrents of beauty and self-determination it brought to the surface of a woman's skin and soul.

Right there and then, at the heart of his first gang bang,

Dominik momentarily understood what it would be like to be submissive and knew that if he were a woman, he would also be a woman who would gift herself to men, to strangers.

He was awed by the fact that a submissive woman could, through the power of her sexuality, almost control such a mad situation.

The young nurse shrieked. Someone had pushed too far. 'Enough,' she protested.

Nevertheless, her blushing face was radiant, ecstatic even.

The men respectfully moved away from her. She slipped off the bed and away from the tangle of bodies.

Spent condoms littered the hotel-room carpet.

'I think I need a shower,' she said. She looked around at the circle of bodies surrounding the bed. 'Wow! That sure was some party,' she laughed, and headed towards the bathroom.

They all dressed and one by one left the hotel room, leaving her behind with just the group's leader, who had initiated the original contact with her and escorted her here.

Dominik attended a further five gang bangs organised by the motley group. None of the men involved knew each other's names, and he soon came to understand the other unwritten rules of the game. Because it was a game, consensual, lustful, sexual. The group provided a need, and surprisingly, some of the women even returned on a few occasions.

Every time, he told himself he wouldn't attend the next event, feeling shameful, guilty, angered by his own compulsion. But every man is led by his dick, and even if he left it to the last minute before confirming his attendance, he would be present at the pub or the bar where yet another new girl would be introduced.

At the final gang bang he attended, back at the hotel near Victoria Station, following forays at the Old Street hotel and the basement in Old Compton Street, Dominik surprised himself by allowing his dark side to take over.

The woman was a librarian from High Wycombe and they were still liberally taking their pleasure with her when a member of the group went to the hotel bar downstairs to fetch some extra drinks and returned with another woman. He had somehow seduced her in record time, or at any rate convinced her to join them all in the room. The newcomer was not taken aback by the spectacle of six naked men writhing lewdly around the pale body of a younger woman, cocks at attention, hair in disarray. She announced she would rather not participate and just wanted to observe.

Right then, the woman who was the evening's main attraction was positioned on her knees on the edge of the bed, feeding on Dominik's cock, who sat with thighs wide apart. He was tiring, losing his hardness. The woman from the bar watched them both, nursing a glass of gin, her eyes eager, her lips moist as she followed their movements. He avoided her gaze, pulled the librarian's face away from his crotch by her hair and raised himself slightly.

'Lick me,' Dominik ordered the young woman in a voice that surprised him. He took hold of a belt that just lay there on the bed, abandoned earlier as part of another sexual variation, and placed it round her neck like a collar.

She obeyed, and for just a moment, he left his body and

became an observer of the scene, watching it all from afar, detached.

This was sex at its most basic.

No need for latex or toys, no need for words, to be called 'master' or whatever.

The rush had been blinding.

A woman between his legs. Another watching.

Ten minutes later, he was dressed, racing through the hotel lobby and signalling for a cab.

'Take me to Hampstead,' he had told the driver.

'Where in Hampstead?' the cabbie had asked. 'It's a big place, Hampstead is.'

'I'll decide when we get there.'

The night traffic was sparse and they soon crossed the Marylebone Road, cruised through Regent's Park and reached Camden Town and then Belsize Park.

'Take a right past the Royal Free,' Dominik said.

'You're the boss, mate.'

He had ordered the taxi to stop when they reached the pond by Jack Straw's Castle.

His mind was bubbling with confusion.

On one hand, he felt downright shocked by his own actions: the senseless sex, the indifference, the emptiness. Images of the women, the men, the cocks, the animalistic sounds of unfeeling lovemaking. On the other, he felt the electricity of dominance rush through him like a drug running wild through an addict's veins.

For a moment, he was tempted to enter the woods by Jack Straw's Castle's car park, an area notorious as a gay cruising ground. He had an irrational desire to explore what it meant to be penetrated, used, as if it would help him better understand the women he fucked. Crazy! He stepped one way, then another, hesitated and finally walked slowly towards home.

Dominik didn't reach the stone steps leading to his door until well past midnight. He could have hailed another taxi, but the walk had calmed his nerves.

A week later, he hooked up with one of his former students, Claudia, and broke all contact with the group. Or maybe it was the other way round and they no longer invited him to attend their somewhat particular events.

The sex with Claudia was good, uncomplicated, healthy in a vigorous way. She accepted his needs, the control he sought, welcoming the variations, the kinks, somehow never questioned them, and for some time he thought he had conquered his dark side, put a brake on his deeper, irrational cravings. Dominik knew, though, there was something missing . . . until he had come across Summer playing her battered violin in the Tube station and the fire inside him had been set ablaze again.

'So how well do you know Summer? And Victor?' asked Dominik, as Lauralynn sat down on the blanket she had brought along and spread out on the grass in Regent's Park.

She'd suggested a picnic and the weather, according to the forecasters, was going to be warm this weekend, a final hiccup of clement sun before the threat of autumn. How quickly the seasons turned, he reflected, making him think of the Vivaldi piece. Almost a year since that fateful afternoon when he'd ventured into Tottenham Court Road Tube and heard the intoxicating music of a violin coming from along the corridor and had within seconds come under the dazzling spell of Summer and her violin-playing and the way she looked when she played.

'Victor has been an acquaintance, a sort of partner in crime, for some years. We met at a party and he offered to help me set up some scenes. He recognised that streak of aggression in me, I guess. He's a dangerous man, you know. He uses people. There's a powerful core of vindictiveness in him . . . But he is well connected. And experienced.'

'And Summer?'

'Only the once after the special concert in the crypt when you had her play naked. I found her – how can I put it? – interesting.'

'You and her?' Dominik enquired. 'Anything happen?'

'Sadly, no,' Lauralynn confessed. 'I don't think she's that way inclined. Maybe some no-strings play, but nothing serious. I know her type, though. Like a moth attracted by the flame. Also dangerous. She thinks she's in control, but is sometimes quite mistaken. She can't see the forest for the trees and doesn't realise what is motivating her. Hasn't quite yet reconciled herself with her cravings. She thinks she is modern and assertive, but it's so easy to lie to oneself. Isn't it, Dominik?'

Once again the malice in her eyes was both overt and complicit.

She took two plastic cups and carefully poured out coffee from the thermos flask she had carried along with her to the park in a wicker basket. Dominik had brought the sandwiches. A stone's throw away from where they were sitting, along the road that bisected the park, files of noisy kids were being led towards the nearby zoo.

'What happened? When she met up with you?'

'We played. I summoned one of my playthings, a sub, a guy. I think she enjoyed it, opened her eyes to some new variations.'

'I see.'

'But as I said, I know her sort. I've come across others like her before. They are their own worst enemy. Left to their own devices, they have a talent for getting drawn in by all sorts of temptations. Their pride leads them by the nose.'

'Really?' Dominik remarked, partly annoyed at the way Lauralynn was articulating feelings about Summer's psychological make-up he was still confusingly attempting to get to grips with himself.

She took a bite from an egg mayonnaise and cress sandwich.

'If you're so attached to her,' Lauralynn pointed out, 'I wouldn't leave her at a loose end in New York, or for that matter anywhere. You'll lose her.'

'Victor?'

'Possibly. But he's not the only wolf in the pack. She is just the sort of sub some of our kind would take a shine to, would want to break.'

'Break?'

'Her spirit. She's strong, I grant you that, but no one is immune to certain pressures. I get the feeling Summer is pretty relaxed about the way she uses or allows her body to be used, so the alphas will go straight for her mind. That's where they will try and bend her to their will. And once broken, you can never put the pieces together again. She doesn't realise, I don't think, that beyond a certain point, there is no return.'

'Very melodramatic, Lauralynn.'

'Maybe . . . But domination comes in many colours,

Dominik. For some, it's the exercise of power. For others, it's merely a game—'

He interrupted her, wishing to make his case. 'I'm not concerned by power, and I reckon with Summer it's more than just a game. I want her to be strong. I have no wish to break her, as you put it. I want to see her grow, assume her nature. That's what gives me pleasure, not the control. The acceptance of her feelings . . .'

'Dangerous ground, Dominik. Some would use a pesky four-letter-word for all that.'

'And you?' he asked. 'With those you play with, control, whatever, what is it you seek?'

'It's a game of wills. Sometimes a cruel game, but a game all the same. See, I thought we were in the same camp, but there is a softness in you, Dominik. I see that now. Most admirable. It's not just your cock leading you.'

'I'd very much hope not. Although neither would I want it to be overly neglected.' He smiled.

'Whatever happens, Dominik, I'd like us to be friends, you know.'

'That would be nice.'

'With Victor, it was always about the next target; he was relentless. At first, I'd find it amusing, but he has an evil streak, a deep-seated desire to bend his subs, his slaves to his will. Beware.'

'I will,' Dominik said.

He had been trying to contact Summer in New York for a few days now, but her phone kept on going to voicemail on every occasion, whatever the time of day over in Manhattan, and he was beginning to worry slightly. She had promised to keep him informed of any adventures there, but so far the news had been pretty prosaic and uninvolving. Incomplete?

'I'm having a small party tomorrow with a couple of my playthings, but was thinking of opening it up. Would you be interested in attending? Watching, maybe?' Lauralynn asked him.

'Wouldn't your . . . acolytes object to a stranger being present?' he queried.

'Not at all. They know how to serve and do as they're told. Though I guess you're not into using guys, are you? A step too far?'

'No,' Dominik confirmed, hiding the fact from Lauralynn that he had given thought to switching, being on the receiving end in order to better understand what it might feel like to be a submissive, rather than out of taste. According to BDSM lore, many doms had supposedly done their time as subs. It helped them understand the dynamic better. The problem was just that he was not attracted to men. Fascinated by their cocks, yes, but not by their faces or personalities. So watching would have been interesting, educational even, but somehow he knew he was not quite ready for this.

'Maybe not this time,' he responded, mindfully not rejecting a future occasion. Right now, his thoughts were of Summer and the bubbling maelstrom of lustful intentions she drew to the surface of his imagination.

'Pity,' Lauralynn said. 'It would have been nice to have some new company. I could teach you a lot,' she continued.

'No doubt you could.'

'My gut feeling tells me that you're not much of a man for toys, are you?'

'Your instinct serves you right,' Dominik said.

'Victor is,' Lauralynn remarked. 'A hell of a lot. Loves his spreader bars, he does. I find that they work well with girls, but guys somehow always get cramps. Most men, that is. Some of them, especially the gay ones, will take anything and more. I don't come across many of them in my business, though; they keep to themselves and their own rituals, I guess,' she added as an afterthought, and Dominik felt there was a note of regret in her voice when she revealed this.

The midday sun was rising above them, with just the flutter of a breeze animating the greenery in the surrounding trees. Lauralynn brushed a breadcrumb from the corner of her mouth.

'Isn't this beautiful?' she said to Dominik, glancing at the sun. He'd taken his linen jacket off. 'Probably the last warm day we're going to have this year. London, eh? I just love the sun.'

He smiled at her.

Her blonde hair unfurled all the way across her shoulders. She stretched, sat up for a moment and in one swift movement pulled off her tight print blouse. She was braless beneath it. His eyes went to her delicately pierced nipples and the exquisite shade of pink they wantonly displayed and then to a blue tattoo, an ideogram in Chinese calligraphy on her left shoulder. She rolled over onto her stomach, kicked off the faded denim hot pants she had been wearing and began sunbathing in just her thong. The mountains of her arse were like a geometric symphony delineating a perfect curve with mathematical precision. The line of the elastic was ever so askew, indicating from her overall tan that she was quite accustomed to sunbathing in the nude.

Male passers-by began to slow down to catch a longer

sight of her as they ambled along the path nearest to the grass, while assorted families spread along the park's lawn threw them angry looks. There was something eminently provocative about the way she just lay there, her bare back and arse cheeks being roasted by the sun.

She was shameless, and she knew it.

Spread like this, legs exaggeratedly apart, in a public park, she would from a distance have onlookers believing she was stark naked.

Before she had turned onto her stomach, Dominik had noticed how the flimsy material of the thong clung to her skin and how the deep cleft of her cunt was visible through it.

He liked Lauralynn and thought they could, given the chance, turn out to be really good friends.

He took off his shirt, his turn to catch the last sun of the year.

Soon, they were both dozing in the arms of the lazy autumn heat.

Dominik dreamed of Summer, though, not Lauralynn.

# 3
## *The Romance of Ropes*

Shadows had begun to fall across the small enclosed garden outside my even smaller window in the East Village apartment, and the remaining light barely illuminated my body in the mirror so that with the corset on, I had an almost mummified appearance, like a strange woman in a Victorian cabaret show.

The garment bit into my skin with all the hard comfort of a steel embrace.

I loosened the laces at the back and leaned forward, carefully unclipping the row of metal hoops from the studs that held the construction together at the front. The boning had left an interesting set of marks on my torso, an art deco effect of symmetrical grooves running parallel round my waist and up to my breasts, vivid red against pale white.

My flatmates and I had just returned from performing a free open-air gig in Union Square, part of a month-long series of informal events celebrating American composers in advance of the upcoming Thanksgiving celebration. It was early November and the sun was beginning to sink earlier from the sky, its absence heralding the arrival of a sharp autumnal chill. We were heading out shortly to one of the rooftop bars in Midtown, to make the most of the evening air before winter brushed her cold hands over the city and banished all but the most determined cigarette smokers indoors.

I had performed while laced tightly into the black under-bust corset that Dominik had bought for me and instructed me to wear to one of Charlotte's parties in London, which kept my chest, as well as other parts of me, warm beneath the thin black knitted shift dress that I wore on top.

It seemed like a lifetime ago now, one of my first experiments in kink, when I had dressed and served as a maid for the evening in an attempt to discover how I felt in a submissive role when following the orders of those other than Dominik.

My behaviour had been impossible to analyse after the event, because clothed in the outfit and attending to the ring of the bell that he had provided for the guests to summon me, I'd felt as though I was following his instructions rather than those of the individuals who had asked for another portion of dessert or a glass refilled.

I missed him terribly, more than I had ever expected, and more than I would ever admit to him. Our communication since he had left had been brief, sporadic. The sound of his voice filled me with such longing that I began to leave my phone switched to voicemail most of the time, so I wouldn't have to face speaking to him.

Dominik had not ordered me to wear the corset beneath my clothes at this afternoon's gig. I had chosen to do so of my own accord, in an effort to recreate the sensation of dominance that I missed so much.

I tried to take advantage of the extra emotion that arose as a result of his absence by throwing my energy into my music, channelling grief and frustration into my violin like a lightning rod, though inevitably, some of the loneliness lingered, and my thoughts were filled with memories of the scenes that Dominik had created in London and fantasies of all the things that I wanted him to do to me. I became irritable and withdrawn, annoyed by the intensity of my own feelings.

I had tried emailing Charlotte for her advice, but she'd either mysteriously vanished or was ignoring me. Chris had completed his short tour with the band in America and had returned to London. He had no plans to visit New York again anytime soon, and besides that, he wasn't keen on Dominik, so I hadn't confided in him. I'd spoken to old friends in New Zealand over Skype, but they were settling down now with office jobs and long-term partners. My life was so different, with the orchestra, New York, Dominik, that I felt at odds with them as well.

Socially, I was at a bit of a loose end, but musically at least, my efforts did not go unnoticed.

Simón, the Venezuelan guest conductor the ensemble had been working with for the past season, had won a post with the orchestra permanently, and he seemed to have taken a shine to me, subtly praising my performance with the odd wink or lingering stare in my direction over the rostrum. I had only begun to notice his attentions once we began rehearsing for the series of Thanksgiving concerts, perhaps because I felt an affinity with the American style; it was influenced by the sound of faraway places, coloured by the infinite variation in cultural backgrounds of composers who emigrated to America to pursue a new life, filled with optimism and collecting the rhythms of new cities along the way, jazz and folk sounds blending with old European traditions.

I had not been sorry to see the old conductor go. He'd

had an academic approach that I felt lacked nuance. Under his control, the string section had been a little wooden. Simón was younger, and his methods were a radical departure from what we had been used to. Orchestral gossip discussed little else.

He had a bit of a bohemian look about him, and at least in rehearsals, he could have passed as the lead guitarist in a rock band, dressing in jeans and loose T-shirts. He was vibrant all the way from his shoes, which varied from comfortable Converse to pointed snakeskin ankle boots, shined to gleaming, up to his hair, which sprouted from his head in a mass of thick, dark curls and bounced with a flourish with his more manic movements. He led the orchestra as if possessed by music, beating time with his hands snapping like the jaws of a crocodile. Every adjustment of his facial muscles responded to internal cues seemingly without thought: a lift of the eyebrow or pursing of the lips signalled an infinitesimal change of mood or tempo.

I hoped that under his direction the string section might be encouraged to display more passion. If our last few concerts were anything to go by, his influence was just what we needed.

Baldo and Marija, my Croatian flatmates, who played trumpet and saxophone respectively, were ambivalent about the change. They had recently got engaged, and the happiness that they found in each other reflected onto every aspect of their lives so that it would have taken a bolt from the sky of portentous doom to bring down their mood.

Following the success of her own romance, Marija had become intent on setting me up, and she interrogated me regularly about the status of my relationship with Dominik with the rigour and cunning of a private eye.

That morning, I had told her about the whole affair, if for no other reason than to explain why I had been so short-tempered at home.

'You know that the best way to get over someone is to get under someone else,' she said prosaically, as we met in the kitchen over a late breakfast, before assembling our instruments and heading off for the concert.

She'd just had a fringe cut into her dead-straight dark hair and the severe line across her forehead lent an authoritative tone to her words.

'But I don't need to get over him. We're still seeing each other.'

'You're not really, though, are you, with you stuck here and him all the way over there?'

'It's not exactly a relationship. We're friends. With benefits.'

'But you're not getting any benefits.'

I had left out the details of our sexual exploits, but had told Marija that we had agreed, considering our natures and the distance between us, that we were both free to explore casual relationships with other people.

'Of course,' she'd said in response to that information, 'if he's not around, that's his problem. A girl has needs.'

She invited me to join her and Baldo that night for a drink at 230 Fifth, the sort of stereotypical pick-up joint that was filled to bursting at weekends with young Manhattanites on the prowl. I really wasn't in the mood for it, but agreed anyway. I couldn't spend all of my evenings locked in my bedroom and strapped up in Dominik's corset, even if I found the company of the two lovebirds bearable only in small doses, and the bar was exactly the kind of pretentious place that I went out of my way to avoid.

When I arrived, I discovered that they'd invited another member of the brass section along, a trombone player called Alex, who had joined the Gramercy Symphonia a year earlier after quitting his job as a divorce lawyer in Wisconsin to move to New York and pursue his dream of making a living from music. Marija had set me up on a double date, and I wasn't thrilled about it.

Alex was pleasant enough, but dull, and he wore a purple shirt that might have suited another, taller, less plump man, but on him, tucked up as he was against one of the bar's mauve suede sofas, just made me think of blueberry pie.

I left them all together on the couches, Marija with her long legs entwined like pipe cleaners round Baldo's shorter pair and Alex glancing up at me wistfully on occasion, and took my drink out to the rooftop garden bar.

The cocktail was average, and the music wasn't my style, but the view of Midtown was magnificent, the Empire State Building looming so close I felt as though I could almost reach out and touch it, leap onto the side and climb up into the sky like King Kong, or a modern-day Jack on his beanstalk.

'Beautiful, isn't it?' said a voice to my left, with a Southern twang to it.

The voice belonged to a blond man in a navy pinstriped suit and a thin tie, with a short glass in one hand and a fat cigar in the other. He had pulled one of the tables up to the side of the bar and was standing up on it, leaning all of his weight against the railing and looking out into the night with the confidence of a person who believes either that he is impervious to the occasional freak accident that results in people plunging off the sides of verandas to their death, or that gravity didn't apply to him.

'Yes, it is,' I replied, inhaling the slight waft of cigar smoke that surrounded him.

He jumped down from his vantage point with surprising grace and stood alongside me.

'Where are you from?' he asked.

'New Zealand originally, London after that, Australia in between the two.'

'You get around, huh?'

'I guess you could say that.'

I watched his eyes flicker at my response, and I leaned a little closer to him, just in case the flirtation in my words wasn't signal enough.

'Can I get you another drink?'

I looked down at the remains of my sub-par mojito.

'Maybe someplace else. Wanna get out of here?'

He didn't need asking twice. Forty-five minutes later, we were back at his apartment on the Upper East Side, the sort of chic, minimally furnished place that I had thought Dominik might favour before I got to know him better and realised that wealth doesn't necessarily equal sophistication, although I still wasn't really sure whether Dominik had money or not. Maybe he'd spent his life savings on buying me the Bailly and lived the rest of his existence on the ordinary wage of a university professor.

The man whom I had pulled introduced himself as Derek, a native New Yorker with a job in insurance. I told him that my name was Helen and that I was a legal secretary. Experience had taught me that most men respond well to secretaries and nurses, and it saved me worrying that they might track down my musical connections and turn up at a concert.

Derek really was called Derek, I noted, glancing at a pile of mail resting on his countertop.

His apartment screamed of money but smelled of recently fried salmon mixed with nicotine. I noticed that most of the windows didn't open. He probably smoked indoors, to save himself the trouble of going out onto the balcony.

'How do you like it?' he asked.

At first, I thought he was offering me a drink, but then realised, as he had made no move to turn on a kettle or get any bottles out of the fridge, that he was referring to how I liked to have sex. The bluntness of the question caught me off guard.

'Er . . .'

He moved forward and broke the ice with a kiss. He wasn't at all a bad kisser, but I couldn't banish the smell of his recent fish dinner.

I considered calling it off, but ever the optimist, hoped things would improve once we got down to it. Besides, I was trying to cut down on taxis to save money, hoping to spend some time travelling later in the year, and if I stayed over, I'd be able to get the subway, or walk home, in the morning.

I barely suppressed a wince as Derek probed my mouth with his tongue, using the sort of deeply exploratory manoeuvres that might be better placed further down.

These thoughts reminded me of Dominik, who did have quite a knack for it, and I wondered if his skill had been dormant since he left New York or if he was having a tête-à-tête of his own back in London. The thought of Dominik with another woman spurred me on. I pushed Derek out of the kitchen and into the living room, where the air was fresher.

'Ooh,' he said, 'a woman who wants to take charge. I like that.'

This was not turning out at all how I hoped.

Derek cautiously slipped the spaghetti straps of my dress over my shoulders and ran his fingertips over my skin as if he were stroking a kitten. Every touch was soft, delicate. Probably the result of reading myriad books about how women prefer liberal doses of foreplay before sex, ideally dipped in chocolate and followed by a warm bath, the sort of nonsense perpetuated in media of all sorts, as ridiculous as assuming that all men want porn, blowjobs and a hot dinner.

I had hoped that Derek might rip the dress off me, push me up against the glass and take me from behind, in Hollywood-movie billionaire style, but the reality was far less exciting. After some wrestling, I managed to unbuckle his belt and his trousers pooled round his ankles inelegantly. I should have taken his shoes off first, as his legs were now locked together, rendering him virtually immobile from the knees down.

We shuffled backwards into his bedroom, and he eased me tenderly down onto the bed and kissed his way softly from my neck down to my navel, looking up and grinning before he buried his head between my legs, oral sex likely his party piece, the trick that he saved for women he wanted to impress. He was eager but gentle. I tried to muster a vision of Dominik in my mind engaged in the same act, but along with his tongue, he'd have four fingers inside me exploring roughly, occasionally probing my sphincter and promising in an ironically polite tone that soon his cock would follow. Dominik and I hadn't yet had anal sex, and I wondered why he didn't just do it, not that I was averse to the anticipation. He seemed to think that it was one of the kinkiest items on the bedroom menu, whereas I thought of anal sex as the type of thing to save for a second date. I took his view on the subject to be sweetly old-fashioned and was looking forward to the moment when he decided the time was right.

My mind wandered back to Derek and I made an effort to concentrate on him, out of politeness. He had finished his oral ministrations and I pushed myself up, moving forward to go down on him, but he stopped me and pushed me down onto the bed.

'No, babe, this is all about you,' he said.

I sighed, an expression that he took to be pleasure.

His cock was big and hard at least, and his torso pleasantly firm against my chest, though I wished that instead of his endless light caresses, he would use his fingers to pull my nipples or lightly constrict my breathing. Perhaps he just needed a hint to push him in the right direction.

I picked up his hand and moved it towards my throat.

'Whoa. You're not one of those girls, are you? I'm not into that kinky shit.'

I could feel his cock softening inside me.

I pulled him down into a kiss, the sexual equivalent of changing the subject, but the moment was gone. He pulled out of me and disappeared into the bathroom. I heard the sounds of the shower running, and later, he returned with two hot chocolates.

'It's late,' he said, handing me a steaming mug. 'You're welcome to stay over.'

He was kind, at least, and versed in the etiquette of casual sex, even if not my type.

I lay awkwardly alongside him until morning and then

set about making my escape early, though I doubted that Derek would ask me for my telephone number.

The street vendors were out in full force around Central Park, heckling tourists who took a millisecond too long to choose between ketchup or tomato sauce. I picked up a bagel and a coffee on the corner of 78th Street and Fifth, and took advantage of a morning off to drop into the Met while I was nearby.

My mind was in too much of a whirl to appreciate art, and in the end I gave up trying to decide which of the vast array of exhibitions to visit and spent an hour in the Asian section, staring at a fifty-century Afghan head of Buddha, hoping to soak up some of the serenity visible on the features of the stone face with its long, loose ears and wide-set sleepy eyes. I took in the symmetrical brows meeting an angular nose and, below that, a plump, sensual mouth with soft lips, which gave the godlike creature a hint of humanity.

I thought about the night I'd just spent with Derek, the last weekend I'd had with Dominik, the weeks before that, with Victor, and the time that I'd gone to the fetish club in London on my own and enjoyed being spanked by a stranger. I reflected on how all of those things, the things that I was certain at least half the world would think of as abnormal, turned me on so enormously, yet a night with someone like Derek, a nice guy, a good catch in the social sense of the word, did nothing for me at all.

Is that what it had come to? Did I need to be restrained or surprised or pushed around to enjoy sex? Did I really want Dominik for the person that he was, or did I just like the way that he made me feel in bed?

Opting for the long walk home instead of the humid

grime of the subway, the sights and sounds of the city that had only yesterday seemed grand and exciting, today reminded me that I was cloistered, hemmed in, trapped among regimented straight avenues and square blocks. I was surrounded by monolithic glass and concrete structures that soared into the sky overhead like so many sentinels, the slice of blue sky in between building tops just a faraway glint, menacing as a guillotine edge floating above me.

I missed London for its underground hideaways, its narrow, twisting streets and darkened alleyways, its cobbled lanes with old-fashioned names like Cock or Clitterhouse a blatant reminder of a time when the streets bore witness to lewdness on every corner, when bawdy houses overflowed with petticoated courtesans, salacious strumpets and perverse politicians, lords and ladies of the night exuberant in their quest to quench appetites of every nature.

More puritan times had reigned since, and some of the ruder place names had been changed to reflect the social mores of the modern day, but London remained a city with desire soaked into its very streets. If the stones could talk, I thought, they'd cheer at the sight of each passing corruption. London was on my side.

That day, New York felt like the company of a disapproving sister.

I was a few minutes late for that evening's rehearsal and Simón gave me a searching look as I slipped into my seat. I played on autopilot, with none of my usual flourishes, hoping that my distraction and the machinelike torpor of my bow hand were not too evident.

That night, I slept with a heavy heart.

* * *

I woke up at 3 a.m., the time of morning that troubles come home to roost, and sent Dominik a text message:

'I miss you.'

I fell asleep feeling guilty, because I wasn't really sure if I did.

The next day, I decided to take matters into my own hands and look around for some kind of kink scene in New York. Every city was bound to have something, I figured. Regardless of yesterday's temporary depression, I knew from my adventures in London that other people in the world thought and behaved the same way I did. I just needed to find them.

A quick Google search wasn't a great deal of use. Perhaps things were a bit harder here for fetish folk. I had heard that in some places, cops took a poor view of public nudity and consensual violence. Or possibly this was just the style of New Yorkers; maybe they were more discreet about their proclivities and you needed to know people to find out where scenes were held. There were a few venues advertising events, but none that caught my eye. A couple of cabaret nights, a foot-fetish party, a men's spanking society.

Eventually, I found an introductory rope-bondage workshop, advertised for noon the following Saturday. I hadn't had much experience of rope, but the pictures certainly appealed, and if my response to the constriction of the corset and the hold-up stockings that Dominik had tied round my wrists was anything to go by, it would be right up my street. Attending an introductory class also virtually eliminated the risk that I might bump into Victor or any of his associates, which was a definite possibility at a club night.

The address wasn't listed for privacy reasons. I sent an email, stating that I was new in town and would be interested in attending, to the info address on the website.

I received a response almost immediately, an email from a Cherry Bangs, her 'scene name', no doubt. She wrote that she helped to facilitate the event and that I was welcome to come along as a 'rope bunny', a volunteer who would be tied by those learning the art of shibari, and that I wouldn't be expected to have a go with the rope if I didn't want to. She suggested meeting for a coffee, as I was new to the New York scene, and we arranged a date for Saturday morning, a couple of hours before the workshop began.

With a potential kink outlet sorted for the weekend, I went to rehearsal that day with a happy heart and a spring in my step. My good mood was apparent in the music and by the end of the session I felt invigorated. I still missed Dominik but was learning to get by without him. Everything was beginning to click into place.

'You played well tonight,' Simón said, not so much a compliment as a statement of fact, but I flushed with pride all the same. His brown eyes shone in the light, still full of adrenaline from the evening's performance.

'Thank you,' I replied. 'I thought you were great too.'

'That's good to hear. It's always tough taking over, especially from someone more experienced. I never know whether to be soft or firm, how to win respect without being the bad guy.'

'Well, I'm enjoying having you here.'

Perhaps it was the excitement from tonight's music that made me keep talking.

'Would you like to get a drink?'

He stared at me, making up his mind. I hadn't ever considered dating any of my previous conductors – they'd all been well into their older years – so I wasn't sure what the ethics were. Besides, it wouldn't be a date, just two travellers having a drink together. I guessed he must be new in the city too.

'Sure,' he said with a grin.

We went to an Italian café on Lexington. I ordered an affogato, vanilla ice cream with coffee and a shot of Cointreau. The waiter, an American Italian with a booming voice and an electric-blue apron, served it on a tray, the ice cream in a stemless martini glass sitting atop a white saucer with a red napkin and a long-handled silver spoon alongside, the piping-hot espresso and the liqueur lined up behind in shot glasses. He poured the liquid over the top of the ice cream with a flourish and then returned with two biscotti on a plate.

Simón eyed my elaborate concoction and then his own simple glass of red wine.

'I feel a little jealous,' he said.

I handed him the spoon. 'Go ahead, please.'

He paused before accepting this gesture of intimacy and taking a spoonful. 'Hmm, it's good.'

I took the spoon back, the stem still warm from the touch of his hand, though the scoop was icy cold.

'In Venezuela,' he said, 'we eat coconut and caramel for dessert.'

He enunciated the 'c' in each word in a way that suggested that he was thinking of something else, hotter than coconut or caramel, but the expression in his eyes was nothing more than warm and friendly. If he was flirting, I couldn't be certain.

'An excellent combination. How long have you lived in New York?'

'I was born here. My mother worked on Wall Street. She met my father on holiday. He was playing in a band. He emigrated to be with her but never managed to settle in, so we moved back to South America when I was a child. They're still there. I spent most of my childhood travelling between the two cities. I studied music in Caracas. Began by learning the violin . . .'

'Oh? Why did you give it up?'

'I wasn't very good at it. I was always distracted when I was playing by the sound of the rest of the orchestra. I wanted to control everything.'

I laughed. 'A natural conductor, then.'

'I suppose so. You play very well, you know. You play like a Latina. You have passion.'

'Thank you,' I demurred.

'I'm not just flattering you. But you're hemmed in by the constraints of an orchestra. Your sound would work better alone, solo.'

'That's very kind of you, but I don't know if I could. I'd be terrified on stage alone.'

'You would get used to it. I think you'd enjoy it.'

He reached out his hand and for a moment I thought he was going to take my hand in his, but instead he picked up the spoon and took another mouthful of ice cream.

Did he mean it? I wondered. My modesty was only true to a point. I would love to play solo for an audience, though the prospect scared as much as it excited me.

We sat in silence for an awkward few seconds. I scraped

the remaining drips of my dessert up with my finger, my focus on the melting ice cream to distract from the sudden discomfort between us.

'I've enjoyed the last few weeks,' I said, breaking the silence. 'I like the American composers. Philip Glass, particularly.'

'That's good,' he laughed. 'Though I don't think everyone shares your opinion. Some find him rather repetitive.'

'Does your family celebrate Thanksgiving?'

'Not really. My mother did, but she's taken up the Venezuelan lifestyle now. I'm actually having a little soirée at mine on Thursday. Just a few other "orphans" in the city who don't have family dinners to attend. You're very welcome to come. There's someone I'd like to introduce you to.'

'I'd love to,' I replied, ignoring a lingering worry at the back of my head that said that encouraging Simón wasn't fair, on either him or Dominik.

A few days later, I was in the same café to meet the woman who had answered my query about the rope workshop.

Cherry looked exactly as her name suggested. Her hair was dyed a vivid pink and cropped into a perfectly smooth bowl shape. She was short, buxom and dressed entirely in pink, aside from a black leather bomber jacket, which gave a rough edge to a look that might otherwise have seemed girlish. Her thick lips were liberally glossed, and her fingers were decorated with a variety of large rings, which shined in the light as she gesticulated. Cherry talked with her hands almost as much as Simón did.

'So you're new in town?' she asked, in a voice that suggested she might originally hail from further north. She told me she was from Alberta, someplace near Calgary, originally, and I guessed that explained why she was going out of her way to help out another newbie.

'Not exactly,' I replied. 'I've been here a few months. Just new to . . . the scene.'

'Don't worry about that. We're all friendly. Have you been tied up before?'

'Not with rope.'

'Well, it's better to learn in a place like this than stumble across a rigger at a party who doesn't know what they're doing or strings you up and leaves you hanging there. I'll keep an eye on you.'

I watched her hands lightly caressing a large cup of iced coffee with all the trimmings. One of her rings, I noticed, was a large spider, its thick body a long, black stone, with eight silver legs that wrapped round her finger like a cage. Another was a skull, with glittering faux-diamond eyes. I doubted she would be the gentle sort, but it's not always possible to tell. If everyone's public behaviour mirrored the way they responded in the bedroom, then I'd presumably have a lot more success in dating.

The workshop was held in a loft space between Midtown and the aptly named Meatpacking District. The room was part of someone's apartment, though the hallway leading to the bedrooms was cut off by a privacy screen, and the living room had been transformed into a 'play space'. It was light and airy, more like a yoga studio than a dungeon. Cushions were dotted around the room, and sitting upon them, attendees in a range of ages and sexes.

A young couple huddled into each other on a fake cowhide bean bag, looking like predictably nervous first-timers. The rest of the crowd were relaxed, chatting together happily. The sound of a continually boiling kettle gave the room a sense of homeliness, and the kitchen was filled with people waiting to pour water into mugs of tea and coffee. A table to one side displayed a range of herbal teas and a platter of fruit and organic chocolates. Near that sat a lone man with long hair and a scuffed leather jacket, defiantly eating a bowl of potato crisps.

Cherry introduced me to a few people, and I took a place beside her at the front, alongside Tabitha, who was running the workshop. Tabitha looked like a pagan goddess, with long, dark hair that flowed over her shoulders like a river, and a floor-length crimson dress, patterned with vivid, tiny blue flowers. She was barefoot, and she wasn't tall, but she commanded the room in a way that made it seem as if she was.

Tabitha began by outlining the safety issues of rope bondage, including how to avoid nerve damage and asphyxiation. (Never put a harness round the neck.)

She held up a pair of blunt rope shears. 'Always have a pair of these handy,' she advised, 'if you need to release your partner quickly, in case of fire, injury or an unexpected visit from your mother-in-law.'

The room tittered.

She demonstrated a few of the basic ties, laying a length of rope out on the floor and slowly folding it into knots.

I followed along, surprised by my feeling of satisfied accomplishment when I managed to correctly fix a single column tie round Cherry's wrist.

She grinned. 'See, it's fun, huh?'

The second half of the session was more advanced, the bit that I had been looking forward to.

Tabitha invited me to be her 'bunny', as she called it, to

demonstrate the tying of a basic box tie, the starting point, she said, for most body harnesses.

'Hold your arms behind your back.'

Her voice, quiet but firm, made me predictably weak at the knees.

She moved my arms into the right place, not straight out in the prayer position that Dominik had effected when he tied my wrists with the hold-up stockings, but with my forearms pressed straight against each other, my fingertips on one hand brushing my opposite elbow.

She began by tying my arms together, looping a single length of rope round the area midway between my wrists and my elbows, and then binding it round the upper and then the lower part of my chest, creating a border round my breasts and pinning my arms to my sides. She ran her fingers expertly along my arm before pulling the binding tight, checking that the rope was placed safely, not trapping a nerve.

The room fell into a hush, all the participants now quiet, listening closely to Tabitha's instructions. She had stopped telling me which way to turn and instead moved me about as if I was a doll, inanimate other than to respond to questions about the tightness of each binding. I began to relax against her body, softening my limbs and holding my shoulders back, allowing her to restrain me at her will. I closed my eyes, conscious of the audience watching.

Tabitha finished the harness and then left me standing in the centre of the room while she walked around the group, checking the work of the attendees who had now secured their partners in similar knots. She returned to me periodically, squeezing my hands behind my back to check my circulation, making sure that I hadn't gone numb. I had begun to sway gently on my feet, as if I'd got up suddenly after having a massage.

I was in a daze by the time that Tabitha returned from instructing the group and began to untie me. The rope brushed against my skin with a soft swish as she loosened the knots. It felt almost as good coming off as it did going on. Freed from the restraints, I stretched out my arms and wiggled my fingers, bringing the blood flow back.

I stared at my forearms, noticing the pattern that the rope had left on my skin, slightly sunken hatched markings, white in response to the pressure of the tie, where the circulation had been cut off, and red around the edges. It was an oddly domestic print, reminiscent of a traditional tablecloth in an Italian restaurant.

Cherry promised me that the marks would be gone in a few hours, which was fortunate as I had another rehearsal that evening. We parted with a promise to get in touch soon and arrange further exploration of the New York fetish scene.

I played well that day, pleased that I had made some new friends.

The marks on my arms vanished so quickly that I wished for their return, some kind of reminder of my pleasant afternoon, but instead I was left with nothing but the memory of the experience to mull over. I had been clothed throughout the tying, a workshop requirement, to ensure that the trainee riggers were not so distracted by naked bodies that they couldn't concentrate on the lesson. Next time, I thought, I'd like to try it naked, so that I could feel the rope all over and not just on my arms.

'Good work tonight,' Simón called out, as I packed the

Bailly away in its case. He was stuck in conversation with Alex, the trombone player.

We'd been back to the Italian coffee shop a second time and were beginning to fall into an easy sort of friendship. Knowing him better had improved my playing. I began to follow movements so subtle that I doubted he was even aware he was making them, interpreting the music exactly as he did, and I basked in the warmth of his praise as he told me that I was continuing to grow.

'See you Thursday,' I replied on my way out.

I didn't feel completely easy about the situation. The time to drop Dominik's name casually into conversation so that Simón would know that I wasn't entirely available had been and gone. He hadn't made any kind of move on me, but I couldn't shake the guilty feeling that I was leading him on.

Too late for that now, as I had just rung the bell at his apartment in a sought-after block on the Upper West Side, a stone's throw from the Lincoln Center, and was standing on his doorstep holding a steaming pumpkin pie. Marija had baked it for me, despite my protestations, as soon as she found out that I had a 'date' with the conductor.

Simón opened the door and relieved me of the pie. He was wearing a gold waistcoat tonight, with matching gold cufflinks and his pointed snakeskin ankle boots, reminiscent of a gangster from a 1930s film. Fitting, I thought, as he sometimes wielded his baton like a machine gun. I kicked myself for not dressing up more. I'd fretted over what to wear and opted for casual, dressing down in soft black leggings, a long J. Crew cardigan and a pair of low-heeled sandals, so that he wouldn't think it was a date. I slipped into the bathroom at the first opportunity to add a pair of pearl earrings and matching necklace, which I'd stowed in my handbag in case the evening turned out to be more formal than I expected.

The other guests were a motley bunch, as most of America was at home with their own families, so Simón had assembled all those he knew who didn't have anywhere else to go: Al, an architect on secondment from a firm in the Middle East, working on a luxurious new hotel complex on Madison Avenue; Steve, a performance poet visiting from England who had performed just before us at the Union Square concert; Alice and Diane, a couple who ran an art and performance space in Nolita; and Susan, a sharp-eyed woman with a ready laugh who Simón sat me next to over dinner. She was an agent, I discovered, who had a range of solo musicians on her books.

Simón spent most of the night chatting to Steve, the poet, leaving me free to make small talk with Susan.

She slipped her card into my hand at the end of the night. 'Keep in touch,' she said. 'Simón speaks very highly of you, and he has excellent taste.'

I was the last to leave. Simón walked me to the door, maintaining a friendly but professional distance between us.

'Thank you again for the invitation,' I said politely.

'You're very welcome,' he replied, inclining his head in a low bow. 'I'm glad you had a chance to talk to Susan.'

His eyes were sharp, unblinking.

'She seems very nice.'

'She is. She's also very good.'

I returned home to find Baldo and Marija awake and sprawled out over one another on the couch in the living room. They were entirely happy to celebrate a Thanksgiving for two.

'Sooooo,' said Marija, 'tell us everything.'

'Your pie went down well.'

'I hope it wasn't the only thing that went down well,' she sniggered.

'It's not like that with him. We work together.'

'Yeah, right. Famous last words.'

I glared at her as I pushed the door open to my bedroom.

She was probably right, though, I thought, sighing as I sank into bed.

My corset lay forsaken, hanging limp over my wardrobe rail, its silver catches gleaming in the glare from my bedside light like a row of tiny moons.

# 4

## *Bourbon Street*

Dominik took it as an omen when a review of a book of essays he had contributed to appeared in an issue of *Book Forum* magazine alongside an ad for a dozen or so major fellowships at the New York Public Library being offered for research purposes to scholars or writers, endowed by a family trust he had not previously come across. He appeared to tick all the criteria listed on the application form he found online as far as past publications and academic credentials were concerned.

He'd been considering a particular book idea for some time now, before he'd been distracted by the arrival of Summer in his life, which would have involved substantial research at the London or British Library. The thought immediately occurred to him that an office of his own in the New York Public Library would be a perfect place to have, and a perfect excuse to spend nine months in Manhattan closer to Summer. The lecturing obligations that came with the fellowship were both minimal and manageable, and the stipend generous. Not that the money was any sort of consideration for him, even knowing New York rental costs.

He applied and was shortlisted by return of post.

The interviews would take place the week before Christmas.

Everything was falling into place.

Summer had informed him about a recent one-night stand she'd had back in New York. He hadn't been jealous. More so reading between the lines of her amused confession focusing on the guy's furniture and apartment colour scheme and how she had giggled when she had revealed that the place had not a single book to be seen. It had obviously not been anything serious, just an itch scratched. He couldn't expect her to remain an unsullied nun in a place like the Big Apple. In fact, he was grateful that she felt secure enough to keep him in the loop about her minor sexual adventures.

She had also informed him that she was planning to attend a rope-bondage class the following week and sounded rather excited by the prospect. He was looking forward to her account of the event and encouraged her involvement.

At the same time, Dominik knew he could not afford to have her loose in America too long.

They had renewed their bond, but it was still tenuous and subject to the whims of distance and coincidence. Dominik wanted to see her again, spend time with her. He was aware she felt the same way and that the relatively innocent one-nighter with a stranger whose name she could apparently no longer even recall was just displacement, a stop gap until they could be together again. All part of the give and take that would be necessary if they were to make their own relationship work.

He rang her and, for once, managed to get through without tediously having to leave a messages or arrange a particular time down the line for an actual conversation to take place.

'It's me.'

'Hello, you.' He could hear the genuine pleasure in her voice. 'I had a feeling you were about to call.'

'Really?'

'Yes. I felt it in my bones.'

'Only in your bones?'

'Maybe somewhere else too,' she added flirtatiously.

'Listen, I've arranged to come to New York in three weeks.'

'That's wonderful.'

'To hold conversations with an institution there about the possibility of taking up a fellowship in New York, which means I could move to the city for a whole nine months. What do you think?'

There was a moment's hesitation, as she no doubt realised this could possibly prove a major step forward in their adventure.

'Hmm . . . it sounds great.'

'I'll tell you more when I'm there, but it could be exciting.'

'Yes.' He could feel Summer drawing back into a shell at the other end of the line.

Dominik had been about to suggest that if the gig came off, they could actually find a place to live together while he was in town working and researching his future book, but he held back on hearing the hesitation in her voice. Yes, it would be a big step. For both of them. An experiment. For which neither of them might yet be ready.

'And . . .'

'And?'

'Just an idea. There's no reason for me to rush back to London following the interviews. I would have no more lectures until well into the new year. I could stay over and we could go somewhere in America for the holiday period. You always mention how much you enjoy travel and there are so many places in the States you've always wanted to try out, no?'

'We have a Christmas Eve concert pencilled in,' Summer said.

'That's fine,' Dominik said. 'We could fly out the following day. Maybe somewhere warmer?'

She failed to respond as he had anticipated. 'Orchestras always get lumbered with crap concerts around the festive season,' she added. 'I hate that repertoire, the second-rate music the public somehow expects. To cap it all, it'll be with a guest conductor who's being flown in all the way from Vienna. Strauss waltzes, pomp and circumstance and all that. Simón is glad he doesn't have to be involved.'

'Who's Simón?' Dominik asked.

'Our conductor. Our permanent one.'

'Oh. I didn't realise he was now with the Symphonia. I read an article about him. From South America, no?'

'Yes. He's doing a great job. Lives the music so intensely.'

'Like you?'

'I guess so. Probably why I like working with him.'

'Good.'

There was a pause on the line. Dominik could feel Summer's impatience building. She hated lengthy telephone conversations.

'So how long have you got free after Christmas Eve?' he asked.

He could hear her moving across the narrow bedroom to consult her desk diary.

'Next set of rehearsals don't begin until 4 January,' she replied.

'Perfect,' Dominik said. 'Keep those days free.'

He heard her sigh.

'I'll make the arrangements,' he indicated, knowing the way she liked him to be firm. He had to be his old self again, and he had every intention of being so.

They'd spent three whole days in his hotel room in New York, interrupted by a couple of four-hour final orchestra rehearsals prior to the Christmas concert that would close their season. Summer had half feared that, just like at the London Proms, the musicians might be asked to wear funny festive hats, don Santa beards or other humiliating extras to commemorate the occasion, but management here seemed less bothered and the only suggestion pinned to the noteboard was for a possible sprig of holly on lapels or dress straps, and even then it was not compulsory. It was bad enough that the concert's musical line-up was essentially muzak, pap for mostly suburban concertgoers who only came out when the bright lights of winter shone, no one really serious. Commuters from Long Island and New Jersey to the big city for a pleasing night out after their frantic shopping at Macy's or FAO Schwarz.

Their lovemaking took place below framed prints of a younger Ingrid Bergman and Marlene Dietrich, which hung on the wall above the bed. Dominik had not managed at short notice to secure a deluxe room with a king-size bed and the double bed in the room was a touch narrow, so they had to sleep spooned together; certainly not designed for anyone overweight, Summer reckoned.

She could have invited him to stay at hers, even though

she had even less space, but the thought made her nervous, as if the intimacy it might involve was greater than fucking for hours on end until they felt raw.

She floated through the rehearsals, her mind a total blank, indifferent to the music and playing by rote, eager to get the chore done and return to the comforting warmth of Dominik's bed.

The room was on a different floor of the hotel in Washington Square from the last time he had been in town, but the room's configuration was the same. The pink room, as she remembered it, even if it was more a light shade of purple when the blinds were not drawn, she noticed now. Strange how memory could imperceptibly shift at random through the spectrum of the rainbow and a curious filter of emotions. The room had become a now familiar, gentle cocoon in which she willingly surrendered to Dominik's arms and soothing words.

His body was a map she had journeyed through before, with parts unexplored and heartbeats in exquisite disarray. Her senses were alert to the sound of his breath across her skin, the touch of his fingers. It seemed to her – a strident thought that raced through her brain more often than not when they were fucking – that there might actually be two separate Summers involved in this game. The one she knew, who wondered why all this wasn't enough, why she harboured this compulsion, this need for more while yet another alter-ego, devilish and provocative, treacherously whispered in her ear that surely there was more to life than this.

The thought never lasted long, however, as she surrendered to his vigorous embrace.

He was her man. For now. His arms pinned her back on

the bed the way she liked men to control her sexually, his cock filled her with an imperious form of roughness, and the sounds he made while inside her were just the right mix of affection and animal lust. It was enough. Summer knew she had to live in the moment. Because those special moments never lasted for ever.

'Tell me, tell me all the things you want to do to me,' she rasped, as another hard thrust turned the fire inside up a notch and she briefly felt dizzy.

'Oh, so many things, Summer. So many. Bad things, wonderful things, filthy things, dangerous things.' His words emerged slightly haltingly. The weight of his body pressed against her ribs, restricting her breath.

Watching her under him, her eyes firmly closed, her skin so soft and pliant, communing with the flow of her lust, Dominik felt a faint wave of generosity course through his mind, overcoming the tyrannical demands of his cock, now buried deep inside Summer's body. At times like this, he felt he could die happy on the spot, in this hotel room with the night glow of the nearby arch shadowed through the gaps in the drawn blinds.

He looked up, the sight of her face almost too much for an instant, and Bergman and Dietrich enigmatically smiled down at him.

He slowed his pace, almost to a halt, and Summer half opened an eye, querying his change of rhythm. He didn't want to come yet. He wanted this to last for ever, inside her, part of her, feeling the implacable force of her surrender. Of her love?

His fingers roamed with delicate attention across her warm flesh. Beneath them, the sheets were crumpled and humid with sweat. He withdrew briefly from her and changed his position, adjusting his stance before penetrating her anew. While her hands moved from his shoulders down across his back, her nails gently scraped against his skin in a parody of massage.

Oh, yes, there were so many things he wanted to do. Not now. One day. With her. He would observe the unease of the initial onset of pain and then the acceptance of the discomfort morphing into pleasure from the metal clamps or clothes pegs he would one day inevitably adorn her dark nipples with. He would gauge the intensity of her breath as his fingers put pressure on her delicate throat and her whole body convulsed wildly under his control. Oh, Dominik, dangerous thoughts, he told himself. He would enjoy breaching her sphincter with toys and then his cock when the time was right, another taboo standing between them still like a landmark . . . Enough, Dominik, enough . . .

His thoughts raced wildly as he continued his thrusts inside her, sensing her own pleasure rise in unison with his, slowing his progress to match hers as best he could, and then felt Summer slipping a finger into his own anal opening . . . FUCK . . . He came instantly and with such violence he was briefly worried that he could have punctured the condom.

Her impulsive gesture had certainly taken him by surprise.

His breathing ragged, he lowered his lips to Summer's and kissed her affectionately, brushing the salt from her brow as he did.

Clearly, he still had a lot to learn about Summer Zahova.

And he would.

The interview with the trustees of the foundation endowing the Public Library fellowship had gone swimmingly that afternoon and he was now confident the position was his. He relished the prospect of nine whole months with Summer in Manhattan. He looked down at her naked body, stretched across the bed, open, pale, exposed in all its intimacy. So much time, so many things they could now do.

The formal decision about the fellowship was expected early in January, and if successful, he would be expected to take up the position shortly after Easter.

He was about to say something to her and noticed she had fallen asleep.

Dominik welcomed the sudden silence, a chance to think.

'I want to display you,' Dominik had warned her.

The Symphonia's Christmas concert was over, which had not proven too excruciating in its excess of jollity after all, and Summer had been asked by Dominik to pack enough clothes for a week. When she had queried where they would be going, all Dominik had said was that the weather was expected to be mild.

'I don't think a bathing costume will be needed, though,' he had added.

Nevertheless, Dominik was unable to keep their destination a secret for long once they arrived at the airport. La Guardia was a teeming mass of people dashing in all directions, as the holiday season was in full swing. You would have thought most folk would, by Christmas Day, already be at their destination, instead of wandering around terminals like headless chickens, but this wasn't the case. Dominik and Summer, opportunistic leisure travellers with no family reunion in prospect, could sense a feeling of panic and desperation in most of their fellow travellers, darting looks at the display boards and grimacing every time an announcement over the tannoy system warned of a delay somewhere on the continent due to bad weather or some other reason.

She would have preferred not knowing where he was taking her, a magical mystery tour, but once they checked in their luggage, there was no escaping the information: their flight (and hopefully their luggage too) was going to New Orleans.

It was a city she had read much about in books and almost felt she knew from the myriad movies in which it had been enshrined, a bit like New York. When she'd first landed in New York, she had discovered that Manhattan and the other boroughs were much more than the sum of their parts, and that between the image and the reality there was a subtle element missing: life and its sounds, smells and colours. And people. She expected New Orleans would prove to be a similar revelation.

Dominik had visited the Crescent City on many previous occasions, but it had been before the destruction Hurricane Katrina had unleashed on New Orleans and he held bittersweet memories of the place. As the cab crawled from intersection to intersection in the French Quarter, attempting to reach their boutique hotel in the pouring rain, the view outside the drawn windows of the vehicle appeared familiar, the lights, the wrought-iron balconies, the terraces hanging with magnolia flowers, the heady blend of music and laughter in the air.

It was only later when they had showered and changed and gone out to enjoy their first meal of the trip that small differences became apparent. Less people, like a film set cutting down on crowd extras, notices on many of the bar and restaurant windows and doors for new personnel, oyster chuckers, domestic help.

'It just doesn't feel like America at all,' Summer remarked, her eyes darting in every direction, trying to find her bearings.

'I know,' Dominik said. 'It's quite unique.'

'I never got the opportunity to visit Europe much – just a long weekend in Paris – but it's not quite European either, is it?' she queried.

She had slipped into a thin white full-length dress with capped sleeves, held in at the waist by a narrow red belt worn with low-heeled sandals. The rain had ceased, and the atmosphere felt close, a touch claustrophobic, pregnant with future storms.

'Just a blend of diverse influences,' Dominik confirmed. 'French, Spanish, Creole, colonial English. Many of the early settlers here were Acadians, all the way from Canada, refugees from religious intolerance. It's a curious historical melting pot.'

'I like it already,' Summer remarked.

'Pity the weather is so dull today. Not the perfect introduction to the city.'

'I don't mind.'

'According to the forecast, we should avoid further rain for the next handful of days,' he said.

'Good.' Dominik not having informed her of their destination, Summer was worried she hadn't brought a proper set of clothes.

'Remember the Oyster Bar under Grand Central?' he asked her, with a gentle smile spreading across his lips.

'Of course,' Summer said. 'You know how much I love oysters.'

'This is the right place for them. And crawfish. Shrimp. Gumbo. We'll have an ongoing feast.'

There was a lengthy queue outside the Acme Oyster House on the corner of Iberville and Bourbon, and both of them had skipped breakfast back in New York and turned down the airline food, so spurred on by their appetite, they moved ten minutes down the main road and found a window table at Desire, the oyster bar of the posh Sonesta Hotel.

The elderly waitress brought them their hot bread and butter while they ordered.

'You'll see,' Dominik said, 'they serve a sauce that is a blend of ketchup and horseradish with the raw oysters. Initially, I was wary of the prospective culinary delights of tomato ketchup, but the combination works wonders. If you want it even stronger, you can add a further dollop of horseradish. It's fierce but blends beautifully with the taste and consistency of the oyster meat. I also indulge in a squeeze of lemon and a sprinkle of pepper.' He demonstrated a moment later when the waitress brought a large platter over to their table. He brought the first enormous oyster to his mouth and swallowed it one gulp.

Having watched him closely, Summer followed his example.

Soon the platter was a thing of the past, a battlefield of empty shells dotted against a background of crushed ice.

She'd also added a few drops of powerful Tabasco to her final trio of oysters and her throat felt on fire as she greedily downed her glass of iced water to sooth the burn.

She looked up at Dominik, saw him wiping the corner of

his mouth with his napkin and devouring her with his eyes. She couldn't help suppressing a smile of her own.

'If I didn't know better, the way you look at me makes me think you want to eat me too, with the oysters just an hors d'oeuvre. I know they're supposed to be an aphrodisiac, but, remember, I'm already in your bed – there's no longer any need to lure me there,' Summer said in jest.

'And don't I know that,' Dominik said.

The following days were taken up by the obligatory tourist activities: taking the tram up to the Garden District and a visit to Audubon Park, a couple of riverboat cruises down the Mississippi to survey the swamps and the reluctant-to-show-themselves alligators, the pilgrimage to countless cemeteries and the scattered voodoo museums, coffee and beignets at the open-all-hours Café du Monde on Jackson Square in the middle of the night after leisurely hours of lovemaking in their hotel room, their tired limbs and souls in bad need of recharging, hunting down trinkets in the French Market and more food, glorious food, and aimless walks up and down Bourbon Street listening to the duelling sounds of music rushing from open bar to open bar, a crazy patchwork of jazz, rock, folk, zydeco, soul and every variation of melody.

On the corner of Royal, the shoe-shine kids tap-danced to their hearts' content, and at the intersection of Magazine and Toulouse, a blind musician played the accordion while a string-like hippie girl with a gallery of tattoos down both her arms accompanied him on the violin. She was not a patch on Summer, in talent or looks, but Summer insisted on leaving her an exaggerated tip, clearing Dominik of all the useless change in his pockets out of solidarity.

Dominik was visibly restless. He'd been here and done all this before. He could sense his unease growing, as could Summer.

There was a whole day to go before New Year's Eve. Dominik had managed to obtain a much-sought-after booking at Tujague's in the first-floor dining room with access to the balcony, a stone's throw from Jackson Square and the Jax Brewery, where the traditional glittering ball would rise all the way from street level to the roof at the stroke of midnight to bring in the new year. It was one of the hottest tickets in town, which the restaurant usually restricted to local regulars and Rotary Club eminences.

Summer walked out of the bathroom, where she had taken a shower, shrouded in a big, white fluffy towel that barely reached the top of her thighs and revealed a teasing glimpse of her cunt. Sitting reading in bed, Dominik's eyes moved up from his page and fixed on her. Summer looked down and realised how short the towel was. She made an effort to stretch the material but only managed to pull the thick white veil of the towel down and her breasts slipped out. Dominik smiled.

'Shy?' he remarked.

'A bit late for that, surely,' she said.

He kept on staring at her, deep in thought, inscrutably pensive.

Summer peered out of the window to check on the weather. The sky was grey, but she knew it would be warm enough to walk around with short sleeves, at least until evening.

'What do you want me to wear today?' she asked him.

His eyes lit up with undisguised mischief. 'Nothing.'

Summer dropped the towel altogether, allowing it to fall to the floor. 'Like this?'

'Perfect,' Dominik said. He pulled the bed covers from his body, revealing his already semi-hard cock, and began stroking himself.

Summer initiated a movement to approach the bed.

'No!'

'You don't want me to help,' she suggested.

'No. Just stand there. As you are.'

He widened the angle between his legs and kept on caressing his extended penis, the thick trunk gripped in his palm, a stray thumb gliding simultaneously across his purple glans. His balls appeared to grow in size as he played with himself, his eyes locked on her nudity. Summer recalled that first evening at his London house, how he had asked her to masturbate. She shivered.

His breath quickly grew halting.

Summer dropped a hand and brought it to her lower lips, but again he ordered her to remain still. He didn't want her to pleasure herself. She must watch him. In silence.

There was a moment, frozen in time, when the light from the window slat landed on the tip of his straining cock, like a line of fire bisecting the mushroom-shaped extremity, his balls full to bursting, and then the moment passed and Dominik came.

He let out a deep sigh.

'Come,' he said, nodding to Summer.

She unfroze.

'Lick me clean,' he said.

He tasted of oysters and horseradish and every sin under

the sun. She was desperately hungry again. Rang the toll for her waistline.

They left the House of Blues on Decatur just before midnight. The band had been good and Summer had imagined herself on stage with them, improvising around their riffs on her violin. It had been months since she'd played anything of a non-classical nature, something improvised, variations, natural. She missed that freedom now that she was part of an orchestra.

The crowds had spilled out across the pavement outside the venue. Out of the corner of her eye, she noticed Dominik in conversation with a bystander, a tall guy with a seersucker jacket and jeans full of strategically placed holes and black leather winkle-pickers. Surely he's not buying drugs, Summer thought. That wasn't Dominik's style.

The two men parted, but she couldn't help seeing them shake hands and a few green notes passing between them.

'Who was that?' she asked as Dominik walked over to join her.

'A local. I needed some information.'

She recognised that glint in his eyes. She'd witnessed it before.

They found a cab on Canal Street, and Dominik whispered the destination to the driver. Summer was feeling drowsy after the deceptively strong cocktails she'd sampled at the club while listening to the music. After a few blocks, she briefly closed her eyes, only to open them again and see they had crossed Bourbon Street well beyond the point they had often reached on previous evening strolls and were now entering a zone of relative darkness in comparison to the well-lit thoroughfares she had so far been accustomed to tramping through.

The cab finally came to a halt in front of an anonymous building with a steel gate. Dominik paid the driver, and as the car began to disappear in the distance, Summer felt the weight of the silence landing on her shoulders. This was all so unlike New Orleans. There was a dimly lit buzzer to the right of the door, which Dominik pressed. The electronic mechanism of the gate clicked and he pushed the door open.

They were now in a large courtyard, with a perimeter of smaller buildings surrounding it.

'Those were the slave quarters,' Dominik said, pointing at the outlying units. 'Many years ago, of course.' He took hold of Summer's hand and led her towards the central building, which loomed out of the darkness and was visibly much larger than the others, a three-storey structure with a wooden veranda, a set of white stairs leading to the porch. Slivers of light peered through the sides of some of the downstairs and first-floor windows.

They walked up the steps and the front door opened. A large, shaven-headed black man wearing an impeccable tuxedo simultaneously greeted them and checked them out. Having passed his scrutiny, they were ushered into the building. On a low-slung table by the stairs that led to the upper levels of the house was a tray with high-stemmed glasses. The imposing greeter poured them champagne and asked them to wait before disappearing through a side door.

'What is this place?' Summer asked, sipping her glass. It was good champagne. Dominik didn't partake.

'A strip club, actually, but a rather private one.'

'A strip club?'

'A very exclusive one,' Dominik added. 'There was a time when anything went in New Orleans, but over the years, things have become both commercialised and tamer. Strip joints on Bourbon Street used to be bottomless, but these days that's no longer the case. They only disrobe as far as G-strings and knickers. It's also become tawdry, exploitative. This place, I'm told, is the right thing.'

'Where anything goes?' Summer suggested, her flesh tingling with familiar desire.

'Exactly.'

'I've attended burlesque shows before,' Summer said, 'and enjoyed them. I just hope it's not too tacky,' she added.

'I've been told it's not,' Dominik said.

A woman approached. She wore a white carnival mask, and her hair was coal-black, falling to her shoulders like a cloak of silk. Her dress clung to her body, a long-sleeved red velvet gown of vintage provenance, which only bared her neck and a strikingly thin pair of ankles over perilous platform shoes.

'I'm your hostess for the evening. This way, please,' she said, and pointed to the stairs.

If there was one thing Dominik hated, it was vulgarity. He was hoping tonight would not prove an embarrassment.

The tables at which the guests had been seated formed a half-circle facing an improvised stage no larger than a boxing ring. There were fifty spectators at most, and Dominik noted that, apart from Summer and him, there were only three other couples in the audience. Each table kept to itself, barely glancing at the others present.

First, there was darkness, then a white spotlight shining like hellfire on the centre of the improvised stage, then for the space of an eye-blink total darkness again, immediately followed by the light flashing on once more and a young woman standing at the heart of the newly created sun, an apparition from nowhere.

She was majestically tall, her head a haloed jungle of yellow-blonde Medusa-like curls, her skin like alabaster. All she wore was an impossibly thin cotton robe that was almost transparent in the fierceness of the spotlight shining on her and that highlighted the doll-like fragility of her waist and the endless avenues of her long legs. She was barefoot.

At first, she was motionless, like a statue, while the spectators caught their breath.

Then there was a faint buzz as the sound system was switched on, with an indistinct blanket of static sound.

'My name is Luba,' they heard the whisper. A Russian accent, a bedroom voice. The sound system surrounded them and it felt to everyone present as if the pre-recorded voice was a personal gift, for their ears only. Dominik felt Summer's hand abandoning her glass and gripping his thigh under the tablecloth. The woman was stunning, as was the sheer theatricality of the event.

Then the music began.

Classical. An impressionistic cascade of soft, delicate notes that reminded Dominik of the sea, and the shimmering surface of troubled waters.

'Debussy,' Summer said quietly.

Luba came to life. An eye blinked; a shoulder moved imperceptibly; one foot lifted off the floor; a hand shifted, fingers unfurling like flowers blooming.

Luba danced with the grace of a trained ballerina and the calculated provocation of a whore, seemingly totally unaware of her audience, as if the art of undressing and teasing was something essentially private that she was doing just for herself, a personal journey to the heart of her pleasure.

'She's in the zone,' Summer whispered to Dominik, both of them entranced by the performer.

Quickly Luba slipped out of the flimsy garment she had been wearing. The fierceness of the spotlight in which she allowed herself to remain captive made her appear whiter than white, the sole touch of colour the delicate pink shade of the nipples of her firm, small breasts and the barely there demarcations of her smooth genitalia, her body pouring like milk through the tremulous melodies of the French composer. Dominik couldn't help noting the small tattoo she displayed barely an inch from her cunt, a small blue flower, or maybe it was a miniature image of an improbable gun, the image seemed to change with every movement of her body before he could focus fully on it. Why would she sport the tracing of a gun there, etched deep into her skin, where her flesh was at its most secret? he wondered.

He knew so little of the lives of others.

But thirsted for it.

What could Luba's story be?

Summer's fingers grazing against the hard knot now tenting his trousers snapped him back to reality. Even she was turned on by the performance.

The Russian dancer contorted into impossible positions with the elegance of a dove in flight, impervious to the amount of intimacy she displayed in the process with such liberal abandon, the puckered light brown circle of her arsehole, the nacreous pink of her inside depths when she was in a spread-eagled position or in athletic movement.

Her face remained ever impassive, majestic in her detachment, superior.

Dominik recognised the final chords of the Debussy piece nearing and sighed, regretful this performance could not go on for ever. Summer's fingers lingered and he could feel the beat of her heart through the heat of her fingertips. He leaned towards her, brought his lips to her ear.

'One day, maybe I'll ask you to go on a stage and display yourself in such a wanton and beautiful way, Summer. Would you like that?'

The heat visibly rose to her cheeks as words tried to pass her lips but were unable to do so; a rushing herd of emotions clearly bubbled inside her. That was answer enough for Dominik.

As the terminal strains of the music faded and Luba's movements slowed in unison, her back straightening, her legs coming together again, her arse cheeks tightening and firming up, out of the corner of his eye, Dominik noticed the hostess in the mask and the flaming velvet dress making her way back towards the stage and approaching the dancer just as Luba finally came to a standstill and reverted to a living statue.

The spotlight abruptly disappeared, plunging the small stage back into pitch darkness.

None of the other spectators at the other tables was showing any sign of moving. The performance maybe wasn't over.

The sound system came alive again. 'Show your appreciation for Luba,' a female voice said, breaking the spell, and the scattered spectators began to applaud the performance, slowly at first, then louder when a small silhouette tiptoed back onto the stage.

It was Luba. The dancer.

She was now draped in a leopard-print robe, the shape of her body obscured, and so much smaller than she had appeared in the dazzling glow of the central spotlight.

'She looks tiny now,' Summer remarked.

'How's your dancing?' Dominik asked her.

'Not a patch on hers,' Summer said.

'I'd like to see you dance.'

'I'm clumsy. I've no sense of rhythm, or grace.'

'I'm sure you'd be great. You're a musician. It's in your blood, no?'

'You'd be surprised.'

Dominik took a sip from his drink. The sounds of Ravel's trancelike 'Boléro' were being piped through the loud speakers as background music, muted, distant. He wondered whether there was to be another performer, or whether the enigmatic Luba would make a return appearance.

He looked Summer in the eyes and knew. Yes. That was it.

The familiar surge of power raced through his heart.

'It was actually quite beautiful,' Summer finally said. 'Not what I expected. I was afraid it might turn out to be somewhat sordid. Not at all.'

She picked up her champagne glass.

The hostess walked by their table. 'I hope you enjoyed the show?' she asked.

'Indeed,' Dominik blurted out. He was at a loss for words.

'We only employ out-of-town artists,' she said. 'Mostly Russians. They are so well bred. Lovely bone structure,' she added. 'Local girls don't have the same finesse. Luba, for instance, looks so at ease with her nakedness.'

'So is my companion here,' Dominik remarked, nodding towards Summer. 'Remarkably at ease.' It just came out, as if the devil made him say the words, cementing his earlier thoughts about Summer dancing.

'And quite beautiful too, I have no doubt,' said the older woman in the red dress, examining Summer with renewed interest.

He couldn't resist it. 'Do you agree to private hires?'

'It could be arranged,' the hostess said.

'Tomorrow maybe? After the New Year celebrations?'

Summer was shifting uncomfortably in her chair. Most of the other spectators were already drifting away.

'We have a dinner booked for the turn of the year, but could be here at one o'clock, say?' Dominik suggested.

'That would work well,' the woman said. 'How much of an audience would you require?' she asked Dominik.

'Like tonight. Not too large. Intimate. Discreet, of course.'

The hostess turned towards Summer. 'And you are willing to play, madam? You realise the choice is yours?'

Summer's knuckles were gripping the edge of the table. She averted her eyes from Dominik's. 'Yes,' she said, as firmly as she could.

'Just a dance or . . . more?' the older woman asked Dominik.

'What would . . . "more" consist of?' he queried.

'You are a man of imagination. I would leave that to your appreciation,' the woman said with a suggestive smile.

Dominik considered. 'I think just dancing,' he finally said with a sideways glance at Summer's pale features.

Summer held her breath.

'Our artists also perform privately,' she said. 'Might that be of interest?'

Summer's heart was now beating wildly, the initial fear subsiding and a new strain of nervousness invading her system.

'I think I would just like to see my companion dance,' Dominik concluded. 'On this stage,' he nodded.

'Good,' the woman said. 'Might we discuss particulars, then?'

She indicated to Dominik that they should walk a few steps away, out of Summer's hearing, to agree the finances.

The negotiation was a short one and Summer noticed Dominik handing over one of his credit cards and the hostess passing it through a small handheld terminal.

Once the transaction had been settled, the hostess in the red velvet dress walked with them down the stairs.

'We will supply Madam's outfit for the occasion,' she said. 'I'm confident we can present her with a varied choice of garments that will fit her most exquisitely. We shall have a full hour to spare until we present her to our public, so there will be an opportunity to adjust a stitch here or there if necessary.'

'Sounds perfect,' Dominik said.

She opened the door to let them out into the darkened stretch of Bourbon Street. It felt much colder now.

'Oh, sir?'

'Yes?'

'Any musical preference?'

Dominik caught the look in Summer's eye, a brightness that bore witness to anticipation and fear, as if she were begging him to say the right thing.

'Vivaldi's *Four Seasons*.'

'A good choice,' the hostess proclaimed. 'I look forward to tomorrow.'

At midnight, after the ball finished its ascent, the fireworks were set off from the barges at the centre of the Mississippi and Dominik and Summer watched from the shelter of Tujague's balcony as the crowds below roared drunkenly.

On the stroke of the hour, he took her in his arms and kissed her. Such a simple act, but it went straight to her heart.

If only things could be so simple, if only this was enough, Dominik thought.

For now, they had an assignment.

# 5
## *Dancing in the Dark*

I wanted to dance naked, but the mistress of the show would have none of it.

She was an imposing woman, still dressed in her red gown and beaked mask. The mask gave me the shivers. She looked like a plague doctor for the wealthy, plucked from the pages of history books, but I followed her anyway, into a dressing-room backstage, where all of the costumes were arranged.

The room was cavernous and painted a rich, dark red, womblike. High-ceilinged and expansive with evening gowns lining every wall in an array of coloured chiffons; there were silk and beaded robes with matching shoes, towering stilettos and elegant ballet pumps alongside dancers' props, feathered fans and even a large, gilded bird cage suspended from the ceiling. Inside the bird cage sat a woman dressed in white, like a dove, surveying the proceedings below with a curious stare.

I stared back at her.

'Pay no attention – she's rehearsing for tomorrow night's show,' said the masked woman impatiently. She cast out her hand, indicating the enormous choice of outfits available to me. 'You must wear something.'

'I prefer to dance naked.'

I wanted to enter the stage on my own terms, not

uncovering myself to satisfy a voyeuristic audience, particularly as I found it so difficult to slip out of a dress and kick it away gracefully. No, if I was going to have to dance naked, I wanted to begin naked, as if I was not removing anything for the sake of those who watched. Even Dominik.

We stood facing each other in a silent stand-off. I held what I thought to be her gaze, though it was difficult to tell in what direction she was looking beneath her mask.

'You will wear these,' she said eventually, ignoring my smile of satisfaction at having won the argument, and presented me with a wooden box lined with black velvet and filled with a variety of adornments: two clip-on nipple rings, matching attachments that fitted onto each of my outer labia and a small butt plug. Each carried a rust-red jewel, almost the same colour as my hair. She held one of the nipple rings up to the light and waved it back and forth, demonstrating the way that the stone glittered and shone.

I baulked at the butt plug, but she insisted. 'Your benefactor would prefer it.' Did that mean that Dominik had instructed her to suggest it to me, or was this her idea?

She fitted each of the decorations to my body, including inserting the plug with a touch more force than was strictly necessary, perhaps a punishment for my insolence in refusing to wear one of her costumes.

If the woman in the cage had watched our exchange, she said nothing, but I was acutely aware of her looking down from above.

The rings ached a little, particularly the nipple clamps, but it was that amount of pain that was just on the right side of pleasure.

I followed the woman through another corridor, which led to a velvet curtain, the opening that would take me to the stage. I held my breath, hoping that if I stood still for long enough, perhaps the whole thing would be forgotten or Dominik would change his mind. I still hadn't planned what I would do once the music started.

The stage mistress laid her hand on my back and pushed me through the curtain.

At first, there was nothing but darkness.

Then a spotlight burst out of nowhere, one bright bolt illuminating my body like the fierce beam from an artificial sun.

The glare was blinding.

I searched for Dominik at our table on the right, but I could see nothing other than the stage light reflecting back into my eyes.

Then the music began.

I lifted my arms immediately, out of instinct, as if to hold a bow and violin.

Then I stood still. I am a musician, not a dancer. Nevertheless, I was rooted to the spot, trapped within the confines of Dominik's instruction, as though he had attached to me the invisible threads of a puppet master. As I thought of him, the threads began to move. First one arm and then the other. I began to sway, to dance, quicker to the rhythm of 'Spring', slower to the beat of 'Autumn'.

It was over before I had begun to lose my breath, and the stage was once more returned to darkness. A cool hand grasped mine and led me away into the dressing room.

'You were very good,' said the still-beaked stage mistress.

I was sorry to see the jewellery go and resolved to buy myself some nipple clamps at the next opportunity. They would be easier to wear under my clothes than a corset, and certainly much less work to put on in the morning.

Dominik's face was slightly flushed when I returned to our table. His greeny brown eyes were glowing as bright as the stage light.

I thought that he might take me in the back of the car on the way to the hotel, under the scrutiny of the driver in the rear-view mirror, but Dominik was a strangely private individual, despite his desire to display me publically. He preferred to have me on his own terms, and that didn't include humping in the back seat of a taxi crawling slowly through the crowd of revellers still bringing in the New Year through the Vieux Carré.

Dominik stared out of the window on his side, drinking up the last of New Orleans, craning his neck to see the final bursts of fireworks erupting outside, fountains of colour lighting up the sky. I took the opportunity to flick through the text messages on my phone, the usual New Year greetings from faraway friends to whom I hadn't spoken for months. One of my best friends in New Zealand was born on New Year's Eve, and for the better part of a decade, before I moved overseas, I had spent every 31 December with her, usually indoors at house parties, drunk on cheap fizzy plonk purchased underage, then in later years moving on to more expensive liqueurs and cocktails of every persuasion once we left school and began working. I had forgotten to send her a birthday message this year, for the first time since we met, and was filled with guilt. I had been avoiding all of my friends from home, worried that they would find me changed, and might not like or approve of the new Summer.

Simón had sent me a message. 'Happy New Year! I hope 2013 brings you everything you ever wanted.'

If only I knew what I wanted.

Dominik leaned over and rested his hand gently on my knee. I flicked my phone off and returned it to my purse. I would reply in the morning.

'You were perfect,' he said, when we got in the door. 'My own bejewelled whore. How did it feel?'

'Strange. As if you and I were the only people in the room, but I couldn't see you. I couldn't see anyone through the light.'

He reached his arm round me, snaked his hand under my dress and ran his finger down the cleft in my arse.

'I couldn't help but notice that anal plug. That was additional to my instructions. Your choice, or the woman's?'

'It was hers.'

'Did you enjoy it?'

'Yes. I was worried that it might fall out, but there was no chance of that.'

'Perhaps I will get you one and make you wear it to your rehearsals.'

'I might have trouble concentrating.'

'You would manage, I have no doubt of that. It would make you think of me while I'm away, wouldn't it?'

Dominik swooped down and lifted me into his arms, carried me to the bedroom and then unceremoniously dumped me on the bed, face down. The bedroom smelled intensely of sex, though the cleaner had come during the day and changed the sheets. Our perpetual lovemaking had flavoured the air, leaving it sticky and sweet, like the humid energy of a hot day just before rain falls.

He pulled the bottom half of my dress up to my waist and stood between my legs, pushed my thighs apart, then dropped to his knees, separated my arse cheeks with his hands and ran his tongue along my crack and around my perineum. His breath was hot, his tongue unyielding. I wriggled, a minor protest at this intimate exploration, but he placed his hand on my lower back and held me down firmly, continuing his licking.

His finger followed, and then another, stretching my arsehole further than the small butt plug that the stage mistress had inserted. Tonight, he was cruel and silent, his soundlessness the result of intense concentration. My face was buried in the blankets, but I could imagine that Dominik was looking down on me from above, probing my pleasure points with what seemed to be curious detachment. He didn't use any lube, besides the wetness of his tongue, which had now moved lower and lapped at my pussy, sending waves of pleasure through my body. As my breathing grew deeper and less even, he withdrew his fingers, gripped my hips and pulled me back against him, burying his cock inside me and collapsing onto my back with a moan without waiting for me to climax.

This was the Dominik I liked best, hard, rough, thoughtfulness overtaken by lust.

We celebrated our last night in New Orleans together with more oysters. I had eaten enough oysters to last me at least until the next time I saw him, but I didn't think that any amount of sex that we could fit in between our last dinner and our check-out would fill the gap of his upcoming absence.

He'd fucked me raw, and me him, but that didn't stop Dominik from entering me one last time before we left. He put his palm on the hotel-room door just as I opened it and slammed it closed again, then held my wrists over my head with one hand, pulled my knickers down with the other and filled me again from behind.

My pussy throbbed for the duration of the flight, a vivid physical reminder of Dominik, disrupting my flirting with the good-looking man in the seat next to me.

We had parted at the airport, as he was on another flight back to London, via Chicago, taking advantage of an extra night in New Orleans rather than returning with me to New York and travelling home from there.

Then we would wait to hear the result of his fellowship application.

The thought of having Dominik permanently in New York filled me half with pleasure, half with worry. I had grown so used to my independence and enjoyed having all the time in the world to rehearse, to meet new people, to spend my days doing whatever I liked, beholden to no one.

Marija pounced on me the moment I got in the door, eager to hear every detail of our few days together. She was very blunt, though considering that she made no effort whatsoever to keep a lid on the sounds of her nightly lovemaking with Baldo, I suppose I shouldn't have been surprised.

'So the sex, is he good?'

'Marija!' protested Baldo from the couch, where he was stretched out lazily, wearing just a tight pair of briefs, his feet resting on the arm of the sofa. He was so hairy, he could have been mistaken for a blanket, which explained why he was so scantily clad in New York in January.

'He's very good.'

'Does he have a big one?' She held her hand against her

crotch and mimed what appeared to be the trunk of an elephant.

I held my hands two feet apart in response.

Baldo jumped up from the couch in a huff and stalked into their bedroom, slamming the door behind him as he left.

He opened it again and called out to Marija, 'Come in here and join me when you've stopped gossiping like a pair of old parrots.'

She winked at me and sashayed across the living room to join him.

The headboard was banging ten minutes later.

I disappeared into my own room and fell into bed the moment that I set down my case. Sleep came as soon as I closed my eyes, as if the cloak of exhaustion that I had been carrying had finally found the opportunity to wrap itself round me, now that I was alone.

In my dreams, I saw myself dancing, hanging suspended from the ceiling in a golden cage. Dominik watched from below, only it wasn't the Dominik, I knew; it was another man wearing a beaked mask.

I woke feeling as though I hadn't slept at all.

Rehearsals began again in a few hours. With the schedule that Simón had set out for us, I would have little chance of a break for the foreseeable future.

At least, thank heaven for small mercies, we had got through all the cheesy Christmas music. I had thought that if I had to play one more hymn, I would throw my violin through a window. For the remainder of January, Simón had us playing a series of Latin American composers; tonight we were working on Villa-Lobos. I always enjoyed the exposure to something new, and the Villa-Lobos had a folk feel to it; if the cello got a bit more air time than the violin section, that was OK with me. Simón seemed to have singled me out for extra attention, which was not always a good thing. He noticed and addressed every flaw in my performances.

That night, I was still tired from the flight and had a touch of the post-holiday blues. Dominik had worn me out, and though I smiled with the discovery of every new ache, it didn't make getting through rehearsals any easier.

Simón approached as I was packing away my Bailly. His body relaxed as soon as the music ended, losing the hard edge he always had when he was behind the rostrum. I wondered how much of his authority was just a show to keep the orchestra in line and how much of it was truly him.

'You have a bit of a tan, Summer – unusual for a winter in New York. Did you manage to get away?'

'A few days in New Orleans . . . I must have been in the sun a bit too long on the riverboat . . . *The Creole Queen*.'

'Did you go with anyone special?'

'A friend. From London.'

'Good. You'll be glad of the rest. We have a busy couple of months.'

'No more holidays planned for a while, then.'

'Oh, it's not so bad, is it? I wouldn't want to wear you out.'

The rehearsal space had emptied, the rest of the orchestra dissolved into the bowels of the night to take advantage of whatever was left of the evening. Even Baldo and Marija had grown accustomed to the extra time we spent chatting at the end of rehearsals and had left us to it.

Simón had moved closer to me, close enough to kiss.

The smell of his cologne drifted around him like a cloud, a combination of musk and spices, so different from Dominik's plain, soapy scent. I had never seen Dominik apply any aftershave.

His hair was electric, even thicker than my own. It framed his face like a dark halo. For a moment, I thought that if we were to have children, they would surely have hair like poodles, but it was a ridiculous thought. I didn't even want to have children.

I moved my violin so that it covered the front of my body, blocking Simón's path if he had planned to make a move, and shifted forward, toward the exit. He picked up his own bag and walked with me to the door.

The blast of cold air outside burned the back of my throat. I rifled through my bag for my mittens.

'Damn, no gloves,' I sighed. The rehearsal space was only a couple of blocks from my apartment. I would be there by the time that I managed to flag a taxi down.

Simón unwrapped his scarf from his neck, took my hands in his and wound the length of fabric round my wrists. It was still warm from the heat of his body.

'Oh, no,' I protested, 'you'll be frozen.'

'I insist,' he said, giving my hands a squeeze through the wool. 'Your hands are much more important than mine.'

'Thank you,' I replied, in the politest, most professional tone that I could muster.

I took a small step backwards, increasing the space between us, and nodded a goodbye.

'See you tomorrow,' he said, turning on the point of his snakeskin boots with the finesse of a dancer and disappearing into the night.

I pressed my hands, still wrapped tightly in his scarf,

against my face to keep warm. His scent followed me all the way home, and, try as I might to forget it, I couldn't help but wonder what his bare skin would smell like. Perhaps it wasn't cologne; maybe Simón, naked, smelled of spices, cinnamon and nutmeg mixed with sweat.

That night, I dreamed of two men. Each time I conjured up Dominik, the sound of his voice, the complexity of his desires, the image in my mind would blur into Simón, the way I imagined his thick hair would feel in my fingers, the warmth of his hands, the rich caramel colour of his skin, so different from Dominik's pale English body. I wondered if he was hairy, like Baldo. I always liked hair on a man, associated it with heat and testosterone, manliness. Dominik had just a soft line of fuzz on his chest, fading to nothing on his stomach and then beginning again at his groin, like a dark arrow leading the way to his cock.

In the end, I gave up trying to separate them and imagined having them both at once, Dominik in my mouth, holding my face against his cock, Simón in my cunt.

Somehow, though, I didn't think that either of them was really the sharing type.

I had given up on any hope of advice on the subject from Marija. She hadn't met Dominik, but mistrusted him nonetheless. Her favour was firmly in Simón's court and she forever nagged me to flirt with him more.

'You're crazy, girl. You could have the world at your feet with that man. Or the Lincoln Center, at least. And what does the English one do for you, eh?'

She had taken up Baldo's habit of wearing just her underwear around the house, with the heating turned up full throttle. She always wore matching cotton sets, in bright colours that covered every shade in the rainbow. No lace or satin for Marija. Thankfully, my share of the rent included bills, so they were picking up the tab for the extra heating. She had the long, thin legs of a wading bird, her thighs about the thickness of my upper arms, I reckoned, though she ate like a horse. Baldo was forever on a diet, but his thick body resolutely maintained its stoutness. 'My chunky monkey,' Marija would call him, chuckling when he scowled at her.

'It's not about what either of them do for me,' I sighed.

'Don't be silly. Of course it is. At least, if you're going to be a fool and date the Englishman, keep it quiet. The conductor will stop giving you favours if he loses all hope of getting into your pants.'

'And here I was thinking that she was with me for love,' Baldo piped up.

'I'm just with you for your body,' she replied, draping her arms over him and nuzzling her face into his neck.

I took my bag and hurried through the door, eager to escape before their display of affection grew more amorous.

I had a date with Cherry tonight. She was performing a burlesque act at a bar in Alphabet City as part of a cabaret. It was a good gig, and she was one of the headliners. The show started at eight and she wasn't on until eleven, so we had a few hours to sit together and chat.

She was already inside when I arrived. Even under the club's low lighting, her bright-pink hair shone like a beacon. She spotted me coming in the door, waved me over to the table and handed me a cosmopolitan.

'I haven't had one of these for years,' I said.

'Not since *Sex and the City* was on the TV?'

'Yeah, something like that,' I laughed.

'You need to catch up. This is my second. The trick with performing, you see, is to find that fine line between drunk and too drunk, then ride it all the way home.'

'Doesn't seem to work that way in an orchestra,' I mused. 'One beer and the conductor would throw me out the door.'

'You should play rock music instead.'

'Too late for that now, I think. Vivaldi pays the bills.'

'How was New Year in New Orleans? Your man came over to visit?'

'It was great. I need a holiday to recover, though. He wore me out.'

'You should consider yourself lucky. Both of my boyfriends are away at the moment, working.'

'Hang on. "Both" of your boyfriends?'

Cherry grinned from ear to ear. 'Yup. I'm a lucky girl, huh? I have two.'

'And they know about each other?'

'Sure do. Pete has another girlfriend. He's away visiting her at the moment. Tony is touring with his band. He just sees me, but he does get quite a bit of interest from his groupies. He's a busy boy.'

I stared at her. 'Don't you get jealous?'

She sighed. 'That's the first thing everybody says.'

'Well, it's a reasonable question. Don't you?'

'Occasionally. I think everybody does. But I've been seeing Pete for five years. We make it work. Tony is sort of like my bit on the side. I don't think I could cope with just having one guy. I get bored.'

'Whose idea was it? Yours or his?'

'Mine, I suppose. We started by going to a few swingers' clubs, just as a way to spice things up. It grew from there.

How about you? What's your story? Are you serious with this English guy?' She held her drink up to the light. 'They never put enough Cointreau in these things. Remind me to tell the bartender.'

Her fake eyelashes glittered in the reflection from the glass. The end of each lash was decorated with a tiny crystal, like the legs of a spider that's just run through snow.

'Well, we sort of see other people.'

'What do you mean, sort of? You either do or you don't. Any kind of "sort of" is dangerous territory. Have you actually talked about it? Worked out what's OK and what isn't?'

'It's complicated.'

'Now, that's where you're going wrong. It's not complicated. It's very simple. Or at least it ought to be.'

'He might be moving over here soon. He's applied for a job in New York.'

'Well, you had better work it out in a hurry, then.' She drained her glass. 'One more?' She checked her watch. It was as big as a golf ball resting on her wrist, a diamanté-encrusted orb, like a disco ball, that flipped open with a digital display inside.

'Why not. Still got a couple of hours.'

I slipped off my stool and lined up at the bar. The lights dimmed as the first act appeared on stage to the tune of Shirley Bassey's 'Goldfinger'. The dancer was tall, slim and clad in a 1950s-style high-waisted leopard-print bikini, with astronomically high matching heels. She was mixed-race, with bronze skin and thick, dark hair teased into an afro. She sang as well as danced her routine, and she owned the stage with the confidence of a young lion that's just knocked out 170 pounds of gazelle for dinner.

'Thanks,' said Cherry, as I handed her a cosmopolitan, heavy on the Cointreau. 'You'd never know she was a man, would you?' she whispered to me, nodding her head toward the stage.

I took another look at the dancer. Yes, she had a distinctive bulge tucked tightly between her legs, but her movements were exquisitely feminine, with a definite hint of the feline. Even in a relaxed pose she looked as though she was ready to pounce on something. Me, I hoped, though that seemed unlikely.

The next act was dull in comparison, a fairly pretty girl doing a strip routine dressed as a man. She didn't quite have the bravado for it and tripped awkwardly over the costume that she was carrying as she left the stage. I felt a little sorry for her.

'Right. That's me. After the next turn, I better go and put my gear on.'

Cherry disappeared through a door to the side of the stage. She was carrying a bag so large she looked as though she might live in it, like a tortoise carrying its shell around.

I barely recognised her when she appeared on stage, following one further strip act, though this time a man dressed as a bear dressed as a man, who stripped down to his bear suit in an act that managed to be absurd and comic in all the right places.

Cherry was dressed entirely in pink, in a floor-length satin gown with a chiffon fishtail, and was carrying a pair of enormous pink feathered fans, each of them almost bigger than she was. She wore towering stiletto heels, bigger than any I had seen before, also bright pink, and covered with tiny crystals that glimmered with each step she took. Besides her stiletto-clad feet, her body was entirely hidden from view by the fans.

I had expected her act to be much like the previous one, another femme fatale slow-stripping song in the background as she elegantly danced down to her smalls, but Cherry's routine was much racier, and performed to the tune of Rick James's 'Super Freak'.

The audience applauded wildly as she shimmied out of her gown and swung her heavy breasts so the nipple tassles went round and round like windmills. She finished the act on her back on the floor, with her legs over her head, demonstrating that she could lick herself out if she chose to.

'Wow,' I said to her, when she returned to her seat. 'That was pretty impressive. I can see why you have two boyfriends.'

She giggled. 'You should come over sometime. I'll show you some moves.'

Her lips were still coated with vivid pink lipstick, which she had enhanced further by adding a layer of glitter and a coat of gloss.

I walked her to the subway. 'Oh, I nearly forgot,' she said, rummaging around in her enormous handbag for an age. 'I got you something.'

'It's not my birthday.'

She pulled out a length of rope, about four feet long, and handed it to me. 'So you can practise. Just make sure that if you tie yourself to a table leg, you either have a pair of scissors handy or you leave the knots loose enough so that you can get out in a hurry if the house catches on fire. Now, that would be embarrassing to explain to emergency services.'

'Thanks,' I replied, stuffing the rope into my purse, 'but you know I'm not really the tying type. I prefer to be on the receiving end.'

'You should learn how to do it anyway. Then you'll appreciate how much work it is for the person who ties you up.'

When I arrived home and glanced in the mirror, I noticed that I had a line of glitter smeared across one of my cheeks, though I didn't recollect kissing her goodnight.

The rest of the week rushed past in a blur. My days had been reduced to rehearsing, eating and sleeping, and that was basically it. I hadn't heard a peep from Dominik yet.

'You look tired,' Simón said to me when I returned his scarf.

'Thanks,' I replied bitterly.

'You should relax more. When I first started here, you played with your whole body. Now you play with your mind. You need to let go again. When was the last time that you left the house, other than to rehearse?'

'Last week. I went to a burlesque show.'

'It's not enough. You can't play with the world in your music if you don't get out and see the world.'

I was too exhausted to argue. I just nodded my head in agreement and picked up my case to leave.

'I have two tickets to the bull-riding at Madison Square Garden on Friday. Want to come? I was supposed to be taking my dad, but he's had to delay his visit, so I have one going spare.'

'Bull-riding?' That wasn't what I expected.

'Don't look like that. It's bull-riding, not bull-fighting. It's not quite how we do it in Venezuela, but as close as you'll get in Manhattan. It starts at four. I'll take you to dinner afterwards, as a reward for sitting through two hours of sport.'

I laughed. 'OK, then. It sounds like fun.'

Marija and Baldo were nestled up on the couch together when I got home, watching old horror films. Marija had her hand over her eyes, opening her fingers every few seconds to peek at the screen and then shriek. Baldo had one arm draped over her, and with the other, he was dipping rice crackers into low-fat cottage cheese and grimacing after every mouthful.

'Have you guys ever heard of bull-riding in Manhattan?'

'You've got tickets for Friday?' Baldo said. 'Lucky you – it's been sold out for months.'

'Ah,' said Marija, taking her hand away from her face. 'A date with Simón?'

'It's not a date.'

'Whatever,' she replied, staring back at the screen and huddling into Baldo as a woman on the television emitted a piercing scream.

Friday rolled around so quickly that I barely had time to get nervous about the prospect of spending a full afternoon and evening with Simón. Every time I looked at him now, I worried that he could somehow pick the thoughts out of my brain and know that, just days before, I had masturbated breathing in the scent of his scarf.

I'd only ever once been on a sporting date before, with a boyfriend in New Zealand, to watch the Kiwis play Samoa in the Rugby Sevens at the Westpac Stadium in Wellington. The game was fast-moving, and I'd been surprised by how much I enjoyed it considering that I don't watch any sport at all, though I had spent most of the match fantasising about being let loose on the players in the locker room afterwards. They were insanely thick-limbed, with bodies like gods and shorts so short I was surprised that someone hadn't complained the game wasn't suitable for younger viewers. We'd had sex after the game and I had closed my eyes and dreamed that I was being taken by first one muscled player and then another – men from both teams, though if I'd been pressed to make a choice between the two, I would have taken the Samoan side. They were better-looking.

Deciding what to wear for these sorts of dates was always impossible. I'd look a fool if I wore high heels to a sports match, but if I was too casual, then I'd feel underdressed at dinner. I opted for a rust-red woollen shift dress, worn with hold-ups, flat lace-up leather boots and my faux-snakeskin handbag.

Simón had come as a proper cowboy, in a white shirt and jeans, with a brown leather stetson perched on top of his curly hair. He wore a black belt with a large silver buckle in the shape of a skull, and a pair of deep-maroon boots with pointed toes and a skull motif on each ankle, as if he had tried to match the flamboyancy of his hair with that of his feet. On anyone else the outfit might have been ridiculous, but Simón was the sort of man who dressed with such aplomb you would never question his taste.

He took my hand and led me through the stadium, down the steps to seats just a few rows back from the front, where we would have a perfect view of the action. Half of the crowd at least were wearing cowboy hats; most of the women were in blue and red checked shirts and jeans. I was the only person that I had seen so far wearing a dress. It was warm inside, with the heat of the crowd, bright lights and the excitement of a show about to start. I could smell the dirt floor where the riders and bulls would soon be bucking in front of us; it had a dusty, coppery scent that reminded me of Northern Australia, where I had worked briefly before moving to the UK.

'You'll have to tell me the rules,' I said. 'I really don't know anything about bull-riding.'

'Forget the rules, just watch. Each ride won't take more than eight seconds, and that's if the rider is good, so there's not much time to explain.'

Simón was right: some of the riders were only on the backs of the bulls for three or four seconds. I imagined, though, that on the back of an animal like that, a few seconds would last a lifetime. The bull never had all four feet on the ground at once, and one bull jumped about four feet into the air, carrying his rider with him, before hitting the ground again and not even pausing for a moment before continuing to buck. They behaved as though the ground were electric, snorting and leaping and heaving like 1,800 pounds of beef on Ritalin.

The riders weren't what I expected. Most of them were short, with bodies like gymnasts. They responded to each move of the bull with an equal and opposite reaction, moving back or forward, left or right with perfect speed and precision, more like a wind-up toy than a man. Several times the rider was thrown and pulled out of reach of the bull's stomping hooves in the nick of time, a hair's breadth from being trampled to death.

Simón watched with shining eyes, hollering and jumping to his feet when a rider managed to hold his ground for more than a few seconds.

'Imagine having an animal like that between your legs,' he sighed.

'Mmm,' I replied, sucking up the last of my Coke through a straw.

'In Venezuela, the riders chase the bulls on horseback and race to be the first to take the animal down by pulling its tail. We call it coleo.'

'That sounds easier than this.'

'That's a very dangerous thing to say to a Venezuelan!'

'I don't mind a little danger, else I wouldn't be here.'

'I guessed that about you. It's not every girl that you can invite to a bull-riding show.' He bent his head towards me as he spoke.

I put my mouth back to the straw.

'Mind if I have a drink?' he said.

'Sorry . . . I've finished it.'

'Never mind. The show is almost over. We can get another drink somewhere else.'

We went to Caracas Arepa Bar on 7th Street in the East Village. It was still fairly early, but the queue to get in snaked out through the door.

'It's worth it, I promise.'

'Don't worry. I can be very patient when the need calls for it.'

'I'm sure you can. You know, I've been thinking . . .'

'A dangerous habit.'

'I know I've been a bit of a slave driver lately, but I think you should go for that solo gig. You're good enough. I can speak to some promoters. I think we can fill a house.'

'I thought you said that I was playing with my mind.'

'Don't be like that. There's always room for improvement. What do you say? I know the rehearsal space you're using is a bit of a hole. You can use my basement. It's sound-proofed. I had the place renovated when I moved in, so it's very comfortable. I can give you some extra lessons.'

'That's very good of you, but . . .'

'No buts. You're talented. Trust yourself. This could be your big break, you know. I'll make sure a few agents get on the guest list.'

'OK.'

'OK?'

'Yeah. OK.'

He threw his arms round me and lifted me straight off my feet, planting a wet kiss on each of my cheeks. His stetson fell to the ground.

'Probably best I take that off now, anyway,' he said, smiling as he bent down to fetch it.

We squeezed onto the end of a table with four others. They were halfway through their meals, and if the expressions on their faces was anything to go by, then the food must be divine.

'Guacamole and chips to start,' said Simón, 'and margaritas – we're celebrating.'

'Please feel free to order the rest,' I said. 'I haven't a clue what any of these things are, and I trust you.'

'You might regret that.'

'I doubt it.'

We ate until I felt as though I would need to be rolled home.

'Did you order everything that was on the menu?' I asked, eyeing the last of the tajadas, fried sweet plantains with salty cheese, and patting my stomach regretfully. No doubt about it, dating is not good for the waistline.

'Not quite,' he laughed.

He walked me back to my apartment. We'd both downed four or five margaritas and were unmistakeably tipsy. I was, truthfully, closer to drunk. It made a nice change not being the only one drinking.

I fumbled in my handbag for the keys to the apartment, leaning against the wall for support.

'I can't be locked out,' I said. 'The front door locks from the outside.'

'May I?' he said. 'I think I'm more sober than you.'

I held the bag open as he tentatively snaked a hand inside.

'Do you actually need to carry around this much stuff?' he asked.

'You never know when you might need a spare pair of shoes.'

He pulled out the length of rope that Cherry had given me after her show. It had been buried at the bottom of my bag ever since.

'Were you planning to kidnap me?' he said, dangling the rope in front of my face.

'I'm a girl scout,' I replied blithely.

'You're certainly full of surprises.' He slung the rope loosely round my waist and, holding each end, pulled me against him. 'Now I've got you trapped,' he said.

Then he kissed me.

His kiss was warm, rougher than Dominik's kisses, probably because he was drunk. He tasted of tequila, and when I breathed in, all I could smell was the lingering spice of the perfume that he wore, like the smell of a kitchen after baking a batch of gingerbread biscuits.

He dropped the rope and buried his hands in my hair, holding my head tightly.

I held my breath, hoping that he would pull my hair the way that Dominik did and kiss me again. I was beginning to feel a familiar warmth running through my body and was tempted for a moment to invite him inside.

Instead he broke away, holding his hands against his sides stiffly.

'I'm sorry – I shouldn't have.'

'It's OK. We have to work together.'

'I know. It's a bad idea.'

'Definitely a bad idea.'

I picked up the rope and returned it to my bag. My keys were gleaming in the side pocket, exactly where I always left them.

'I'm sure I saw you put your hand in that bit,' I said accusatorily.

'I did. I was just trying to stall you.'

'Thank you for dinner and the bull-riding.'

'Thank you for joining me.'

He was back to his usual persona, friendly, professional, flirting but as if he didn't really mean it. Though, if his kiss was anything to go by, he really had meant it after all.

'I'm going inside now.'

'And I should be getting my beauty sleep. Rehearsals tomorrow. And we can start planning your solo show.'

'Goodnight.'

'Goodnight.'

I left him standing on the doorstep and shut the door.

I still hadn't heard from Dominik, but I could feel the weight of his disapproval from across the ocean.

# 6

## *An Island on Spring Street*

The formal offer of the fellowship arrived through Dominik's letterbox a fortnight after his return from New York. Having been given the initial impression the answer would reach him earlier, he had spent an awkward week moving between anticipation and a curious form of mild depression, waiting for the trustees' decision.

It was, as he had fervently hoped, a positive response and he had been granted the fellowship and attendant stipend, and was expected to begin his period in Manhattan after the Easter break. He was being supplied with a small office within the New York Public Library precinct and electronic and physical access to all its materials, against which he would be required to give a monthly talk of no more than an hour on a subject of his choice. How long he spent on actual research in the imposing building on Fifth and 42nd with the stone lions was up to his discretion.

Dominik now had under three months to make all the necessary arrangements: organise for his sabbatical from the London job, assist in finding someone to stand in for him in his absence and, most importantly, find accommodation in New York, as the library was unable to assist in the matter.

He rang Summer.

'It's finally come through. I have the fellowship.'

'That's great. Really wonderful.'

'I will arrive straight after Easter.'

'Oh . . .'

'What is it?'

'I'll be in full rehearsals for the solo gig.'

'No problem. I'll find somewhere, a place, where you can play the Bailly at all hours of day and night, without fear of disturbing neighbours.'

'That would be so nice,' Summer remarked. 'Until then, I'm mostly restricted to a small room in the bowels of the Symphonia's locale. Not a very inspirational bolthole. Plus it has to be booked days in advance, as so many of the other musicians require extra rehearsal time. Simón has offered me the use of his apartment on the Upper West Side, but I'd feel uncomfortable taking advantage of him.'

'You're right.'

'Anyway, I like to be alone when I'm preparing,' Summer added.

'What about me? No more private recitals?'

'Ah, that's another matter altogether,' she said.

Finding rentals in Manhattan, even with the most generous of budgets, is always an uphill task, particularly at a distance. Online searches were an initial waste of time, so Dominik finally went through a local property broker and found a loft space in SoHo on the fifth floor of a building on Spring Street near the corner of West Broadway.

Summer surveyed the place for him and declared it absolutely perfect. It was vast, she reported, fabulously lit, and the acoustics were incredible. Although it was furnished in a particularly minimalistic style, she was confident that Dominik's books, and the way he so quickly accumulated them, would soon provide the loft with some extra warmth and personality.

The rental contract was for a whole twelve-month period and it was arranged for Summer to move in a full month ahead of Dominik's arrival in New York, to take advantage of the place. She was initially reluctant to abandon her Croatian friends, but soon began to look forward to escaping their joyful rutting sounds and its insistent distraction at night.

She would describe their exploits to Dominik when she spoke to him on the phone; hearing about the adventures of the lusty Croatians always made him laugh heartily. Later, a pensive Summer invariably reflected that she had seldom seen Dominik laugh in the flesh. She wondered why.

Dominik had only seen photos of the loft, so Summer, once she had moved in, described the space to him.

'Apart from the bedroom, which has been partitioned off on one side, it's all one large area, with shiny wooden floors. It feels like a ballroom.'

'Really?'

'The kitchen is so hi-tech. I've never had a kitchen like that, with granite worktops and all the latest gizmos. Space-age stuff! Not sure if I'll manage omelettes and beans on toast there, though – it would feel like an insult to cooking technology.'

'We can eat out,' Dominik said.

'No,' Summer said. 'I want to cook for you. I've so seldom done that for a man, a lover.'

'Good. So no more corsets or vintage violins now, I see. I'll have to get you cookery books full of abstruse recipes, no?'

Summer chortled. 'There are huge bay windows. So much light. But no view: it just looks out on the vast grey façade of the building opposite. No windows there whatsoever, pipes and metal grilles. A bit ugly. As a result, though, it's deathly silent at night, even though there are so many restaurants on the street outside open late. Eerily peaceful.'

'And private?'

'Totally,' she confirmed.

'Wonderful. I'll want you to rehearse naked, of course, when I'm around.'

'I was beginning to think that was the only reason you chose the place.'

'Exactly,' Dominik confirmed.

Unbidden and without his knowledge, Summer had already quickly grown into the habit of wandering the loft in the nude, whether playing the Bailly or just hanging out. It felt right, on the edge of arousal, natural, the loft a new garden of paradise, a playground of innocence.

She liked the space's bare atmosphere, its minimal lines and white walls, and the naked brickwork peering out artistically between the steel ceiling beams and at regular intervals like splashes of dark paint in the landscape of the immense walls.

Summer bought a few orchids, which she scattered around to bring a shy touch of colour to the loft. She hesitated about whether she should bring one of the tropical plants into the bedroom. She was unsure how Dominik felt about flowers. She still had so much to learn about him.

What would living together be like?

By arranging to come to New York, Dominik had confronted her with a brand-new situation altogether. It had been a major decision to live with him, although Summer couldn't quite remember actually consenting. It had sort of happened, out of sheer inertia, as if her body had made the decision without consulting her brain.

It had been ages since she had lived with a lover. She had for years shared apartments on her travels: Australia, London, New York . . .

Would it work?

Could it work?

'It'll be nice to have you here,' she said.

'I'm looking forward to it,' Dominik responded.

A thought occurred to her. 'Are you shipping some of your books out, for your research?' she said. 'Maybe I should get some shelves, at Ikea or somewhere. I'm happy to look for some.'

'No need,' Dominik said. 'There will be everything I need at the Public Library. More than I require.'

'OK.'

'Just a month to go,' Dominik said.

'Yes.'

'One thing, though . . . You know our understanding. If you feel you have to go with someone during these coming weeks . . .'

'Yes?' She skipped a heartbeat.

'Go to theirs or elsewhere, not the loft.'

'I understand.'

She was unsure whether it was an instruction or encouragement.

The best intentions are often confounded by coincidence. The woman in the window seat on his left on the flight from London to New York was reading *The Great Gatsby*, which gave Dominik the perfect opening for a conversation. It was a book he could almost recite unaided from memory end to end, having pored over it for so long on many occasions. Her name was Miranda.

Would the conversation have quickly become so flirtatious had it been another book, or had Summer's amusing tale about her one-night stand in Manhattan not lingered in his brain, festering quietly for a few weeks now?

Dominik knew he was not a jealous man. He was a realist.

This was the reason he had made the terms of their current relationship perfectly clear to Summer and agreed to this form of non-exclusivity, but the heart sometimes denies reason.

Unlike Summer, it seemed, he did not go out of his way to initiate matters (and the fact that she had, to a large extent, provoked the meeting with – what was his name, Gary or Greg?) and preferred to let the ebb and flow of life and human interaction intervene instead. Many years ago, when he was still in his early twenties and funds were so limited he couldn't afford the full-price plane fare between London and Paris, he had used a cheap coach service operating between the two cities, from Waterloo Coach Station to the Place de la République, and had found himself sitting next to Danielle, a young French girl with dark hair. Maybe she had also been reading a book he was familiar with; he couldn't recall. The conversation had been easy.

She was returning from London, where she was in the process of conducting a long-distance affair with an Indian medical student that was now seemingly on its last legs. Dominik was between relationships. They had both enjoyed their chat and exchanged phone numbers and addresses before going their own way on arrival. It was obvious she was somewhat promiscuous and carefree. Within a week, he had called her up and they had ended up in bed and became regular lovers over an eighteen-month period. Or, at any rate, Dominik had joined the list of her numerous lovers, as Danielle granted her favours with uncommon generosity and was quick to admit he was not the only man she was bedding on a regular basis. There was even one night when another man came knocking at her door as they lay exhausted in bed, in her small flat near La Santé Prison, and she'd gladly invited him in and they had ended up all three between the covers, both men taking turns to mount her as she moved from one to the other.

After he'd returned to live in London, he'd lost touch with Danielle until she'd called him in a panic one afternoon while he was still working, having somehow been thrown out on the street by another man she was sleeping with because she'd stolen his wallet. She was now penniless and badly needed Dominik's help. In dire straits, alone in London and with not even spare clothes, as the man had held on to her suitcase, she'd been desperate and had even attempted to whore herself in Soho backstreets, with no success. He'd found her a small hotel room in Bloomsbury at two in the morning and loaned her the money for the fare back to Paris the following day. It had been too late for him to get home that night, as he no longer had enough cash on him for a taxi, so he'd joined her in the narrow hotel room and they'd fucked until the early hours, Danielle in tears for most of the time. One thing had led to another, as they both knew this would be the last occasion they would see each other, and they had had anal sex. His first time. He'd left early in the morning as he had to be at work, Danielle soundly asleep in the bed, her make-up smudged, the dark areola of a breast peering above the messed-up sheets. She'd always been an intense lover and sometimes her recklessness scared him. He didn't even say goodbye, a fact he would regret for years.

He'd always suspected that Danielle would end up badly somehow, but a decade later, out of curiosity, he'd Googled her and found out she was now teaching sociology in Bordeaux and had even produced a thesis on some highly specialised academic subject that he had, however, little interest in reading.

It had been total coincidence that their coach tickets happened to have sequential numbers and this had thrown them together and eventually, unexpectedly, led to his first experience with anal sex. Ever since, Dominik had been relaxed enough to allow life's currents to take him in all unplanned directions, never resisting the flow.

Did he carry the smell of books with him that so many of his chance encounters had academic connections? Miranda, his seat companion on the flight to New York, was an administrative assistant at Hunter College, uptown. Dominik had always been a quietly charismatic public speaker. It was one of his strengths as a lecturer. If he felt in tune with the subject, he could happily improvise for ages, spinning theories, random thoughts and left-of-field ideas with particular aplomb without ever falling into pedantry or being a show-off. When it came to Gatsby, he was very much on home territory, so the flight went by painlessly as he engaged in light-hearted banter and conversation with Miranda. The seven hours quickly fell away. Less time to think about Summer and how they would manage to live together in New York.

Miranda wore a grey business ensemble, her skirt

reaching to her knees, but gradually moving up to mid-thigh as she shifted in her seat. Her tight white blouse gaped a little between buttons, stretched by the black bra she visibly wore underneath. Her neck was wonderfully delicate, flushing ever so pink as the flight progressed and the heat in the plane rose.

She was divorced and lived alone on the Upper East Side, Dominik learned. Absorbed in their conversation, she would regularly extend her fingers and touch his lower arm when trying to make a point and even, on a couple of occasions, his knee. Dominik was no expert on body language, but knew it was something he often did himself, quite innocently and instinctively. Only with women he was attracted to, however.

On arrival at JFK, they swapped details and agreed to stay in touch. Dominik wrote down her number on the back of one of his business cards. He was planning to get a new phone for New York, as his London number would not be practical here, which left the ball in his court, Miranda-wise. He had deliberately not informed her he would be living with another woman during his stay in the city.

By further coincidence, their respective luggage arrived almost together on the carousel. The smile on Miranda's face as this happened was worth a thousand words. It appeared she also believed in coincidences.

Pretexting geographical distance, Dominik insisted in the taxi rank that they should take separate cabs. Deception comes easy.

This time, the driver was Vietnamese and struggled to understand Dominik's English accent when he asked for Spring Street.

The road unfolded. A familiar litany of outer boroughs, the Southern State Parkway, the obligatory detour by Atlantic Avenue, followed by the Van Wyck Expressway and its cortege of concrete pillars supporting the AirTrain, then Jamaica Hospital and the final rush towards the Midtown Tunnel. How many times had he taken this road and survived the traffic jams in either direction?

Dominik took a deep breath.

This time it would be different.

Summer was at the end of the journey.

By the time the cab reached SoHo, a spring shower had broken. There was no shelter between the taxi and the unprotected front door of the building. Dominik rang the bell.

'It's me.'

Summer, as planned, was home and she buzzed him in.

The elevator was already on the ground floor, doors open, industrial in appearance. Years ago, he had learned, the building had been host to floors full of workshops peopled by migrant labourers, until the schmutter business had moved further uptown to what became the Garment District. The vast empty spaces had been occupied by artists attracted by the light and by cheap property values. Today, few artists could afford SoHo lofts any longer, and they were being swooped up by investment bankers, hedge-funders and business folk.

The fifth floor had been divided into three apartments, and the one Dominik had arranged to rent was at the end of the corridor when he exited the elevator.

The door was half open.

Gripping the handle of his suitcase, he pushed it further open with his foot. The varnished wooden floor led up to a slight ramp, which ran in parallel to the outer corridor, to the right of which was the kitchen area. Beyond it was the wide open space of the loft, all the way down to the bay windows, through which a curtain of rain cushioned today's grey skies.

Because of the inclement weather, Summer had switched on the lights. A series of recessed spotlights ran the full length of the ceiling, bisecting the loft space.

At the very centre of the loft's living area, bathed in a puddle of light, Summer stood.

Naked.

Holding her precious violin in one hand, by her side.

A knowing grin spread across her face.

Dominik's eyes rushed from her painted lips to the explosion of curls crowning her head, then to the shocking red of her nipples. She had used lipstick to enhance herself, just as he had done all those months ago.

His gaze fell lower. Her pubic hair was growing back, but he could see she had also painted her lower lips.

His heart skipped a half-beat and he let go of his suitcase.

Summer ceremoniously brought the violin to her chin, a slave to this private ritual they both recognised as their very own, and began playing.

The second movement of Vivaldi's *Four Seasons*.

A wave of emotion swept over Dominik.

He stood still, overcome by a complex maelstrom of feelings.

Startled by her offering. Her greeting. This overture to their future time together in Manhattan.

Every single note was both familiar and new to him,

evoking memories, past events, visions of Summer in all her splendour. Oh, how tender this spring would be . . .

As the music swirled across the walls of the loft, and Summer retreated into the music, she closed her eyes. As ever she needed no partition. The Vivaldi notes were now a part of her. Of them?

Dominik kicked off his shoes. He was wearing black stretch socks, as he always did. He pulled them off; these wooden floors were made for bare feet. Stepping closer to Summer, he felt the gentle heat radiating outwards from her body, the underlying green smell of her perfume, the faint undercurrent of sweat breaking through to the surface of her skin as the violin-playing warmed her measure by measure.

He took a deep breath.

Circled her. Her back was white as snow, but Dominik couldn't help imagining past marks, faint and dull across her back and buttocks, like a long-forgotten lattice of minor tattoos moving in straight and perpendicular lines across the pallor of her flesh. How he imagined the ropes she had told him about would have briefly marked her.

He moved closer, his whole body just inches from hers. He placed a delicate kiss on the soft tip of her ear.

Her eyes still closed, Summer shuddered, the involuntary movement causing a slight shimmer in the flow of the melody she was playing. Her back straightened.

Dominik moved a foot or so back and circled Summer again, now facing her.

Without impeding the movement of her arms as she played on, he ran one finger from her shoulder down her side, twisting his hand to trace her bikini line and skirt the edges of her painted lips. He kneeled before her, using both hands to widen the gap between her legs. He moved his face closer, almost touching, but not quite. He was aware that with the violin in place she could not see him, not see his tongue as it slowly approached her wet, inviting lips.

Summer continued playing, although he was aware that every cell in her body was screaming for her to throw the precious instrument aside and grab Dominik and provoke him into exploring her body faster, harder. She knew he was teasing her. Playing with her. Tempting her to stop concentrating on the violin. Become more active. She was aware how unsteady the music was becoming, how unprofessional. The musician in her was appalled by the poverty of her music, but the woman inside just couldn't help it.

Dominik stopped for a brief moment, savouring the moment, savouring the taste of Summer. The waxy taste of the lipstick she had used was sweet and cloying and no doubt emigrated to his lips. He'd probably look a bit like a clown should he see himself right now in a mirror, he reckoned, light-hearted. Summer was terribly wet and he felt her react to every sweep of his tongue inside her, but she kept on playing regardless. He buried his face into her intimate parts, the extremity of his tongue flicking her clit, feeling it harden, and taking it between his lips, pressing it, massaging it, repressing a strong desire to actually bite her. She adjusted the angle between her legs without missing a beat of the melody, inviting him deeper into her. His hair brushed the inside of her thighs as he gladly accepted the invitation and dug deeper into her, his lips tasting the flow of her juices.

Summer came with a deep shudder rising like a wave from the core of her stomach just as the music reached its appointed end.

The rain outside had stopped and there was a long moment of total silence, Summer standing to attention like a statue of salt in the centre of the loft space, eyes still firmly shut, and Dominik on his knees, facing her. Both hesitating as to who should speak first, say something, as if the decision might have terrible consequences.

The silence was broken by Summer's staccato gasps as she now struggled to steady her breathing.

Dominik rose from the hard wooden floor, glanced around him and noticed a length of rope lying on one of the kitchen area's granite worktops alongside Summer's handbag, her pink mobile phone and a set of keys. Something from her workshop, maybe?

'Stay there. Keep your eyes closed,' he said, walking over to the worktop and picking up the short length of rope, weighing it in his hands. It was just long enough, he estimated. Just right.

He stepped back to Summer.

He stood by her side and delicately passed the piece of rope round her neck and secured it with a loose knot fixed in place.

He could feel her nervousness as she attempted to control her breath, slow it down.

'Come,' Dominik said.

He pulled gently on the improvised lead. Summer brought her legs together, hesitantly put one foot forward and followed in the direction the rope was stretching.

Dominik led her to the bedroom.

Dominik had been in New York a whole fortnight and he and Summer had fallen effortlessly into an easy routine.

He fitted in his hours at the library with her rehearsals

and so far there had been no conflicts, although they were both aware that it would soon prove more difficult as her solo gig approached. She would require further hours to practise and had agreed to have some extra-curricular coaching with Simón, the orchestra's conductor. Dominik had suggested they all have dinner together, but Summer had been hesitant to organise this, under the pretext she wished to keep her personal and professional lives strictly apart.

'We can't keep to ourselves all the time,' Dominik remarked.

'Can't we?'

'It feels as if we are prisoners of the loft. Just you and me against the world.'

'Isn't that what being together is all about?' Summer said, with a hint of irritation.

She wasn't sure what to expect when she had agreed to move in with Dominik. She was unsure whether she was ready for this domesticity. True, there were still moments when he surprised her, was unpredictable, connected with her inner slut, when he took control in unforeseen ways she craved but couldn't always express. And Summer also knew it was unfeasible to sustain that feeling day after day. On one hand, she felt a captive of the necessary routine of their relationship, while on the other, she endlessly yearned for some sort of additional challenge. Oh, damn, it was all so complicated . . .

He was curious about her time with Cherry, the rope workshop, the mild scenes she had got herself involved with. Maybe she should introduce him. Surely it couldn't be harmful.

'There is a friend I've made – you know, when I tried out

the rope. Her name is Cherry. Maybe we could meet up, have a drink. I think you'd like her.'

'Absolutely. Why not?'

Summer picked up her phone and made the arrangements. They would meet up at four at a bar she knew on Bleecker Street. They would have at least a couple of hours, as Cherry was performing that same evening at a joint on the Bowery.

Bleecker Street was its customary early evening bustle of bohos, wannabes and tourists. They'd walked there, crossing Houston and passing a million other bars along the way.

'Why the Red Lion of all the places around?' Dominik had asked Summer.

'It's English, isn't it? We thought you might enjoy a touch of home.'

As a non-drinker, Dominik had never been a 'pub person', something that Summer seemed unaware of. All their non-sexual encounters had been in small cafés or Italian espresso bars dotted across London.

As it happened, there was a big European football match being broadcast live on TV that same evening and the Red Lion was packed to the rafters with a loud crowd of expatriates and curious Yanks, so they were forced to move on further down Bleecker Street to Kenny's Castaways, a folk club that had survived from the Greenwich Village heyday of Baez, Dylan and others, where the bar was quite empty and there were still tables available and a modicum of privacy.

Dominik was struck by how short Cherry was, not what he would have expected from a burlesque performer.

She was small and compact under her pudding bowl of shocking-pink hair, and the bulging canvas bag she was carrying, slung over her shoulder, dwarfed her frame.

'My gear,' she pointed out, as she lowered the heavy bag to the floor. 'I always seem to pack more than I need. A spare outfit, accessories, half a dozen pairs of shoes . . . It's just the way the job is – you never know what you might need,' she said apologetically, pulling her ring-laden fingers through her dyed hair to straighten it out.

Dominik had forgotten to ask the barman to go easy on the ice and his Coke arrived ultra-American style, smothered in the stuff. Both of the women ordered pink cocktails in homage to Cherry's hair. Not the sort of thing Summer usually drank, Dominik observed, particularly as the bar had a selection of Japanese beers behind the counter.

'So you're Dominik?' the pink-haired buxom friend of Summer's said, checking him out. Her black leather jacket was frayed at the edges and patched up in places. She was wearing a skin-tight pair of leopard-print leggings and glittering skyscraper heels, an outfit that would be better suited to a cabaret act than a pub.

Dominik had forgotten to ask Summer how much she had disclosed of their relationship and past to her new friend.

'The one and only.'

'Very British,' Cherry remarked.

'And you're Cherry, the rope lady.'

Summer smiled, observing their initial sparring.

Cherry raised her glass. 'To new friends,' she proclaimed.

They followed suit.

'I'm no good on American accents,' Dominik said. 'Where do you come from, Cherry?'

'Canada, actually,' she exaggerated her drawl to emphasise the point.

'Ah. My humblest apologies.'

'I'm from Turner Valley, Alberta, a small town just south-west of Calgary. You've probably never heard of it, but I'm guessing it's exactly what you expect. Wild country, not a skyscraper for hundreds of miles, and certainly no cabaret bars. I got out at the first opportunity I was given. Topless waitressing to start with, and that's where I met a few girls who taught me to dance. Soon as I had enough tips saved, I hit the Big Apple. Ain't never going back.'

'New Zealand backwaters, Alberta and London,' Summer remarked. 'We're all exiles, strangers in a strange land.' She felt uncomfortable, relying on clichés now to keep the conversation going, unsure whether bringing Dominik and Cherry together had been a bright idea after all.

'I'll drink to that,' Cherry said.

'So you're here alone? Your family are still in Alberta?' asked Dominik.

Summer shifted on her seat, becoming more and more uncomfortable with the direction in which the conversation was headed.

'Not exactly alone. My boyfriends keep me warm at night, but they're both out of town at the moment. One travels with his band and the other with his work – he works in sales and is on the road a lot.'

'You have two boyfriends?' Dominik smiled and raised an eyebrow quizzically.

'You'd think I wouldn't spend as much time alone as I do. Maybe I should look into hooking up with a third.'

'Would you like another drink?' Summer interrupted, an

attempt to stop any further talk about Cherry's multiple partners.

'My round, I think,' Cherry replied, balancing her weight on the table as she lowered herself to the floor. It was a long way down for her short legs, and she paused for a moment to check her stability before putting all of her weight on her heels and teetering towards the bar.

'Your friend is an interesting woman.'

'Yes, she's . . . different. But I like her. She's honest.'

'Does it work, do you think, her with her two boyfriends?'

'It seems to. I haven't met either of them yet, but she seems happy enough. I don't know how she does it. With all the rehearsing, I barely have time for one. She says the trick is in the diary management.'

'I know you're busy, but I hope you will manage to find enough time for me.'

'Oh, no, I didn't mean it like that. Of course I have time for you.'

'Not interrupting, I hope?' said Cherry, easing a tray with two pink cocktails, full to the brim, and a glass of Coke onto the table. 'I noticed you weren't keen on the ice, Dominik, so I watched the bartender like a hawk. I hope this is OK for you.'

'Perfect. That's very kind of you.'

First, they had to find the right dress for Summer's solo performance. Dominik had insisted she wear something brand new for the occasion, not her old fallbacks. Price was no object, he added. His suggestion they spend a weekend visiting the fashion stores dotted across the lower reaches of Fifth Avenue and below Houston on Broadway was quickly dismissed by Summer. She knew she was unlikely to find the right garment in such stores. An afternoon wandering through SoHo darting in and out of designer boutiques was similarly unsuccessful. The styles were just not right for her, Summer felt, let alone the extortionate cost of most of the dresses on display, despite Dominik's insouciance when it came to money. She felt so much in debt to him already, and this concert was to be her hour of glory and she was conflicted about his involvement. He had paid God knows how much for the Bailly, and she knew the rental cost of the loft was pretty exorbitant. She had insisted on contributing, but knew the amount she paid wasn't close to half. Enough was enough. It was pride, she knew, but damn it, she was who she was and had no intention of changing now and becoming a kept woman.

There was only a week left to the gig, and Summer was bone-tired from the rehearsals, Simón's persistence in pursuing her and Dominik's silent looks of disapproval when she returned to the loft after dark, hours later than he had expected, exhausted by the mounting pressure of the impending concert and her own insecurities about how good she actually was and whether she deserved the solo gig. She knew she was not easy to live with these days.

They took their meals in silence, then moved to bed, where the lovemaking had become prosaic. All this time, Dominik kept to himself too, never talking much about the research he was doing at the library, handling Summer with kid gloves. He hadn't told her he had made contact with Miranda and was planning to see the Columbia administrative assistant a few days later for lunch, the old demons inside him striving to be rekindled.

As the end of June approached, the temperatures in

the city were rising. On a lazy Sunday afternoon, they'd resolved to take a walk, maybe amble over to Washington Square and sit by the fountain to listen to the musicians, have an ice cream and get away from the prison of the loft and their own awkward silences. There was a street fair in full cry across a couple of blocks along Waverly Place and the north side of the park. Smells of food drifted on the air – kebabs, fried onion, burgers, Mexican fajitas – and there were stalls galore with trinkets, pashminas, leather goods and T-shirts, plus lemonade and smoothie vendors and a parade of tables full of old, dog-eared books. Dominik was automatically drawn to the bookstalls, while Summer noticed across the way from them a tent-like marquee with old vintage clothing scattered randomly across its length. It was a veritable jumble of colours and fabrics, but her attention was quickly drawn to a slightly crumpled dress hanging askew from a railing towards the back of the improvised awning.

A black dress.

Summer approached the garment with a tingle in her fingers.

Surely not?

It was made from a double layer of chiffon, almost but not quite see-through. Daring, but just modest enough to pass the eagle eyes of the concert organisers. It had a very low back, thin spaghetti straps and a turquoise beaded strip that snaked down the front, providing extra cover for the wearer's more private areas and also highlighting the curves of a feminine body. The bottom of the dress was beaded in the same colour, weighting the dress down so that it would hold its shape and swish with each movement. It came with a pair of full-length fingerless gloves, with the same beading running from a delicate strap that fitted through the index and middle finger, to just past the elbow.

The stallholder, spotting a possible sale, was quick to approach. 'It belonged to an English burlesque dancer. She had it made for her. Only dress like this in the world, and she had a body just like yours.'

'It's beautiful. Just feel the material – it's so soft to the touch.' She called Dominik over and displayed the second-hand dress to him.

'It is,' he confirmed.

Summer turned the dress inside out, looking for a label with an indication of its size. There was none. 'It would just be too much of a coincidence for it to be my exact size,' she pointed out with a sigh of resignation.

'How do you know?'

'It's unlikely.'

'Try it on,' he suggested.

'There's nowhere to change,' Summer pointed out, waving at the crowds milling around them in the shadow of the Washington Square Arch and, just a few steps away, the children's swing enclosure, where tiny voices screeched and laughed.

'I know,' he said. 'So what?'

'I can't,' she sputtered.

'Of course you can.'

Before leaving the loft, she had slipped into a loose, casual flower-print summer dress for the walk to the park. She wasn't wearing a bra, as its top held her breasts tight.

'Dominik . . .'

'Since when are you shy?'

'It was different, the other times,' Summer protested.

'I know. It was sexual. Here it's not. Anything but that.

So just do it. It's straightforward.' His tone was now peremptory, severe.

She looked him in the eyes and recognised that familiar glint of mischief and authority that sometimes changed him into an entirely different person, the welcomingly evil and demanding Dominik, a man she now knew well.

She tried to retreat a few steps under the canopy of the improvised tent to pull her dress off, but she heard Dominik tut-tut.

'No . . . Where you are right now will do.'

Avoiding the glances of the many passers-by, Summer gripped the thin straps of the summer dress she was wearing and pulled upwards, the cotton fabric bunching between her fingers, and pulled it swiftly above her head. All she wore underneath was a thin pair of low-waisted black panties.

She was in a New York street, strangers slaloming across her, virtually naked. Out of the corner of her eye, she saw the glances, the surprise, how some even stopped to take a closer look, while others diverted their gaze. She held her breath and took hold of the black dress, her cheeks on fire, and dropped it across her head. The fit was perfect, even round her uncommonly slim waistline. The material felt like silk next to her skin, and soothed the terrible heat racing through her at the thought of all these strangers witnessing her undressing and catching more than a glimpse of her body. There was both an element of shame and one of intense arousal, reminding her of the occasion she had first been naked and turned on in public, at the fetish club in London all those months ago.

It was maybe just a few inches too long, but she knew that with needle and thread that would easily be rectified.

'You see,' Dominik said.

With a smile she nodded.

Dominik paid the stallholder.

Summer was about to suggest she could walk the short distance home in the new black dress, but Dominik asked the stallholder for a plastic bag in which they could carry it and indicated she should change back into her loose summer dress. Once again, Summer stripped under the lubricious gaze of the crowds who had slowly gathered around the clothes stall to watch.

'You liked that, didn't you?' Dominik suggested.

'I like the black dress we bought,' Summer defiantly said, refusing to take his bait.

The new dress had been dry-cleaned and its length shortened and Summer was ready for her solo gig. At Dominik's predictable insistence, she wore nothing underneath. It felt exhilarating. She wondered what Simón would think of her if only he knew.

He was conducting tonight, as usual.

The concert, which was being held at Webster Hall on 11th Street between Third and Fourth, would begin with the full orchestra playing Mussorgsky's *Night on the Bare Mountain*, in the Rimsky-Korsakov orchestration. Summer would then follow with Korngold's Violin Concerto in D major, and the gig would end with the orchestra giving a performance of Shostakovich's Symphony No. 5 in D minor.

Simón had chosen the pieces as perfect showcases for the new dynamics he had brought to the Gramercy Symphonia and felt the Korngold was ideally suited to Summer's temperament and talent.

Dominik arranged for a cab to pick Summer up, as she had to be at Webster Hall sometime ahead of the concert. He would travel there later, separately. He knew the venue, having once attended a performance there by Patti Smith, and had arranged for Summer to get him a place on the balcony, where he knew he would have a superior view of the stage.

There was a buzz in the air as the orchestra and Simón, who was a veritable bundle of energy, curly hair in motion with every movement of his arms, took a bow at the end of the first short and sometimes pyrotechnic Mussorgsky piece as the audience anticipated the arrival of the violinist whose first concert this had heavily been advertised as. It was at Dominik's insistence that a headless photo of Summer holding her violin against her bare chest, with just stray strands of her fire-red hair visible, had adorned the posters for the event, thus keeping her identity a mystery until the actual day of the performance. It was a photo a friend of hers had taken back in London and which he treasured for the private memories it evoked. When the idea had been suggested to the concert's promoters and the orchestra's management, they had proven surprisingly enthusiastic. Even the *Village Voice* and *Time Out* had picked up on it, and the event had, as a consequence, become a sell-out.

The lights dimmed and Summer walked onto the stage. The murmurs in the audience faded.

Summer adjusted her stance, brought the bow into position and launched into the soaring opening solo of the Korngold, the '*Moderato nobile*', which ran into two octaves over five notes.

The new black dress clung to her like a second skin.

Watching from above, Dominik felt a knot in his throat.

He was transfixed by the beauty of both Summer and the music. There was a lush sensuality in the way the jungle of her hair, tousled and luxuriant, was accentuated by the concert hall's lighting, the pale skin of her bare arms contrasting so strikingly with the black fabric of the dress and the background darkness of the suits worn by the rest of the orchestra.

He closed his eyes, imagined her nakedness, the way she played for him, wanton and beautiful, the way the sight of her body lost in the music made his cock shiver and could almost bring him to orgasm, a willing victim of lust.

Around him, the whole world disappeared.

Time slowed but still flowed on and on, lullabied by the sublime sounds and the virtuoso performances of the rest of the orchestra in which the brass section had particular bravura measures, including her Croatian friends, who both displayed broad smiles as they attacked their instruments full-cheeked and teeming with calculated aggression.

All too soon – the Korngold concerto was barely twenty-five minutes long at best – the '*Romanze*' section was over and Summer fell into the opening staccato jig of the final movement, the '*Allegro assai vivace*'. It was the most demanding part of the composition, one over which she had laboured rehearsing for hours on end, but she made it look so easy now, her body in tune with her instrument and the music.

The next time Dominik opened his eyes, the final echoes of the concerto were fading into the distance and the audience were on their feet, applauding wildly, as Simón on his rostrum grinned wildly at Summer as she took her first bow.

Dominik, from his high vantage point, focused on

Summer's face, ignoring the other spectators on the balcony all standing and jostling him as they clapped enthusiastically. There was the faintest of smiles on Summer's face, as she modestly kept on bowing to the audience, and the orchestra members behind her on the stage rose altogether in unison and joined in the applause. It was a smile in which Dominik could read quiet satisfaction but also sadness, as if she had now come to the realisation that tonight she had reached a crossroads and that her life would never be the same again.

A concert-hall attendant walked out of the stage wing and presented Summer with an enormous bouquet of flowers. For a moment, she just stood there, confused, not knowing how to take hold of it, still nervously gripping her violin by her side. Simón approached and, whispering something into her ear, gently relieved her of the Bailly. She now held the flowers, and without glancing up to the balcony, she was led off stage, her retreat delayed by the unending applause.

It was her night, her triumph. She would no doubt want to spend the rest of it with her fellow musicians, celebrating backstage, Dominik knew. Shortly before the tumult quietened down and the orchestra was led into the final piece of the concert, the Shostakovich, he moved to his feet and retreated from the balcony seats. He walked downstairs and left Webster Hall to return to the loft alone.

# 7
## *A Prelude to the Road*

All I wanted was some peace and quiet, a place to sit in solitude and feel the residual post-performance energy ebb and flow from my body, but backstage was like another concert, a cacophony of well-wishers and congratulations.

Marija threw her arms round me and I stiffly hugged her back, her hard body pressed so firmly against mine I worried that she might break one of my ribs.

'You were amazzzzing!' she cried.

Baldo stood next to her, applauding. 'You better come get the stuff you left in the flat,' he said, laughing. 'Marija is planning to sell it now that you're famous.'

She let go of me and turned to give him a smack across his backside.

In the background, I heard the pop of a champagne cork and one of the percussionists squealing as the fizzing liquid threatened to erupt over her dress. A moment later, someone pushed a glass into my hand.

I panicked when I realised that I was missing my violin. Now, of all times, I wanted the instrument in my hand.

'Don't worry,' Simón said softly into my ear. 'Your Bailly is safe. I put it out the back with my things.'

He removed the glass of champagne from my hand and replaced it with a bottle of beer.

'I thought you might prefer this.'

'Oh, thank you. You're too kind.'

'No, I'm really not. You were incredible out there. Truly.'

'Thank you. I just wish . . .'

'What?'

'I don't want to be ungrateful, but I feel as though my head might explode. I just want to sit down.'

'I know what you mean. Come with me.'

He took my hand in his and led me away through a side door into one of the adjacent rooms, then down another corridor, and then through another door, which opened onto a flight of steps leading straight downwards, another unknown door looming out of the murk at the bottom. I hesitated. The steps were wooden instead of stone and lacked that scent that attaches itself to ancient things, but other than that, it reminded me exactly of the crypt that Dominik had taken me to, where we had had sex for the first time.

Dominik. I should be celebrating with him, not Simón. If he hadn't happened upon me playing Vivaldi at Tottenham Court Road Station, more than a year ago now, then I probably wouldn't be here. Most of the events that had happened since would likely not have occurred without him; our chance meeting was like the current that had swept me away from one course and sent me full speed down another.

I hesitated.

'Don't worry, there are no ghosts down here. Just an old store room, but the one place in this building that we'll go totally unnoticed, at least for a few minutes.'

I followed him down the steps. We wouldn't be long, and Dominik would still be waiting, I hoped.

The room was nothing like the crypt – just a few shelves full of cleaning products, some packing boxes and a few buckets and mops.

Simón overturned a yellow bucket and sat down on it, his long legs stretched out awkwardly in front of him.

'Plain black shoes tonight, I see?' I said, amused at the way the formality of his suit contrasted with the dusty surroundings of the store room and bright child's colours of our impromptu seating.

I tipped over another bucket and sat down alongside him, careful to dust off the bottom so that I wouldn't get any dirt on my dress.

'Just one of those things,' he said. 'There's always going to be parts of me that are better kept from view in polite company. Not everyone approves of orchestral conductors wearing snakeskin boots. Though I see you've skated further to the edge than I dared, with that dress.'

He could probably see from this distance that I wasn't wearing a bra.

I shrugged. 'Sex sells,' I said. 'When was the last time you saw a frumpy musician do well? Classical music is all about sex these days.'

'Classical music has always been about sex. And not just the women either.'

'Fighting your way through the groupies, are you, to get back to your dressing room unscathed?'

'I wouldn't go that far, but it can be a bit like that. I don't date much any more. I can never tell whether a woman is truly interested in me or just likes the idea of dating a man who leads an orchestra. And you? Did your English friend pay a visit to see you in concert?'

'Yes. He's in New York for a few months, actually. We're living together.'

'He moved quickly, then. Can't say I blame him.'

I stared at my shoes, avoiding Simón's gaze. 'I should probably get back soon. He'll be wondering who I'm celebrating with.'

'I suppose you should. Why didn't you invite him to join us? Tonight of all nights, you could probably have invited a troop of elephants backstage if you wanted to.'

'I don't know,' I muttered. 'Just seemed like something to keep separate. It's not a good idea to mix business and pleasure.'

'Yes. I worked out your feelings on that point already . . . Now, before you disappear, there's someone I want you to talk to.'

He had pushed himself up to standing, and reached his arm down to help me up. I took hold of his palm and relaxed, letting him pull me to my feet, inhaling as he did so, enjoying the scent of his cologne. He'd piled it on thick tonight and had some kind of pomade in his hair, taking some of the frizz out of his curls and adding a light shine. With his glossy hair, black coat-tails and stiff white shirt, he looked like a magician from a travelling fair.

He pulled the door ajar and held it open for me politely so that I could walk ahead of him up the stairs, though I suspected that he was motivated more by voyeurism than good manners, as Dominik had informed me before I left the apartment that in the right light the back of the dress, which had no beading, was almost completely see-through, giving any onlooker a perfect view of my bare behind.

In the dull light at the top of the stairs, I saw a flash of bright pink, the only splash of colour in the corridor.

'Looks like I was wrong about the anonymity of our hiding place,' Simón remarked. 'You seem to have picked up a stalker already. She looks like the crazy type too.'

'Simón,' I said, introducing them, 'this is Cherry. Cherry, Simón.'

Cherry extended a hand politely. Despite her towering heels, Simón had to crouch to meet her hand with his own. She was wearing a bright-yellow satin cocktail dress and matching shoes, and with her shock of pink hair on top, she looked like something that had escaped from a nuclear power plant.

'Don't tell me you're hiding from your fans, Summer?' she said. 'You were incredible. You should be out front, basking in the glow.'

'We were just finding a safe place for her violin,' Simón interrupted.

'Right,' Cherry replied, her eyes darting between the two of us suspiciously.

'And I'm afraid that I will have to steal your friend away again, as she needs to meet some of her admirers.'

He took my hand again and pulled me through another maze of corridors, to one of the bars, which was fortunately relatively quiet. I felt a little self-conscious, as the lights here were much brighter than the dim electrics backstage, and I was suddenly aware of my nudity beneath the thin slip of a dress, which on stage was all part of the show, but off stage might seem rather shocking. I kicked myself for not bringing a change of clothes. An amateur's mistake, which I wouldn't make again.

'Remember the agent at my dinner party, Susan?' Simón hissed into my ear. 'Now's your chance. Go and talk to her.'

I nodded as he put a hand on the small of my back and pushed me forward.

I leaned against the bar alongside her, as if I just happened to be there, waiting to buy a drink. She was elegantly put together, in a stylish but demure plum-coloured pencil dress and perfectly coiffeured hairdo, just the right look for someone who was half at work and half at play. Susan was a natural redhead, which I counted as another mark in her favour. She had a BlackBerry in hand and was furiously tapping away, as if oblivious to her surroundings, but her eyes lit up the moment she saw me.

'Summer! I'm so glad that I bumped into you again. You were wonderful out there, an absolute triumph.'

'Thank you. Er . . . I like your shoes.'

I berated myself for not thinking of something more intelligent to say before I approached her.

'Oh, thank you. They're high-heeled boat shoes. I haven't seen any in New York. I bought these in London.'

I nodded.

'Look, I'll get straight to the point. I know you must have legions of admirers waiting to congratulate you, and you're probably dying to get away from them all and get home, but I think you've really got something. I want to take your show on tour.'

'On tour?' I gulped.

'Yes. Just you and a few members of the string section. I think you've got just the right element of skill and sex appeal to pull off a solo act. And not just in America. I want to take you all over. Is that an Antipodean accent you have there?'

'Yes, I'm from New Zealand originally, but lived in Australia for a little while too.'

'Great. The local promoters Down Under will lap that up. They do seem to love anyone who has made it overseas and comes home for a visit.'

'I would love a trip home,' I replied, 'and anywhere else that you'd want to send me, of course,' I added quickly, emphasising my enthusiasm.

'Good. That's settled, then. Don't go talking to any other promoters, will you? You can come into my office on Monday and we'll organise all of the paperwork.' She took a card from one of her pockets and slipped it into my hand. 'This is a big deal, you know, Summer. You'll be relaxing in a beach house on Long Island before you know it.'

'When would you want to begin?' I asked, dreading her response.

'Now, of course. Time is absolutely of the essence in these situations. Did you see the crowd out there? You've got to ride the wave, because you never know when it might disappear again. The public are impossible to predict. You just never know what the next big thing is going to be. And it's you at the moment. Take advantage for as long as it lasts.'

'OK. Thank you,' I said, careful to paint a smile onto my face. I felt overwhelmingly tired. I just wanted to go home to Dominik.

It was one in the morning by the time I got home. Dominik was already asleep. He had thrown the covers off, a point that I would remind him of in the morning, as he always complained that I kept stealing the blankets.

His white English skin looked even paler against the black sheets. He preferred his bedding the same colour as

Lauralynn's, I remembered, and I had told him when he bought them that the colour was impractical and would soon be covered with stains. He bought them anyway, of course, though didn't put up a fight when I changed them over to a cream set of my own. We had reached an unspoken agreement now and rotated between the two. I was just grateful that he didn't have a penchant for stripes or anything floral.

He slept naked, as I did, and he looked strangely vulnerable curled up on the bed without any covering at all. He lay almost in the foetal position, with one leg bent at a right angle, and the other leg straight, his flaccid cock on display. It looked small and shrunken, but still rather beautiful. I leaned over and stroked it very gently, surprised at the softness of his skin in this place that in my mind I always imagined permanently hard, a weapon, the seat of his power. I had never examined a man's cock when it was soft. It made me wonder what else about men, and Dominik in particular, that I had taken for granted.

I had been meaning to wake him up with a blowjob ever since we moved in together, but he inevitably woke up before me, leaving at least one and sometimes three cups of coffee going cold next to my side of the bed before I stirred.

His skin had been browner when we met, I was sure. Must have been a holiday, rather than the result of some Mediterranean heritage, I thought, dropping the dress to the floor and crawling under the covers that he had kicked away.

There was still so much I didn't know about him, so many things I had never asked.

I resolved to be a better girlfriend, starting tomorrow. At

least, for as long as I could before I had to leave him alone in New York, as now seemed inevitable if I were to believe Susan.

In the event, it was Dominik who woke me with oral sex the next morning. I hadn't had a shower before I went to bed, and I pulled his hair gently with my hand as soon as I felt his head between my legs, endeavouring to dissuade his attentions until I had a chance to bathe. He batted me away and continued. There was no point arguing with Dominik, either silently or conversationally. Sometimes I thought he liked me more when I hadn't washed, as if it gave him a feeling of power to arouse me when I felt undesirable.

I had just begun to relax and enjoy the firm stroke of his tongue when he shifted himself up and kissed me.

'My favourite breakfast,' he breathed into my ear. 'You taste even better now that you're famous.'

I laughed. 'Now you're just being ridiculous.'

'No, I'm not. You should have seen the men in the audience. I reckon every single one of them had hard-ons by the final movement, especially your precious Simón.'

I bristled. 'It's not like that.'

'No,' he said, 'I like it, that they want you. I can't blame any of them, and I'm the one who's got you, right where you belong.'

He shifted his pelvis up and lowered his cock into me. The feeling of him inside me, where his tongue had been just moments before, was enough to drive away every other thought in my head. I moaned with pleasure, fears about the future forgotten, as he took hold of both my wrists and held them tightly as he thrust, ignoring the sound of the headboard beating against the wall.

'I suppose I need to be careful of your hands now,' he said. 'Are you going to have them insured?'

He stifled my laugh with a kiss.

'The missionary position is underrated,' I remarked, nestling under his arm, after he had come inside me. We'd both been through the rather unromantic but necessary rigmarole of discussing sexual histories and birth control. I had begun to enjoy the shocked response of sexual health doctors as I recited my relationship history. It was worth every moment of embarrassment to enjoy the feeling of Dominik's hot semen dribbling down my legs without any residual guilt or worry that there might one day be the pitter-patter of little feet, an eventuality that I was keen to avoid.

I left it a day before broaching the subject of the tour, at Toto, the sushi restaurant on Thompson Street that had become our regular port of call. I had figured that in public, and happy with the prospect of raw fish for dinner, Dominik might take to the idea more warmly.

I was wrong.

'You're leaving?' he said, incredulous. 'I've just arrived. We only have a few months together. Can't the tour wait?'

'My agent says that time is of the essence.'

'Oh, I bet he does.'

'She,' I corrected.

He screwed up his paper napkin viciously. 'Right. And what am I supposed to do while you're gone?'

His voice was calm, but I noticed that he was gripping his glass tightly.

'Carry on with your research, I suppose. Look, the first few months aren't so far away. I'll be able to come back and visit easily, between concerts. I'll need to anyway, to change my clothes and things like that.'

'Did it not occur to you to consult me before you decided all this? I didn't move here to be your laundromat, you know.'

'I didn't mean it like that. I'll miss you, really, but don't you see I can't pass up an opportunity like this? It might never come round again.'

He sighed. 'I know. I can see that,' he said, spearing another piece of fish with alarming violence. 'It's just that it wasn't easy to arrange to come to New York, and the whole point of the exercise was so that we could spend some time together. I'm not particularly enjoying the research, you know, and I might point out that you haven't asked me how it's coming along, not even once.'

'I'm sorry.'

'OK. Fine. You have to go. Let's not quarrel now and ruin our remaining time together.'

We sat through the rest of the meal in silence. The sashimi, normally one of my favourite meals, stuck in my throat, and even a bottle of Asahi did nothing to wash it away.

The agent's office was a few blocks from Central Park. It was small but stylish, with bright fittings in primary colours and a series of plants dotted around, the sort of décor that a feng shui expert might recommend as the perfect blend of professionalism and friendliness to gain the trust of an inexperienced client. She had a dog, an old Bassett hound, which sat on the sofa across from me on a worn red cushion, staring at me through heavy-lidded eyes.

I found the presence of the dog comforting. I tend to

trust people who own animals, particularly dogs. If I had known that Dominik didn't have pets before I arrived at his house in Hampstead, I might have held it against him. As it happened, though, we had already had sex by the time I visited him at home, so it was too late to include this character fault in my initial judgement.

I figured that Susan must be nice enough at least for the dog to want to hang around, which is why I gave up reading the ton of paperwork she gave me after the first few pages and just signed everything. It was all long words and percentages, nothing I saw that I had any real choice about. I was beyond lucky, I realised, to be in this position at all, and certainly not in any position to negotiate. That might come with my next tour, if this was a success. Aside from the dog, I trusted her instinctively. She was calculating, but genuine with it.

I had arranged to meet Cherry after signing the papers with the agent, as she worked nearby. As a primary-school teacher, I discovered.

'How does your private life go down with the school board?' I asked her over coffee at Lenny's on Second Avenue.

'Oh, God, they don't know a thing. That's why I use my stage name for everything. Only my family and my work colleagues call me by my real name. I have two lives, basically. You get used to it. And you should probably do the same, if you're going to be in the public eye and continue with any kind of kink life.'

'I don't think I could call myself anything else. It would feel dishonest.'

'You're not all that honest, though, really, are you?'

'What do you mean?' I was a little offended. Frankness

was something that I had always prided myself on. I disliked people who I felt were hiding themselves. I thought it a sign of weakness, a lack of courage.

'Your two men don't know about each other, do they?'

'They're not my two men. I'm not seeing Simón.'

'Doesn't look that way to me.'

'Well, you don't see everything, do you?' I felt my blood boiling. It had been a stressful few days, days filled with criticism and hurt from Dominik, and I didn't need to hear the same from Cherry.

'Look, what you do is your business, not mine, but I don't think the way you're operating is ethical. It's not non-monogamy; it's cheating.'

'I haven't touched Simón!'

'Haven't you?'

I didn't have much to say to that. I'd kissed him, but that was it.

'What I have with Dominik, it's not like you and your two . . . boyfriends. Who don't seem ever to be around,' I added cattily.

'I'm just sayin'. I can see why you'd want to keep Simón happy – it's obviously doing wonders for your career – but don't sacrifice Dominik for it. He's a good guy. You might regret it, that's all.'

'Are you saying I'm using him? For my career?'

'No, not at all. I'm sure that without a wealthy benefactor to buy you a fancy violin and a famous young conductor pushing you in the path of agents, you'd do just as well, eventually.'

I had told her how Dominik and I had met, and suddenly wished that I hadn't. She didn't understand.

I picked up my purse and threw a note down on the

table, covering the cost of the drinks with a more than ample tip, though I felt a little mean as I walked away, aware that underneath it all, she had a point, and in any case it wasn't fair to rub my new-found fortune in her face. Too late now, though, I thought, slowing my storming pace to a walk as I realised that I was now in Central Park and had no idea which direction I'd come from or where I was headed, as I'd been so angry I hadn't paid any attention to my surroundings.

The park, rather than being the place of solitude and respite that I had hoped for, was full of screeching children. I had arrived near the Alice in Wonderland statue, close to 74th Street, so at least I now knew where I was.

Parents and nannies were out in full force with their offspring, who were climbing and cavorting over the giant mushroom that Alice sat on, its bronze surface smooth as marble, perhaps by design, but aided by myriad toddlers, who had been running their hands overtop for decades, hoping to find the magic button that would drop them down the rabbit hole.

I wanted to tell them to forget about fairy tales, stranger things happen in real life, but I doubted their guardians, stressed to the point of explosion, would approve. A little girl wearing a red jacket and matching red shoes with yellow laces was trying to remove the top hat from the Mad Hatter's head. She cried when her mother pulled her away.

I sat down on the grass and tried to imagine what my life would be like if I had chosen the road more travelled, if the little girl in the red jacket were mine, if I had a house with a yard and a Bassett hound to go home to and a regular job that didn't involve late nights in concert halls or now tour buses.

I could have it, if I wanted it. Probably not with Dominik, but with Simón, or any of a dozen other cookie-cutter men with whom I might think myself in love for a time, and might get bored with eventually, but whom I could introduce to my friends and family, and go on dates with, and have family holidays with, and perhaps grow old with, if we were lucky.

The thought filled me with dread.

Life with Dominik in the SoHo flat was probably further from normal than would suit most people, and choosing life as a touring musician would drive an even greater wedge between any possibility of my ever living an ordinary existence, but it was the life that I had chosen, and one that suited me.

I had always been the type who preferred swimming upstream, even if it was harder that way.

My new-found optimism waned quickly over the next fortnight, as the two weeks before the beginning of the tour that Susan had quickly set up disappeared in a flash, as if life were so keen to throw me down this new path, it was moving at double speed to get me there faster.

Only a handful of musicians from the Gramercy Symphonia were able to join me on the tour and no one I knew well. I realised through the audition process how self-absorbed I had been since I had arrived in New York, as besides Marija and Baldo, I really hadn't formed a bond with anyone in the orchestra. I had spent most of my time talking to Simón. He and Susan cobbled together the other musicians from acquaintances, recommendations and the range of professionals that she had on her books. They were all accustomed to touring and used to working with new players at short notice.

We spent hours rehearsing together, this time taking advantage of Simón's offer to loan us his basement as a rehearsal space, it being a far more pleasant space to spend an afternoon than the shabby old building that we had been renting, which was nearer my old shared apartment, but dark, dingy and full of draughts that crept in somehow no matter how tightly the windows were shut, as if the walls were asthmatic.

Our first stop on the tour was a few nights in Calgary, followed by Toronto and Quebec City, before moving down the East Coast of America, where I would be closer to home and able to drop in on Dominik.

I'd barely seen him for the past ten days. He had been reclusive since I announced the tour, insisting that he was behind on his research and lecturing commitments and spending more and more time at the library. We hadn't had sex, not since the morning after my concert, and my efforts to point him in that direction had backfired severely.

One afternoon, when he had expected me to be out of the flat, rehearsing, I had come home early to surprise him after one of his occasional talks. He opened the door to find me in the kitchen, baking an apple pie and wearing a schoolgirl's outfit, which I had ordered online, complete with bobby socks, tartan miniskirt and suspenders, my long hair pinned into ponytails. I had meant it as a joke, though of course I had hoped that he'd find the idea arousing as well as amusing.

'Sometimes I wonder whether you know me at all,'

he had said, taking one scathing look at me before disappearing into our bedroom and slamming the door behind him.

I threw the pie away and turned on the kitchen area's extractor fan to get rid of the smell.

After that, I stopped trying and just let him sulk, although every night as I slid between the sheets next to him and he turned his back to me, I felt as though we had both been cryogenically frozen, separated by a wall of ice between us that didn't belong there.

I wanted to reach out a hand to touch him, to make it better with a warm embrace, but my arms were pinned to my sides as effectively as if they had been plastered there.

By contrast, Simón was eager to spend more and more time with me, and I wondered whether he engineered the availability of the other musicians so that they always had to rush to leave for another appointment the moment rehearsal finished, leaving the two of us alone together in his basement while I packed away my sheets of music and gathered my things. He wanted to know every detail of the tour, the music planned for each night. I had left all of the organisation to the wings of Fate and my agent, who had every last detail planned with the efficiency of a covert CIA operative, so I didn't even know the answers to most of Simón's questions about where I would be staying and for how long.

I had begun to tire of his attentions. His spicy cologne gave me a headache. The frizz in his hair tempted me to leave a bottle of my hair gel in his bathroom cabinet. Even his vast array of shoes lined up by the front door, which I had once found charming and elegant, now grated on my nerves.

After each rehearsal, I rushed home, hopeful that

Dominik would have forgiven me, would be his old self again, at least for our last few days together, but the loft was empty, and the longer I spent in it alone, the lonelier I became.

When I couldn't put it off any longer, I started packing, taking as little as possible with me in an attempt to reassure Dominik that I wouldn't be away for long. I packed my performance costumes, the long black dress that he had bought for me for my first solo gig, a couple of shorter cocktail dresses for smaller, more intimate venues or those that might be too conservative to cope with a see-through dress.

On the night before my departure, Dominik was out, working.

Simón called to wish me good luck, as I was flying out first thing in the morning. I let the phone ring to voicemail and didn't pick up his message.

In a last-ditch effort to make things up with Dominik, I laced myself into my black corset, as tight as I could without any assistance, and decorated myself with the night shade of lipstick that he preferred, in the same way that I had for our first night together in the loft, the way that he had painted me when I played for him and his secret audience, painting my nipples and then my labia a vivid shade of red.

I turned off all the lights in the apartment, other than one spotlight in the ceiling fixed directly over the wooden living-room floor.

Then I held my violin and my bow in position and waited.

And waited and waited.

The clock struck midnight and still he didn't come.

Had he been any other man, I would have expected him to arrive drunk, but Dominik didn't drink, meaning that wherever he was, he knew what time it was and that it was my last night in New York before the tour.

Was he with another woman? Unlikely, I thought. He would be alone, surrounded by his books probably, drowning out his anger with a flood of words.

I climbed into bed and closed my eyes, not bothering to unlace the corset or to wash off the lipstick.

He woke me before dawn, the time when only birds, garbage men and women, and teenagers on their way home from the night before are still up and roaming the city.

'I was waiting for you,' I said sleepily.

'I know.'

He took hold of the laces at the back of the corset and pulled me up onto my knees. His breathing was heavy, catching in his throat.

I felt the almost imperceptible current from his arm lifting into the air before his hand came down on my rump with a loud slap, first one side, then the other.

I jumped in shock, then lowered my chest down further onto the bed, pushing my arse into the air to give him better access, like a dog waiting to be mounted.

How I had missed this, the heaviness of his hands on my body, which washed all other thoughts out of my head, the chance to show him that there was nothing that I wouldn't do for him, the delicious expectation of the things that he might ask me to do for him and how much his requests turned me on. It was as if he was surrendering to his lust for me when he got into this sort of mood, allowing his passion to drive his actions despite whatever reservations his brain might hold. That ability that I had to drive him to submit to his desire gave me a heady rush of power, even when I was the one on my knees.

He stroked me gently, easing the sting, and then nudged my legs apart. 'Spread your legs.'

He ran his finger between my lips, wiping the moisture up to my arsehole.

'You missed me, I see.'

'Yes, very much.'

'Put your hands behind your back.'

I leaned further onto my haunches so that I could balance, with my arms behind my back and hands clasped together in prayer position. I regretted giving up my yoga classes of late, as I hadn't had time with all the rehearsals. My shoulders ached, but the aching just made me more aroused. I wanted Dominik to take me further than he had before, to wipe away all the discomfort of the last few days with his touch.

I heard the rope before I felt it, the swish of the length unravelling. It felt rough against my skin, the frayed edges brushing my wrists. He bound my arms tightly together, handcuff style.

'Bring your knees closer to your chest.'

His voice was quiet, calm, firm, a tone that from previous experience, I knew was a prelude to much rougher treatment.

He wound the rope round my ankles, tying my legs to my wrists so that I was on all fours in front of him, face down in the covers and completely unable to move.

Then he raised his hand again, bought it down on my rear with another hard smack and then another, and another and another, until my eyes began to water and time folded in on itself. The stinging blended into another sensation altogether and my initial yelps of surprise and hurt became cries of pleasure.

For a moment, I felt as though I was a part of his body, that somehow through the act of his palm meeting my flesh we had become conjoined in a way that was sexual but more than sex could ever be, both of us journeying together into unknown parts of our psyches in an act that was as intimate mentally as it was physically.

Then I heard the unbuckling of his leather belt, and the soft swish as he pulled the length of leather through the tabs of his trousers, the very slight creak as he folded the two ends together and then the soft current as his makeshift paddle flew through the air and landed on one butt cheek and then the other. It felt remarkably similar to his hand, and soon I could not distinguish between the impact of his skin and the belt.

Occasionally I felt a brush of cloth against my feet as he leaned against me, still fully clothed, and in the morning I would imagine how we might have looked to a curious neighbour or a fly on the wall. Some might say beautiful, others immoral; others still would call us ridiculous. A tired man in a crumpled suit and a naked girl on her knees and bound in front of him. I would bear the marks of his hand and his belt for the better part of the week, would have a sharp reminder of our last hour in bed together each time I sat down.

For now, though, I just let my mind swim into the sensation of his hand against my arse, the wetness seeping down my legs a vivid reminder of my body's response to this strange form of lovemaking that bound the two of us together as tightly as the rope round my ankles.

He paused for breath, resting his hands gently on my rear cheeks, and leaned forward, squeezing my hands to check that they weren't going cold, turning blue. I wiggled my fingers to confirm that I was OK, about the only movement that I was capable of at that moment, as the spanking had sent me into a trance.

He ran his hands over my body, caressing my legs, sliding his fingers inside me again, feeling no doubt the slickness of my lips, the lubrication that he had created; then he dropped to his knees and buried his face between my thighs, nibbling at my lips, fucking me with his tongue.

I heard the squeak of the drawer of his bedside table opening, a sound that during sex gave me the same thrill as the fizz of a can of cola opening on a hot day. It was a sure promise of something pleasant to come.

The lube was icy cold against the skin of my arsehole, though warmed quickly as he inserted first one finger and then another. Another man might have commented that I was tight there, but Dominik was ever silent, though his breath grew more and more ragged. I couldn't hear his heart beating, nor could I see the expression on his face, but I imagined that he was as lost in lust as I was, eyes closed and mouth smiling in satisfaction at the responses that he was eliciting from me.

He ran his cock up and down the cleft in my arse, the head of it soft and silky, slippery with lubricant, both of the chemical and the natural variety. He rested it against my arsehole and began to press, tentatively, then seemed to change his mind. He bent down hurriedly and untied my feet and ankles, his hard cock banging against my thighs as he did so.

The blood rushed back into my feet and hands, and I wriggled both, easing the inevitable pins and needles.

'Are you OK?' he said, stroking my limbs, warming the parts of me that had threatened to go cold without the benefit of circulation.

'Yes, please don't stop.'

There's something about anal sex. It's a sensation that I had experienced only a handful of times, but which always gave me the feeling of being owned, of giving myself to a man entirely.

Dominik returned his attentions to my opening. I held my breath as he pressed slowly, then harder, going deeper with every push, as I relaxed, opened myself up to him. I grasped the covers in handfuls as he pumped inside me. He had given up his silence now, and his pleasure was audible with each thrust.

He grasped a handful of my hair and pulled me up, using it like reins to help him push harder as his movements became steadily quicker and less controlled, accelerating to frantic levels until he came inside me, collapsing onto my back, his warm come filling me and dribbling down the inside of my leg.

He lay inside me until I felt his cock soften, his breath hot against my ear.

It was daylight in New York.

I began to shift, moving to get up, clean myself.

'No. Stay,' he said. 'I want you to feel me inside you like that.'

He curled up behind me, spooning, with his hand wrapped over my chest, holding my breast in his hand, until my alarm sounded, time for me to leave, as the limo booked by Susan would arrive at any moment to take me to the airport.

He was in the kitchen, making me a coffee when I woke to find bruises blooming over my body and the sheets smeared with shades of red, like blood.

The remains of my night-time lipstick, the colour that I used to make the transition into my evening person, had spread over the bedding, harsher than harsh in the day-time.

Midnight in Calgary, where the men all seem to wear cowboy hats. My hotel room here could have come straight from a catalogue of hotel rooms from the 1950s. Functional, grey, depressing in its colour scheme. The windows double-glazed so that not a sound from outside could make its way in. A pocket of emptiness and an empty girl standing at its centre.

Life without Dominik again.

The imagined marks of his hands across my body, like a road map of our relationship.

Just as I was leaving New York, on a mad impulse, I had packed the short length of rope into my case.

I tightened it round my neck as I wandered naked around the desert of the room.

I lowered my fingers to my midriff and beyond and touched myself, the image of Dominik imprinted on my mind, wishing for him to materialise by my side, take hold of the rope and just pull and tighten it until I came, or fainted, or died.

New Zealand, Australia, London, New York and now, of all places, Calgary. On the road again.

# 8

## *Infidelities*

In theory, Dominik had been granted the fellowship so that he could research a possible project, a paper at least but maybe even a book on American expatriate writers and musicians in Paris in the immediate post-World War II years. It was a subject he found interesting and that offered extensive opportunities for genuine scholarship, as it had been pretty much neglected by other academics. However, the more he investigated the theme, the more he was losing interest in it.

He suspected he might find more research material about the subject in sources in the French capital than New York, and on a few occasions when his mood moved from indifferent to foul, during Summer's frequent absences in the course of her tour, he even contemplated flying out of Manhattan for a week to investigate this further in France.

A thought occurred to him, though, and he fished out the paperwork he had been given after the fellowship had been agreed and checked on the specific terms underlying it. He remembered from the ad in *Book Forum* that it was initially on offer not just for academics and researchers but also to novelists in need of financial assistance to complete an ongoing project. His fellowship had actually been one of a dozen, but he'd only come across the other recipients at the cocktail party that had greeted the beginning of their residence in New York. Two of them – a thin blond guy from Portland, Oregon, and a squat, short-haired, heavily accented Finnish woman – had actually been fiction writers.

Maybe he could turn all these ideas and facts into a novel. Not only would it be a great challenge, but also something money couldn't buy. He could invent a handful of new characters and have them mingling with all the real-life protagonists who had been in Paris during the golden years of Saint-Germain-des-Prés and Existentialism: Miles Davis and the jazz crowd, Juliette Gréco, Boris Vian and Jean-Paul Sartre. Blend fiction and reality, and inject a dash of racy romance.

It could work, he reckoned. He had longed to write a novel for some time now, and had often fantasised about getting published.

This cheered him up no end. He'd been hoping Summer would call him that particular morning. She'd been in Maine, where she had played the previous evening, and often rang him early the following day after she had re-charged her batteries, to let him know how the gig had gone. He had stood by the phone like a teenage fool and she had never called. This was the second time this week this had happened. Following the concert in New Hampshire, she hadn't been in touch for a couple of days. Half of Dominik felt sad and neglected, while the other half dreamed of the punishments he might inflict on her, elements of humiliation they could both get off on. Somehow, though, it felt as if his imagination was drying up.

After returning to the loft from Summer's triumphant début at Webster Hall, he had cancelled his assignation with Miranda, pretexting an imaginary out-of-town obligation, somehow sensing the time was not right for an infidelity.

It's your fault, Summer, he thought to himself, as he checked out the business card on the back of which he had scribbled Miranda's number.

'The elusive travelling man of letters, I see,' she said when he called her.

'None other. Still want to meet up?'

'Would love to,' Miranda replied.

He suggested they have early evening drinks at Balthazar on Spring Street, just a few blocks down the road from the loft. With Summer away so much, he'd grown into the habit of going there for a substantial daily breakfast, which then allowed him to avoid any further meals until dinner.

He'd barely had time to set the phone down on one of the granite tops of the kitchen unit where he usually left it when it rang. Summer, finally? Maybe, at a distance, she had sensed how unsettled he was and guessed he was planning to see someone else. Good or bad timing? he wondered.

'Hello.'

'Hello, stranger.'

Not Summer, but a familiar voice.

'Hi, Lauralynn.'

'I'm in town.'

'Really. Just passing through or here for longer?'

'It depends on quite a few things. Anyway, don't want to bore you with all that now. Would love to see you, exchange some juicy gossip, hear how you're getting on in the Big Apple. I've been reading about our Miss Summer – seems she's been making something of a splash, quite the little celebrity. I'm rather jealous and beginning to regret I took up the cello and not the violin when I was offered the choice at only eight years old, but at that ripe old age you just have no idea what is sexy and what isn't, do you?

Dominik smiled.

'So, what do you say? I'm totally free tonight.'

'I'm not.'

'Summer keeping you on a tight leash, is she?'

'Not at all. She's out of town, touring Canada. She was in Toronto somewhere yesterday, or maybe it's Quebec now – not sure. What about tomorrow instead?'

'Can't. I'm auditioning for a three-month maternity-cover gig out in Connecticut. A chamber orchestra affiliated to Yale University. I'd be based in New Haven, but it's only an hour or so by train from the big city, I gather. One of the girls there is having a baby. Victor gave me the lead.'

'Victor?'

'Yes. He seems to know everything that's going on in our circles. Nice of him to tip me off. Haven't you two met up since you're both in New York?'

'We haven't,' Dominik replied.

He was still uncertain what role Victor might have played when Summer was on her own in Manhattan. When he asked her if they had made contact, she had always proven evasive. Shifty even. He guessed something had happened, but part of him didn't wish to know exactly what. You can't rewrite the past, he knew.

'Anyway, I'm taking the train from Grand Central to New Haven tomorrow afternoon and then will have three days of auditions and practice with the other guys. After which they will let me know if I'm good enough to join them. That's why I thought that maybe tonight . . .'

Dominik really felt like seeing Lauralynn. She had always intrigued and attracted him, even though he knew he was not her type and she preferred women. Her sense of fun was infectious. He reflected and then suggested, 'Listen, I'd arranged to meet up with someone. Why don't you join us? We'll see how it goes. If we all hit it off, we can move on to dinner, make an evening of it. If it doesn't click, I'll know soon enough and you and I can go our own way. It's just a woman I met on a plane and thought was interesting.'

'Oh, you naughty man,' Lauralynn chuckled on the other end of the phone line. 'I like it. Don't tell me she's also a musician?'

'She isn't. What makes you think I'm fixated on string players? I might also have a soft spot for the brass section, you know.'

'Wicked, but I'd steer clear of percussionists if I were you. I'm told they're true cock-teasers,' Lauralynn said.

Arrangements were made. In order not to embarrass Miranda, they agreed that Lauralynn would walk into Balthazar a quarter of an hour after Dominik had planned to meet Miranda and pretend she came across them by pure accident. He knew she was enough of an actress to pull it off and make the reunion seem like a happy coincidence.

Miranda had excused herself and walked over to the washroom. They were already on their third round of drinks.

'She likes me,' Lauralynn said.

'Does she?' Dominik queried.

'I can tell. We gals have a special kind of radar,' she added.

'Like guys' gaydar?' he asked.

'Exactly,' Lauralynn whispered, leaning closer to Dominik over the glass-laden table. 'She likes you too. Just observe the way she keeps on making contact with us when she's animated, brushing her fingers against your arm, my leg, sweeping her hair back. A terrible flirt, she is.'

'A flirt is one thing,' Dominik said.

Miranda was sashaying her way back from the depths of the café, just a touch unsteady on high-heeled feet, a broad smile on her lips, her billowing white skirt contrasting with her black silk blouse, as she neared their table and squeezed herself on the banquette between Lauralynn and Dominik. Lauralynn wore her familiar cruising outfit of white T-shirt, jeans and black leather boots, and looked like anything but a demure cello player.

'You two are so much fun,' Miranda said, her hands resting gently on the thighs of the two drinking companions on either side of her, almost grazing the thin material of Dominik's trousers, where his cock rested, in passing. He knew this was no accident.

Lauralynn was right. It wasn't just the alcohol speaking; it merely served as an additional encouragement.

Dominik exchanged glances with Lauralynn as Miranda downed the rest of her glass of red wine, the first Beaujolais nouveau of the year.

Lauralynn's eyes sparkled with undiluted mischief.

She shifted in her seat until she was leaning against Miranda. 'Miranda?'

'Yes?' Miranda turned her head towards Lauralynn.

Lauralynn brought her hand to Miranda's chin, held it there briefly and then languidly approached her lips to Miranda's and kissed her. The American woman blushed but didn't steer away from the unexpected and intimate contact. Her eyes darted around and fell on Dominik, then moved on, checking out who else might be watching, waiters or other café customers. Her hand on Dominik's thigh firmed its grip. The kiss continued. Just inches away from the two young women, Dominik could see from the tremors coursing through their cheeks that tongues had now met and were recklessly mingling. The knot in his stomach tightened, a familiar vibration riding along his crotch and slowly moving upwards.

The world froze.

Finally, the spell was broken and Lauralynn and Miranda's lips parted reluctantly as they both came up for air. Dominik noticed that Lauralynn's right hand was digging deep into the folds of Miranda's white skirt, touching her, orchestrating her desire almost.

The three remained silent for a while. Picking up their glasses on automatic pilot, even though two of them were already empty.

Lauralynn smiled, her theory now confirmed and a mild triumphant look spreading across her luminous face.

'Shall we?' she said.

'Why not?' Dominik confirmed.

Miranda just nodded.

'Where?'

Miranda wriggled out of her squashed position between the two of them and rose. 'Why not go to mine?' she suggested.

The yellow cab they found waiting just outside Balthazar took Park Avenue going north and then crossed East through Central Park. For once the traffic was light and they found themselves at Miranda's Upper East Side apartment in under twenty minutes.

It was a small and elegantly furnished studio, with a thin Japanese-like screen separating the study from Miranda's bedroom.

As Miranda turned back towards her front door to both lock it and fix the metal latch, Lauralynn backed herself up against the American woman and, slipping her fingers behind the elastic that held up her voluminous white skirt, pulled it down.

She was wearing a red lacy thong.

Moving back towards the two women, Dominik distractedly caressed the soft skin of Miranda's voluptuous arse with one hand while slipping out of his beige linen jacket. She had tan lines circling her waist, the bikini bottoms she had recently worn out in the sun having evidently covered a larger area of flesh than the minuscule undergarment now covering her mid-section.

Miranda raised her arms and, Lauralynn having undone the top two buttons of the black silk blouse, pulled it over her head, parting the brown curtain of flowing hair as she did so. Her lacy bra was also black and for a moment Dominik was surprised to observe the clash of colour in her underwear. Most of the women he had known had always been careful to match their colours.

The two women pressed against each other and kissed again.

Standing beside them, Dominik was at something of a loss. What should he do now?

Being with two women, or even just watching two women having sex, was allegedly a major male fantasy and was well documented in the annals of pornography, but it had never somehow attracted Dominik in a serious way. It wasn't something he had ever actively sought out, and as a result it had never happened to him. Until now.

He moved nearer and kissed Miranda's neck, close to her pulsing artery. Then he shifted slightly and began chewing on the lobe of one ear. Dominik was uncertain as to how he should approach Lauralynn now, knowing as he did that she was not primarily into men.

Noting his hesitation, Lauralynn, still fully dressed, separated herself from Miranda, took his hand in hers and placed it against Miranda's bare back, intimating he should undo the clasp of her brassiere. Dominik suppressed a gentle laugh in his throat, remembering the very first time, ages ago, when he had found himself undressing a woman, or rather a girl, who had been seventeen to his childish sixteen years old, and how long it had taken him to master the art of undoing a bra. A painful memory, if a humorous one in retrospect.

Either the engineering of women's undergarments had grown more efficient over time or his IQ had mysteriously been raised to new levels, but all it needed now was the gentle pressure of a single finger and the straps separated and Dominik was able to liberate Miranda's heavy breasts from the dark, lacy material of her bra.

With a nod of her head Lauralynn indicated he should undress as the trio took a few stumbling steps towards the bedroom. There were teddy bears galore spread across its pink cover. Lauralynn leaned over, impatiently brushed her arm against the cuddly toys and pushed them over the side onto the varnished wooden floor.

They fell onto the bed, all three of them.

And Lauralynn took charge.

Dominik's first threesome.

He would later reflect on the curious nature of the encounter and its manifold frustrations, the fact he had at no stage been able to enjoy the experience fully. Too self-conscious. He recalled riding the pliant form of Miranda in the missionary position and feeling Lauralynn's lazy fingers caressing his ball sack and teasing the stem of his cock as it travelled in and out of the American woman's vagina, distracted by her overly affected girlie moans and the hoarse whispers of Lauralynn's encouragement as she squatted behind their rutting duo, his mind unable to concentrate on the lovemaking as he imagined how vulgar or even ridiculous the spectacle of the two of them fucking like animals must look like to Lauralynn, from her vantage point. At one stage, he knew, Lauralynn had sucked him – was it to make him harder before he'd penetrated Miranda or afterwards, or at some later stage in their excesses? He'd also gone down on Lauralynn as she did the same to Miranda, and the symmetry in their geometry had struck him as particularly apposite. Lauralynn had tasted strong, a flavour new to him but elusive in its savage strength.

He'd watched as the two women had ground breathlessly against each other, observed Lauralynn's agile musician fingers slip into Miranda's cunt and almost go deep enough to fist her, while he sat behind Miranda's head and allowed his cock to brush against her cheeks, teasing her mouth, feeling her staccato breath against his wide open thighs as she fought the tide of desire that Lauralynn had triggered. At one stage he had come over Miranda's breasts, and observed Lauralynn's pleasure as he did so.

Then he had switched off, just become a spectator, lost his hardness and allowed himself to drown in post-coital feelings of helplessness and indifference. He'd kept on watching as the two women on the bed persisted with their grinding and caresses, conducting their pleasure as if he wasn't even present. True, they were both beautiful, in their own way. Miranda a paradigm of softness, and Lauralynn's legs went on for ever. Her Amazonian broad-shouldered proportions as they unfurled across the bed were a delight to watch, as was the unfeigned cupidity of her mouth as she went down on Miranda over and over again. Had he regained his erection, he could at some stage have attempted to mount Lauralynn as she leaned over Miranda with her buttocks on full display, an open invitation. Dominik was unsure, though, whether taking advantage of the situation might not have broken the spell, so he merely kept on gazing at the two women writhe and moan. He had been used and now they were busy with their own business. He had no complaints, though.

Eventually, he stepped out of the bedroom, quickly washed himself, dressed and left the apartment.

Neither woman called him back or even suggested he rejoin them.

It was a balmy New York early summer night and he followed the outer perimeter of Central Park until he reached Fifth Avenue, the Plaza Hotel towering on his right. He decided to walk all the way downtown. He looked at his phone. No messages. What does one do in Maine at night? he wondered.

'I fucked another woman.'

'So what?'

'Does it bother you?'

'No.'

The line was so clear that Summer could have been at the

other end of the loft; her lips sounded just a breath away from his ear. Her voice emotionless and so close.

'Don't you want to know who and how it happened?'

'It happened, didn't it? No.'

He desperately wanted her to be jealous. Angry.

'Actually, there were two women.'

'You don't have to provide me with the technicalities.'

'I suppose not. How did the gig go?'

'It went well. A much more provincial audience. Very formal at first. Took them a long time to relax, I felt. But the booking agent had warned me, which is why the repertoire changes slightly according to the venue. You adapt. Small-town and big-city tunes, so to speak. They warmed up. I always do *The Four Seasons*, though.'

'Good.'

The first part of the tour, in Canada, only featured Summer and a small string ensemble. Having the whole orchestra to accompany her would have proven too expensive, what with the travel logistics it would involve.

'I'll be passing through New York in a couple of days. Just a few hours, an opportunity to drop off my dirty washing, I suppose, and get some changes of clothes,' Summer said. 'Thursday, late afternoon. It'll be nice to see you, as I'll be away for another two weeks after that.'

A few hours, with a rented car waiting for her downstairs, thought Dominik, what's the bloody point? I came to New York to spend my time with you! We now spend more time apart than together. On the other hand, he knew she was also sacrificing a lot; it was her career and this was the time to capitalise on the Webster Hall concert and the terrific acclaim it had received.

'I'll try and be in,' he said. 'Summer?'

'Yes?'

'If you feel lonely, you know . . .'

'I know – I'm allowed to go with others. You've told me before.'

'And have you yet?' he asked her, a knot constricting his throat.

'No. I'm just too tired by the time we get back to the hotel.'

'I want you to.'

'Do you?'

'I do.'

'And you want me to tell you all about it?'

'Yes.'

There was a silent interruption to their conversation. Dominik couldn't imagine what the Maine landscape might look like from her hotel-room window. Fields? Hills? The sea?

'I have to go,' Summer said. 'The others are expecting me downstairs for breakfast. I'm told they make great pancakes here. With maple syrup.'

'*Bon appétit*,' he said, trying hard to keep a smile in his voice.

'I'll see you on Thursday.'

Dominik knew already he would not be at the loft on Thursday, as he had agreed to give one of his talks at the library. He hadn't yet decided what the subject would be. He never had more than a dozen or so people in attendance anyway. He was good at improvising. It was one of the conditions of the fellowship, but neither the library nor the trustees did much to advertise the events, bar a couple of hastily computer-designed posters on notice boards at unstrategic points in the public areas. The only consolation was that none of the other fellows in this year's intake, which even included a Booker Prize nominee and a National Book Award winner, so much more famous and with a longer list of publications to their credit, attracted significantly more of a crowd.

He was wrapping things up, inconclusive but light-hearted ruminations on the various movies that had been made from Fitzgerald's *Gatsby* and the actors who had played Jay, Daisy and Nick. A latecomer shuffled into the small lecture room and sat himself down in the back row. Dominik recognised him. It was Victor.

He knew the man was in New York too, but had still made no effort to track him down.

How could he have found out about this small event? Then Dominik remembered briefly mentioning it to Lauralynn. That must be it. Was she still in New Haven, and had she successfully negotiated the auditions there?

'Have you been avoiding me, dear boy?' Victor said, walking up to Dominik as the other spectators trooped out of the room. In the months since they had last seen each other, he hadn't changed. Short, grey-haired, tidy, trimmed beard, urbane and at ease in his skin. He appealed to women, although Dominik couldn't pinpoint a reason for this attraction. Maybe his air of superiority and the unflinching gaze of his steely eyes.

'Maybe I have, Victor.' His tone was cool but civil.

'I thought we were friends?'

'So did I.'

'What is it, then?'

Victor wore a seersucker jacket, white with blue stripes,

black trousers and a shirt with a button-down collar. Despite the warm weather, he still insisted on wearing a tie, an odd brownish confection with an oversize knot. He had a strange way of dressing, his Eastern European heritage betraying him, more in the manner of a formal party apparatchik than a debonair academic, though perhaps it was just the style that he had grown up with. We're all a slave to our origins to some degree.

Amused by Dominik's lack of response, Victor volunteered. 'The girl? The violin player?'

'Exactly.'

Victor guessed Summer hadn't come completely clean with Dominik about what had happened between them once she had arrived in New York. 'So Lauralynn has told you, hasn't she?'

'That you suggested the crypt, pulled our strings as if we were puppets, Victor. That was rather deceitful, you know.'

'Just a game, Dominik. Come on, we both enjoy playing those games, don't we? We understand each other.'

'Did you get involved with her once she came to America?' Dominik asked. Victor considered. If Dominik was asking, it meant he was unaware of it all. He smiled quietly. 'Of course not. I saw her around; we move in the same circles, after all. It's unavoidable – this little world we're involved in is so small. Almost incestuous, you might say. I knew she was your thing, though . . . Look but don't touch, eh?'

'My thing?'

'Your pet, no?'

'You have a strange way of putting it, Victor.'

'A pretty one, she is. And a wonderful violin player. Quite the little celebrity now, no?'

'Yes.'

'You are together again? Is that why you are in New York?' Victor asked.

'Together? Not quite,' Dominik lied, 'but we still see each other.'

'Wonderful.'

'Back at your place, when you kindly allowed me to watch her playing . . .' Victor hesitated, no doubt imagining the occasion when Dominik had requested Summer perform naked and blindfolded while a stranger – Victor – watched. Dominik thought of how one thing had led to another and how he'd used her in front of this very man.

'What?'

'She has too much pride. As much as she appears to be a slave to her lust, there is something about her – you can see it in her eyes, her posture. She's fighting her own urges, her inner nature.'

'Is that so?' Nevertheless, Dominik recognised the truth in Victor's words.

'Like a wild horse,' Victor continued. 'Some women have to be broken. It's all part of the ritual. They have to accept who they are, deep down, and then you can build them all over again, reassemble the pieces. Except now you have become the one in control.'

'Hmm . . . I know Summer well,' Dominik remarked dismissively. 'I don't believe I will require any outside help.'

'It wasn't a suggestion,' Victor said. 'Just a remark. Anyway, it's good to see you again. Do you have any plans? Right now? I know a wonderful Ukrainian restaurant on Second Avenue near St Mark's Place. Their pierogi and stuffed cabbage are just like back home. Why don't I take you there? My treat. We must become friends again.'

Dominik looked at Victor and the broad piratical smile spreading across his face, his carefully trimmed grey beard a perfect shape. He realised Victor had something at the back of his mind, but he didn't care. The game could continue, surely.

'Why not,' he replied.

Summer had visited the loft, taken most of the outfits from her rail in the built-in wardrobe and filled the washing machine, which was still on its final spin and dry cycle when Dominik got home. She had not left a note commenting on his absence or even to say hi.

She had rested in their bed a moment at least, though, as the smell of her perfume still lingered.

He dreamed of her that night.

And of wild horses.

Was it Summer's way of torturing him, punishing him for his tryst with Lauralynn and Miranda?

She couldn't have imagined a better way.

Curious, Dominik looked through Summer's wardrobe again and noted that the corset was no longer there. It had been previously, he knew, while she was on the Canadian leg of her tour. For the East Coast, she had taken it along.

So, he guessed, she would be following his instructions and finding herself another man for a night or two. Wearing that corset for someone else, though, was another thing altogether, a message of betrayal. Like twisting the knife. Damn you, Summer!

They had divided the wardrobe: her garments on the left-hand side, his on the right. His own wardrobe was functional and fairly monochrome – mostly black trousers, a handful of suits, all but one black, a ton of T-shirts, a couple of dozen shirts ranging from white to black, and most blue in between, a few dark cashmere sweaters and the obligatory tuxedo for dreary functions. He pulled it off the hanger.

Victor had invited him to a small soirée in Brooklyn that he was organising.

'A bit formal, my friend,' he had said, 'but I'm confident you will enjoy the evening.'

The brownstone was five minutes' walk from a stop on the F Line on a leafy street, past a parade of diminutive ethnic restaurants, a towering two-storey suburban building complete with fake colonial wooden porch and rising steps.

Dominik was greeted at the door by a mature woman with her dark hair styled into a chic bob. She was wearing a long, flowing blue evening dress, and every single finger on her hands was weighed down by a heavy ring. A pearl necklace hung from her neck. She was rather beautiful, despite – or perhaps because of – the lines on her skin that betrayed her age.

'I'm Clarissa,' she introduced herself. 'You must be Victor's friend.'

'I am. Delighted to meet you. Is this your house?'

'It is,' the older woman said. 'We've lived here for years now. It goes back several generations in the family,' she indicated. Clarissa opened the door wider and showed Dominik in.

'It looks vast,' he said.

'There's only two of us living here now,' Clarissa said. 'A bit of a waste, though we'd never think of moving,' she added.

There was a pleasant smell of food cooking wafting

through the hall. It seemed to be coming from the basement, where the kitchen must be.

She led Dominik up the stairs to the first floor and into a large lounge bordered by an extended bay of tall windows that looked out on a long, unkempt garden. There were a dozen or so other guests already present, sipping champagne from long-stemmed crystal glasses, mostly couples, chattering softly.

'Victor not here yet?' Dominik enquired.

'He and his companions should be here any minute now,' Clarissa informed him. 'Come,' she said, pointing to a salt and pepper-haired older man standing by the piano in a corner of the room, 'let me introduce you. This is Edward, my husband.'

Edward was wearing a brown houndstooth waistcoat and a deep-brown dinner jacket. A cummerbund circled his waist. His thin moustache was trimmed neatly like a wartime hero in a 1940s movie, and a diamond shone in his right ear lobe. Quite the dandy, Dominik thought. There was something energetic about the man, even when he stood still.

His grip was firm and confident as they shook hands.

'Victor has told us all about you,' he said.

'Has he? In that case you have a distinct advantage over me.'

The front door's buzzer rang and Edward excused himself. He and Clarissa were taking it in turn to go downstairs and greet newcomers.

Dominik walked over to the table and helped himself to a glass of mineral water, then looked out of the window into the garden, where roses grew wild in the borders, shedding petals in the breeze like red, pink and white butterflies. At regular intervals the greenery was interrupted by a series of stone slabs, like altars or small tombstones.

For an instant, Dominik's imagination tripped the light fantastic with all sorts of crazy thoughts, inspired by his previous knowledge of Victor and the crowd he ran with.

Indeed, this was the sort of isolated garden in which much could happen, he reckoned, the high wooden fences circumscribing it, shielding it from view with canny perfection.

Just as his thoughts were about to take an even wilder turn, he felt a hand quietly tap his shoulder.

'Hello, stranger.'

Dominik turned round.

It was Lauralynn, and standing next to her, with a shy grin on her lips, Miranda. Both women wore exquisite evening dresses that bared their shoulders. Statuesque Lauralynn's tanned arms emerged from a cocoon-like second skin of shimmery white material, and she stood, high-heeled, a whole head and a half taller than the American woman, whose outfit was scarlet and altogether looser from the waist downwards. Both women were evidently braless and Dominik could not avoid gazing at the hardness of their nipples straining against the fabric of their dresses.

He caught hold of himself.

'You've escaped New Haven?'

'Indeed. And convinced Miranda to join us . . .'

She was about to say something more when Dominik noticed Victor, fully tuxedoed and standing rigidly straight, at their side.

'Good evening, Dominik. Thank you for coming.'

'Hello, Victor,' Dominik said. 'I see you know both these remarkable ladies already.'

'Lauralynn is a friend of long date,' Victor replied, 'and Miranda has come along as her special guest and kindly consented to entertain us, haven't you, dear?'

Miranda lowered her eyes.

'I didn't realise you were acquainted with Miranda,' Victor said.

Of course he did, Dominik knew. It was obvious Lauralynn kept no secrets from him. He was up to his games again. Was this a set-up of some sort?

The women walked across to the table to pick up drinks.

Victor leaned towards Dominik. 'I think she's Lauralynn's new plaything. Our Lauralynn switches so comfortably from men to women, you know.'

There was a lot more Dominik wanted to ask Victor about the coming evening and its participants, but they were joined by some of the other guests to the dinner party and introductions had to be made and the necessary small talk about who he was and what he was doing in New York. It seemed one of the men was also a trustee of the fund that endowed his fellowship and knew much about him already. Another coincidence? Victor's fixed smile remained as enigmatic as ever as he negotiated all the conversations. A perfect circus ringmaster.

The women returned and joined them. Lauralynn was holding Miranda by the hand.

They were asked to move to the dining room across the landing as dinner was served.

There must have been a professional chef at work in the basement kitchen, as neither of their hosts appeared to be busy with any cooking. An impassive black-liveried butler straight out of P. G. Wodehouse served.

The meal began with coquilles Saint-Jacques, the soft,

sponge-like scallop bathing in an unctuous mushroom-flavoured béchamel sauce, followed by the lightest-of-light lemon sole, exquisitely filleted and flash-grilled with a dash of butter and parsley. The wines accompanying the meal were on the right side of perfection if one was to believe the others at the table, and again Dominik felt a touch self-conscious of the fact he did not drink.

He sat between Lauralynn and Victor at the round table, with Miranda on Lauralynn's left, and he noticed the blonde young woman's hands regularly delving under the table and playing with an increasingly fidgety Miranda.

The meal ended with a varied selection of soft and pungent European cheeses and strawberries and cream. All simple choices but presented with great finesse.

The two women excused themselves as the coffees were set down and Victor gave them a nod of his head. Across the table, the endowment-fund trustee was quizzing Dominik about the progress of his research and he had to confess that the documents he was investigating in the library holdings were beginning to orientate him away from his initial project and towards a work of fiction.

'Ah,' his interlocutor said. 'Novels are always so much truer to life, aren't they?'

'It would be a new discipline altogether for me,' Dominik replied.

'I'm sure you'll do a great job.'

'I hope so, but I haven't reached a final decision yet,' he added.

Those left at the dining table moved back to the lounge.

Lauralynn was already there, sitting on the piano stool, quietly playing a melody he recognised but couldn't put a name or a composer to. Next to her, Miranda sat, now without the red dress she had worn earlier and wearing just an opaque camisole that finished at mid-thigh level. She also wore a dog collar, which connected with a loose metal lead to one of Lauralynn's wrists.

'Ahh . . .' Victor said, leading Dominik to one of a row of chairs that had been laid out across the room, facing the piano area and the two women. The other guests all took their places too.

'Our evening's entertainment. Lauralynn is going to put the newbie through her paces.'

'Her paces?' queried Dominik.

'Nothing very extreme,' Victor said. 'Not at this stage. Just enough to test her resolve in joining our little group.' Once Dominik had sat himself down, Victor stepped over to the two women and Lauralynn ceased her playing, closed the piano lid and rose gracefully from the stool in all her splendour. Victor set a hand on Miranda's shoulder and indicated to the young woman that she should kneel by the now-vacated stool and drop her head to its seat. Miranda's movements were hesitant, as she realised what was likely to happen, but she slowly obeyed the instruction. Once she was in position, Victor, with a flourish for the audience, took hold of the bottom edge of Miranda's camisole and pulled it up, uncovering the woman's bare backside and upper thighs. Lauralynn pulled on the lead and Miranda was obliged to keep her head straight, staring in the opposite direction as Lauralynn bunched up her hair and tied it with a band so that it no longer obscured anybody's view, unveiling the vulnerable back of Miranda's neck in the process.

Suddenly, Victor placed himself between her legs and pushed them further apart. Miranda was forced to adjust the position of her knees on the wooden floor, exposing the dark opening of her anus for all to see.

From the top of the piano Lauralynn picked up a small paddle and handed it to Victor.

He raised it high and with a triumphant wave wacked the white orbs of Miranda's arse.

Her first shriek was one of pain and surprise. How much had she been told in advance about what would happen to her? Surely she must have given her consent. Dominik was not fully acquainted with BDSM practice, save for what he had read about, but from what Lauralynn had told him, it was key that all participants be informed and willing.

By the end of the evening, her arse cheeks were almost as scarlet as the dress she had worn earlier. Following the spanking, Lauralynn helped her up and she stood unsteadily, her running eye make-up a confused mess, instinctively taking hold of the camisole, which was still bunched up above her waist and rolled it down to protect her private parts. She averted her eyes from all those in the audience and was led out of the room.

Edward and Clarissa were now mixing with their guests, offering liqueurs.

'So what did you think?' Victor asked Dominik.

'Fascinating.'

'A new experience for you?'

Dominik hesitated, considering things. 'Not quite,' he replied. 'Summer, the violin player, once told me she had been to clubs on a few occasions and been spanked, whipped, I'm not sure . . .'

'Did she really?'

'I was never present,' Dominik added, 'but I know she took much pleasure in it. It intrigued me. Must say that I've never been tempted to be on the receiving end of corporal punishment myself. I fear it might have an adverse effect on my hard-on.'

'How funny,' Victor said. 'But enjoyable to watch, no? As you see, sex is not always automatically involved in our scene, our little circle. It can be, of course; this is just one side of the coin.'

'I see,' Dominik remarked.

'Would you like to see more, be involved?' Victor asked.

'Maybe.'

'My New York contract comes to an end in three months, so I intend to leave for parts unknown, maybe even return home for a bit. I thought I'd hold a grand party. The party to end all parties. I have a wonderful centrepiece in mind, a real star, not quite ready now, but I know how to make her agreeable. I am confident you will take a shine to her too,' Victor said. 'You'll like this pet. You should come. I dearly wish to make it rather unforgettable, come the day.'

It was getting late. Maybe Summer had left him a message from her hotel room. Dominik was ready to return to Manhattan.

'Quite possibly, Victor. Quite possibly.'

But he knew already that when Victor whistled, he would come, get involved. It was uncanny how Victor recognised Dominik's taste in women. He was already fascinated by the mysterious nature of the star attraction Victor had in mind.

In Maine, on the East Coast leg of her tour, Summer had excused herself from the celebratory drinks in the dressing room with the other musicians following the evening's highly successful concert. She didn't feel like company, or drinking. She'd taken a cab straight to her hotel and slammed the door behind her.

Here, she undressed, showered in steaming-hot water, dried herself and moved naked to her bedroom. The suitcase was under her bed. She pulled it out and took the corset from the plastic bag she had hastily stuffed it in when she had, on impulse, taken it from the shared wardrobe at the New York loft. By the time she had poured herself into the corset and fastened it as tightly as she could, she noted it was already one in the morning. From her window on the fifteenth floor of the luxury hotel, she could see the lights of the principal railway station beyond the road and, in the far distance, the quiet shimmer of the waters of an immense lake.

She'd been doing all this in darkness and now switched the room's main light on and turned to face the full-length mirror on the inside of the wardrobe door. The black corset imprisoned her already-thin waistline, its bones pressing hard against her pale skin, underlining her breasts, pressing them out like an offering, dark nipples at attention, hard as cherry stones; below, she was quite nude, her bush a small, now unkempt core of flaming curls. This is me, she thought, the corset's embrace emphasising her sexual parts, the slut within her. The whore? she wondered.

A wave of unexplainable guilt swam across her mind.

Right now, she felt like she had to be punished, spanked until her arse cheeks burned like embers, fucked senseless. She knew the feelings made no sense; she truly had nothing to feel guilty about. Sexual cravings were just that. You either gave in to them of your own free will and indulged and learned to ride the pleasure or you denied them. That was all. Guilt was not an issue.

She briefly toyed with the idea of phoning Dominik, but part of her resisted it.

She took her trench coat from the hook on the door, the long, loose-fitting mac she usually wore to travel to and from concert venues, as it concealed her evening gowns from view and helped her avoid undue attention, and then slipped on the first pair of heels she could find in the mess of clothes and shoes scattered across the hotel bedroom.

She buttoned up the coat, the rough material scraping against her uncovered nipples and brushing the forest of her pubic hair, and rushed down the floor's long corridor to where the lift was waiting. Outside, she went left and reached the bottom end of the main street.

It was a street that went on for ever, in turns busy, well lit and affluent, and further up, shady, clandestine and even seedy, as the high-class restaurants and shops made way for bars, dubious dives and bargain stores, most of which were closed at this time of night. After wandering north for half an hour, Summer stopped. She stood in a pool of darkness.

She held her breath.

She unbuckled and then unbuttoned the beige trench coat, exposing herself to the night.

Just a few yards away, as she leaned back against the steel shutters of a closed store, exposed in full view under a flickering streetlight, cars raced by on the main road. None slowed down, as if she were not even present or worth a moment's attention.

Her mind was blank. Her cunt was on fire, or was it her face, her heart?

Slowly the silhouette of a passer-by walking south in her direction came into focus. It was a guy. He was visibly swaying, drunk, clutching in his hand a brown paper bag from which the neck of a bottle emerged. As he arrived at her level, he slowed down. Gazed at her. Stopped.

'Fuck me,' Summer said to the drunk stranger. Begging him, forgetful of her dignity, desperate.

The man just looked at her, dazed.

'Please.'

What else must she do? Get on all fours, uplift her arse, hold herself open?

The man hiccupped, his eyes still hypnotised by the provocative nature of her display, a thin smile across his lips, leering at her nipples, her exposed pussy. Then he took a step forward, and another, and moved on down the street.

Ignoring her.

Ten minutes later, still fixed to the same spot in front of the store's metal shutters, Summer realised how she had somehow become a parody of a dirty old man lifting his mac open to expose his genitals, and shuddered.

She pulled the flaps of the trench coat together, buttoned herself and tightened the belt. There was a crumpled bunch of banknotes in one of the pockets. She stepped to the kerb, hailed a cab and was dropped off at her hotel.

She took another shower, washing away not just the dirt but the memory of her despair, and determined never to wear the corset again.

She fell into a deep sleep.

She was woken in the morning by a call from her agent. Was she willing to extend the tour, which was scheduled to end a few weeks hence, with a further fortnight's travelling in Australia and New Zealand?

# 9
## *A Homecoming*

Few other experiences made me feel as happy as walking through the large wooden arch at Auckland Airport that signalled the end of the landing corridor and the arrival into New Zealand.

It's the sound that always got to me first, the recorded Tui birdsong that played around the arch just before passport control, a ceremonial gateway carved with traditional Maori figures that separated my home from the rest of the world.

When I reached that point, I had to restrain myself from breaking into a run to get through the front doors and kiss the earth like the Pope does, an action that in practice would probably have me chased through the airport by customs officials and a pack of well-trained hounds on the hunt for any sign of forbidden fruit and vegetables in my luggage.

I always felt a little daft about my attachment to New Zealand, considering that I had left of my own accord, visited rarely and wasn't sure if I would ever return for good. It was the land that I missed, more than anything. There was nothing else in the world that made my heart sing as much as the sight of Aotearoa appearing through the aeroplane window.

Aotearoa, the land of the long white cloud, a strange

name for a country not characterised by clouds but by hills, which bubble up from flat plains like the bellies of pregnant women, oceans as clear and bright as a fish's eye and rivers that wind lazily from one end of the country to the other, smooth golden water filled with eel and trout, a permanent reminder of hot afternoons and weekends spent floating on my back in the Waihou.

I had managed to negotiate a few days before this leg of the tour to visit my family in Te Aroha, the little town in the North Island where I was born, a couple of hours' drive south of Auckland.

My high school had got in touch and asked me to do a short speech at the morning assembly, a fact I found ironic, as my grades were never great and I had dropped out of university after studying music for only a year. I had also been asked to play a short homecoming gig in the school hall, and my mother had informed me proudly that my picture was in the local paper. Fortunately, not the picture that had appeared on the New York posters, in which I wasn't wearing any clothes.

I collected my luggage and burst through the sliding doors to the arrivals hall, looking eagerly for my brother, Ben, who had agreed to come and pick me up. He worked at the steel mill near Pukekohe, but had taken the week off to come down to Te Aroha and visit me while I was there.

He was nowhere to be seen.

My phone buzzed in my pocket.

'Hey, sis! Come outside. I'm driving round and round to save on the parking.'

Typical.

I flagged him down after about his fifth lap of the pick-up area.

'Hey, bro!'

'Hey, little sis!'

Ben leaped out of the car and flung his arms round me. He smelled of sweat and grease, and had changed very little since I had last seen him, though his shoulders were a little broader since he'd started working at the mill, and a few flecks of grey were apparent in his dark hair.

'Jump in, quick, before they catch us,' he said, nodding his head towards the sternly worded signs that just stopped short of promising certain death to anyone who lingered in the pick-up zone.

He laid my violin case down on the back seat as gently as if it were an infant.

My brother had owned the same car for as long as I could remember, a red Toyota station wagon that he had bought second-hand for less than the cost of a bicycle and patiently restored until it ran with the sort of smooth efficiency that would make a Formula One driver jealous.

'Zero to sixty in fifteen minutes,' he had proudly reminded me when he first managed to get it started.

I sank into the passenger seat with the familiarity that comes with a fond return to something that hasn't changed despite a long absence. My brother and his station wagon were both as reliable as the setting of the sun.

A gentle rain had begun to fall and the windscreen wipers made a steady scrape, scrape against the glass.

It was winter in New Zealand, but still fairly mild, much warmer than a New York winter. Despite the grey skies, it looked much more tropical than I remembered.

I stared out of the windows at the palm trees lining the road that led to the airport.

'Wow,' I said. 'I don't remember it being like this. It looks like an island.'

'It is an island,' Ben replied sensibly.

'I mean a proper island, like a Pacific island.'

'Did you go to school? I guess the big city hasn't made you any smarter, eh, sis? All that pollution wrecked your brain?'

I leaned over and smacked him across the leg.

Ben had only left New Zealand once, to visit Brisbane for a weekend of surfing. He didn't see any reason to leave.

'Wanna put a tape on?'

He still had a cassette deck in the Toyota, and the front passenger footwell was littered with tapes. I rifled through them.

'Sade?' I teased.

'She's good. Better than Beethoven.'

I stared out of the window again and marvelled at the lack of cars, and the fields spreading out on either side of the lanes of traffic. The last time that I had been in Auckland, it had felt like a rat race, a heaving jam of people and machines everywhere, and now even the busiest parts looked downright parochial to me.

'So did Mum tell you I'm getting married?'

'No! I didn't even know you had a girlfriend! When did that happen?'

'About a month ago. Her name's Rebecca. Bex. She lived in London for a while, so you'll have something to talk about.'

'Wow. Good work, bro.'

'And she's pregnant.'

'Bloody hell. Why doesn't anyone ever tell me anything?'

'You never answer your phone!'

'You could email.'

'I'm not telling you I'm having a baby by email. Anyway, you'll meet her at your concert. She's in Tauranga at the moment visiting her family.'

We drifted into silence. The rain was coming down harder now and the traffic was slow, the usual queues of city workers escaping to more tranquil parts for the weekend.

When was the last time I phoned home? I thought about them a lot, my family, friends, New Zealand in general, but I hadn't actually picked up the phone since Christmas, six months ago, and that was just to talk to my mum and dad. I hadn't spoken to Ben for more than a year.

'It's good to see you, big brother,' I said, filling up with sadness, my mood suddenly as grey as the weather outside.

'And you, little sis. We missed you.'

We spent the rest of the journey chattering about old friends and acquaintances. Nothing had changed particularly, other than the inevitable run of marriages and babies in the younger set and divorces in the older. I was always surprised to hear of couples that I knew when I left who had actually managed to stay together.

My parents had made it, married for more than thirty years. They had always seemed fond of each other, though I had never thought that they were really in love. My brother and sister disagreed with me on that point: they thought our parents paragons of romanticism, proof that two people could stay together through thick and thin. I thought they had made it last because staying together was easier and more pleasant than the alternative of dealing with breaking up and then simply being alone. I'd always been the cynical one.

*

I anticipated the onset of Te Aroha before we passed the 'welcome' sign informing us we had officially arrived.

The town had always seemed to me to be cloaked in a light that was slightly darker than the surrounding neighbourhoods. I had always felt as though we lived in the shadow of the local mountain, Mount Te Aroha, and its shadow spread far longer and wider than it ought to, over the whole town. The rest of my family thought I was mad; they thought that the light in Te Aroha was just the same as it was everywhere else. I found it oppressive, like sleeping in a bed with the blankets tucked too tight.

The mountain loomed up in the distance, a dark blot on the horizon no matter what the season. It was both the reason for the township and the first route that I found out of it.

I'd climbed it when I was a toddler, with my father. I'd given up somewhere near the bottom because the ground was so muddy and the ascent ahead so overwhelming. My legs couldn't find any purchase in the earth, so Dad had picked me up and put me on his shoulders and carried me all the way to the top.

When I looked out and saw what I imagined was the rest of the world spread out in front of us, I'd felt for a few moments that I was finally free of the shadow that the mountain cast, and from that day on, I saw everything outside the town borders as the Promised Land. I'd left after my last day at school, and never looked back besides the occasional visit.

I was the youngest, and always the odd one out. My older sister, Fran, worked at the local Bank of New Zealand. She'd been in the same job for the past ten years and had no intention of leaving. My brother had studied by correspondence through the Open Polytech and had a diploma in engineering, but I was the only one to go to university, even if I hadn't lasted.

I had never been able to explain the itch I had to keep moving all the time. New York was probably the most settled I had ever been, and my comfort there, and in London, probably had a lot to do with the fact that the two cities were always changing and in both places I was surrounded by constant movement, enjoying the peace at the centre of the storm instead of forever running around trying to create my own tornado, just to ease the ever-present boredom of life in a small town.

As a kid, my mother informed me, I had been excited beyond belief by a troupe of gypsies who passed through Te Aroha on a tour of the Coromandel Peninsula. They offered carved trinkets for sale, tarot readings, fire-dancing shows and visits of the brightly coloured customised house trucks they lived in.

All I had ever wanted to do was run away and join them, play fiddle for the fire-dancing girls whom I thought so exotic, with their bare feet on the grass and the gracious swaying of their hips, their hands swinging pois dipped in gasoline with the ends ignited so quickly that they seemed to set the air on fire.

It was just beginning to grow dark when we pulled up outside my family home, the place where I'd lived for seventeen years. We'd always been somewhat short of cash, and not materialistic in the slightest, so it hadn't changed much during that time.

There was now a new carport, the garden had been landscaped, and the fence given a lick of paint. The lemon tree in the yard remained, a fact I found oddly comforting, perhaps because its fruit had been gracing the top of my pancakes from the time that I could hold a knife and fork.

The flap in the front door was swinging back and forth, and my mother's two bulldogs, Rufus and Shilo, were growling deeply, their short legs only just managing to land on each of the front steps without toppling them head over feet. My mother was a short way behind them. She'd come racing to greet us the moment she heard the throaty hum of the Toyota coming up the street.

I could see the faces of my sister and father through the kitchen window, both grinning from ear to ear. Fran lived a few blocks from my parents in a small cottage that she had bought together with a friend.

Fran had been determinedly single for years, and there had been no sign of romance on the horizon the last I had heard, though with Benji's announcement, I wouldn't have been surprised if she'd turned up at the door with a man in tow and a pair of toddlers trailing behind her. My mother would have been thrilled to hear Ben's news. With my sister and I both claiming to be sworn off romance, she had feared she'd never see any grandchildren.

'Hello, love,' she said, her arms tight around me. She was wearing a cream apron well used and covered with splotches of food stains, overtop a pair of jeans and a pale-pink sweater. She'd put make-up on for my arrival, just the lightest touch of mascara and blush. My mother had let her hair go grey, though it was still thick and long. She had never been one for vanity. She was a bit plumper than she had been when I last saw her, but it suited her, as did her grey hair. I always imagined her like a tree, just continuing to grow peacefully in whatever way nature intended. I'd never heard her say a negative word about herself, nor to my knowledge had she ever been on a diet, which was probably why my sister and I both had fairly unshakeable self-esteem.

Fran was the only one of us with short hair. She'd cropped it when she was a teenager and dyed it bottle blonde in the biggest rebellion that had occurred in our family before I dropped out of university and moved to Australia, and she'd kept it cropped ever since. We looked nothing alike, I thought, but other people said that our mannerisms were the same. Even having spent several years apart, we could still finish each other's sentences and pick out each other's clothes.

Fran was like a pixie, tiny and lithe with a sharp nose and a wide smile. She rode a bicycle and wore heavy plastic frames, even though she had perfect vision. She looked like the sort of girl you would see cycling around London's Shoreditch, and the fact that she'd opted to stay in Te Aroha was always a mystery to me. Initially, I had thought she stuck out like a sore thumb, but she'd been here so long that the town had sort of enveloped her until she seemed like part of it, like a barnacle on a ship.

Fran's hug was stiff and quick. She'd never been comfortable with affection. With all the talk of the Brits being standoffish, I had been surprised to find that they were much more tactile than the Pakeha in New Zealand, for whom it wasn't common to greet friends with anything more than a smile or a gentle teasing.

My father stood behind them both, waiting patiently. He was still in his overalls, a uniform that I had so rarely seen him out of, it was like a second skin, as familiar to me as seeing my mother in an apron. He picked me up off the ground with his hug and held me for so long I thought I might fall asleep in his arms like a child.

The door opened again and another shape loomed behind them the doorway.

Mr van der Vliet. He wasn't as tall as I remembered, though he was just as thin and still hanging on to the last wisps of hair either side of his head. He must be in his eighties now, but his eyes were as hard and bright as ever, his expression as piercing as a magpie that's just alighted on a silver spoon.

'Well done, my girl,' he said, as I gave his hollow cheek a soft kiss. He patted me gently on the back.

He didn't live near my parents, or socialise with them on a regular basis, so he must have come over just to see me. I suddenly felt as if I would burst into tears.

Fran saved me from that eventuality.

She cleared her throat. 'We should probably go inside, guys. No point standing out here, is there? Even the dogs are getting hungry, the greedy bastards.'

My mother must have been cooking for weeks, as the table looked close to collapse under the weight of all my favourite foods.

'For the last month I've been cooking in batches and freezing it,' she said proudly.

The vegetables were from the garden, which my father kept a close eye on, and the meat from a local farmer. Dad had apparently swapped some truck tyres for an entire cow, the corpse of which was cut into pieces and stored in our big chest freezer in the shed.

We had L&P and Speight's beer to go with it, and hokey-pokey ice cream on homemade apple fritters for dessert, followed by Pineapple Lumps. I noticed when I went to fetch the salt and pepper that the pantry was filled with three different sorts of Vogel's bread.

'We weren't sure what you'd miss most,' Mum said, 'so we got everything.'

Her eyes were getting misty, but she was still smiling.

'I'm never going to be able to eat it all before I have to leave,' I protested.

'Oh, yes, you will,' she replied. 'I'm going to make you.'

'There's food in New York, Mum.'

'Not like your mother's cooking, though, is it?'

'No, that's for sure,' I said, giving her shoulders a squeeze as I slipped back into my seat.

Benji saved me from more nagging, though I knew her gentle ribbing was just a sign she missed me.

'So, sis, tell us about life in the big city. What's it like being famous, eh? Do you get your own dressing room?'

I laughed. 'Nah, it's much less glamorous than it sounds. I love the performing, but get sick of the hotel rooms and living out of a suitcase.'

'Living out of a suitcase?' Fran said. 'Sounds right up your alley. You're never going to come home for good, are you?'

'I will one day.'

Mr van der Vliet was the next to help me out of an awkward spot. 'Where are you playing next?'

'Well, I was lucky to get a free week here first. Then I'm going down south and working my way up. Christchurch, then Wellington, then Auckland and flying out again a day after the last concert to Melbourne, then Sydney. But only a few days in each. A bit of a flying visit. I'm playing with local orchestras on each occasion, part of the selling point, and it also keeps costs down, so I'll be spending a fair bit of time in rehearsals.'

Fran burst out laughing and poked me in the ribs. '"On each occasion,"' she repeated in a mock-English accent. 'Listen to it. When did you get so posh?'

One of the dogs barked his agreement in the corner.

Mr van der Vliet ignored them both. 'They're working you hard, then?'

'Yes, very much so, but I know how lucky I am. Most violinists only dream of it.'

'I read that you were playing with the Venezuelan conductor Lobo?'

'Yes, Simón,' I replied quickly.

'Are you blushing?' asked Fran, who'd been watching me closely. 'What's going on with the conductor, then? Tell us.'

'Nothing, honestly. We're just friends.'

'Oh, God, don't move to South America,' my mother interjected, her hand flying to her face in shock. 'New York is far enough away as it is!'

'Venezuela is closer to New Zealand than New York is, Mum, but don't worry, I'm not moving there.'

'Who are you living with in New York, then? Do you have a home to go to on your breaks?'

'I was flatting with a Croatian couple who play in the brass section, but I moved out when the tour started. I just crash with friends when I'm back for the odd night, and do my washing at the laundromat.'

I was staring at my food, becoming more and more uncomfortable as the conversation wore on. I wasn't really sure why I didn't want to tell them about Dominik. I could easily have mentioned that we were dating, without adding that I liked it when he tied my wrists behind my back or made love to me with his hand wrapped gently round my throat, just like every other person doesn't discuss the details of their love life in polite company, even if they didn't get any more kinky than doing it at the foot of the bed.

My father barely said a word all night, though he didn't once drop his beaming smile. He had nabbed a guest ticket to every concert that I was playing, planning a bit of a tour of it himself, he said.

My mother couldn't make it to all of them, though the whole family would come to watch me play in Auckland, at the Aotea Centre on Queen Street. 'Someone has to watch the dogs,' she said apologetically.

It wasn't until I crawled into my neatly made-up single bed in the same bedroom that I'd had throughout my childhood that I began to feel desperately lonely.

I had become so used to traffic rushing by at all hours that the sounds of the city were as soothing to me as a CD of whale song or the rolling waves crashing on the shore, and here there was barely a noise outside. The intense silence was suffocating, as though I was trapped in a sensory-deprivation tank.

I opened the window, despite the rain that had begun to fall again outside, and kneeled on my bed, staring into the dark. I expected to see stars, but there were none tonight.

Usually the sky was full of them in New Zealand, the air so clean that they shone like beacons.

People said that I was a traveller, but how could anyone from my part of the world be anything else? The desire to seek out new things beats fast in our veins. I could understand why we come back home, of course. I'd never shake my love for the place, no matter how long I was away, but I could never understand the people who didn't want to leave at all.

I wondered if Dominik was the same. If he'd come to New York just for me. If we'd ever really be able to be together. On the one hand, it seemed doomed. I wasn't sure if he'd ever really forgive me for leaving him behind and going on the road. On the other hand, I couldn't stomach the thought of being without him. I had tried all sorts of things to mimic his company, most of them daft or dangerous, or both.

I'd lately avoided tying the rope round my throat in private, because the implications frightened me so terribly, and the fact that my fear turned me on scared me even more. Even Dominik wouldn't like that, I thought, though the chances of me tripping over on something, catching the rope and strangling myself were virtually nil.

I still had it in my suitcase. My heart rate had quickened as I'd gone through customs, imagining all of the excuses that I would need to use if they searched my case and found it. Rock-climbing, or girl-scouting, as I had told Simón when I kissed him goodnight.

Perhaps I'd be honest and whisper that I just liked a spot of bondage, and where was the crime in that? But my bags had gone through without any questions every single time. I hadn't taken the rope from the case. It sat in there like a snake hidden in sand, the prospect of danger ever present but hidden from view.

How on earth had this happened? I mused, staring out at the moon, my face and the windowsill now wet and chilled with rain. Trees whistled in the breeze, gracious companions to my thoughts, and the odd animal scuttled across the ground in the shadows.

Even the dark seemed darker here, with only the odd streetlight to cast a glow. I shut the window and surveyed the contents of my bedroom, unchanged since I had left it.

I had thought that with us kids gone, my parents might move into a smaller house to save themselves the maintenance, or perhaps get a boarder in to make a little extra money. At the very least, redecorate our bedrooms as guest rooms, or use them for storage. Instead, each was unchanged, exactly as we'd left them when we left home, like the architectural equivalent of a time capsule.

I'd been a minimalist as a kid. Just a few books, piles of records, cassette tapes and CDs, a globe that I used to spend hours spinning and staring at, imagining all the places that I was going to visit. There was my first violin, child's size, still in the original case with a tiny bow alongside, most of the strings broken. A white vase with an oriental pattern painted onto it, tiny cherry blossoms, which my father had given me one day, not for my birthday or for Christmas, but because he had seen it in a shop and thought of me. 'For when you go to Japan,' he had said. I still hadn't been.

The sun finally came out again on the morning of my talk at the former school. It was the strangest thing in the world, addressing kids who looked so much younger than I ever thought I was at the same age. They were waist-height, babies. I had been terrified that they would heckle me or throw things, but instead they sat there sullenly staring into space as if they had never been so bored in their lives.

The corridors and school buildings were almost exactly

the same as I had remembered them, and many of my old teachers were still there. I was invited into the staffroom for the first time and was surprised by the warm responses from teachers I had thought hadn't liked me at all. Even my maths teacher, Mr Bleak, who had always seemed like such a gruff man, frustrated to the point of explosion by my inability to understand algebra, smiled from ear to ear when he saw me by the water dispenser.

'Good for you,' he said. 'You went out into the world and made something of yourself. If only half the kids here would do the same.'

His face fell again as he enunciated the last words and he turned away, mug and teabag in hand. He hadn't waited long enough to add hot water.

I took my mug and looked for a seat, nearly bowling straight into the man standing behind me in the process, knocking my hand and splashing scalding coffee up my arm.

'Oh, God, I'm so sorry,' he said, flustered. He dabbed at my wrist with his own shirtsleeve and then pulled away again as if he were the one who had been burned.

'Graham?' I whispered.

Silence enveloped the room like a wave. He was the only person, I realised, whom I had called by his first name, instead of his last. 'Mr Ivers', it should have been, just as I had called my maths teacher 'Mr Bleak' and still called my music teacher 'Mrs Drummond', though she had laughed and insisted I call her Marie. I just couldn't get into the habit of calling my teachers by their first names.

Mr Bleak cleared his throat and kindly began a loud conversation about the weather with the person standing next to him. Soon, the normal sounds of chatter resumed as the staff forgot their interest in our moment of intimacy and carried on as they were.

Graham was my old swimming coach, and the man to whom I had lost my virginity.

He'd caught me masturbating in the girl's changing rooms one day after swimming practice and had asked me if I would like to feel a man inside me, to which I had responded, 'Yes.'

I hadn't told anyone about it, not even Mary, my best friend at the time, though I think she had always suspected.

The only person who knew about it was Dominik, but I hadn't told him the full story – that I had continued to swim and swim for Graham, enjoying the discomfort of every length completed under his watchful gaze.

My mother had been thrilled with my new interest in the sport, believing as she did that I was developing an unhealthy obsession with my music. There was even talk that I might compete in the Waikato Swimming Championships. I had invented more and more reasons to stay late after coaching sessions, late enough for all the other girls to leave so that I could masturbate with the door open, hoping beyond hope that the swimming coach would come in and fuck me again.

The other girls began to gossip about it, of course, and perhaps that talk had spread to the staffroom. One day, I came to swimming practice and we were told that Graham had been transferred to a neighbouring school. His replacement was a bow-legged middle-aged woman who wore a green swimsuit that made her look even more like a frog than she had without it on.

I had dropped out of swimming classes and renewed my vigour for violin-playing.

'I'm glad you're back,' Mr van der Vliet had said, even though I hadn't missed so much as an hour of violin rehearsal. 'I was beginning to worry.'

I had never been angry with the swimming coach, though I should have been. I had just been sad that he hadn't wanted me again. Rightly or wrongly, I'd enjoyed it. At the time, I had imagined myself an adult, though looking at the girls around me, with their fresh faces and lunchboxes, who looked as if they should be in bed by 8 p.m. watching Disney films, I was shocked by how young I must have been.

I couldn't help feeling responsible, that the whole thing had been my fault. Mr Ivers should have known better, but I would never say that he had done anything to me that I hadn't wanted, enjoyed and been in a position to say yes or no to.

He certainly hadn't made me this way, just blown air on a flame that had existed from birth, as much a part of my make-up as my red hair. He was as responsible for the way I'd turned out as the sand is responsible for catching a wave that falls on the shore.

All of a sudden, my stomach churned. I excused myself and headed to the girls' toilets.

In the mirror, I looked as grey as the corridors outside. I splashed water across my face to regain my composure and wiped my mouth wearily.

I checked my watch. The minutes were rushing by, and I was late to meet the senior music students, with whom I would be playing that evening at the concert. I had the rest of the day rehearsing with them.

Time to pull myself together.

Graham was waiting outside the girls' toilets as I emerged.

'Probably not the brightest place for you to hang out,' I remarked, impatient now to get to my rehearsal.

His face turned a blotchy shade of crimson. He had lost some of his youthful athleticism and was beginning to gain a double chin. His thick hair was receding, giving his forehead the appearance of an egg protruding from the backside of a duck. He had taken up smoking and was surrounded by the odour of stale cigarettes. I held my breath.

'I'm sorry,' I added. 'I shouldn't have said that. Are you coming to the concert tonight?'

He nodded.

'See you then,' I said breezily, and made my way to the music room to meet the musicians who'd been lined up to play with me.

They were decent, and not nearly as nervous as Mrs Drummond. I'd sent them the suggested music in advance. I'd spent hours planning it, trying to bring classical music to earth for a town that for the most part probably hadn't listened to a note of it.

Most of it was Enzso, the Split Enz and New Zealand Symphony Orchestra collaboration. Starting with 'Message to My Girl', the song that I had played in the Washington Square hotel room, after leaving Victor, when Dominik had reappeared like magic in my life. The song made my heart ache, even by the tenth time we played it.

I threw in a couple of the instrumental themes from the *Lord of the Rings* film, which the kids seemed to particularly like.

The Te Aroha College assembly hall, low key though it

might be, was my first chance to put my own spin on things, and despite the informal setting, it was the concert that I had most been looking forward to. The music for the other shows in the main centres would be more formal and included mostly classical standbys, as well as the Vivaldi, which had become something of a theme tune.

The hall was brightly lit, no spotlight here or dimming for the audience. I could see the faces in the crowd whenever I looked up. Though I tried to lose myself in the music as I usually did, it wasn't as easy as when I was playing into a larger, darkened room, where even with a thousand people in front of me, I felt as though I was alone on stage because I couldn't catch any of their eyes.

I was much more alert during this performance, conscious as I was on encouraging the music students, some of whom had been as pale and quivering as white sheets on a washing line on a windy Wellingtonian day before we went on stage, and it was the first time I'd played publicly for my friends and family since I was in high school.

My family had dressed up in their fanciest gear for the occasion, and even my friends Cait and Mary, who had travelled down especially for the occasion, had pulled out their smartest frocks, though they both looked bemused, being more accustomed to nights out in Auckland and Wellington. The thought of not living up to their expectations filled me with much more trepidation than the presence of the classical world's sharpest critics.

The first set went well, and we had a brief intermission, a fifteen-minute break, to catch our breath. I didn't have the heart to make my way through the room, accepting the congratulations of well-wishers and the curious stares of the locals who wanted to see how I'd turned out. My agent had told me that I needed to make more of an effort to engage with my audience, but I thought that even she would forgive me my reticence this time.

I scrabbled through my bag for my mobile phone, feigned receiving an important call, then snuck out through a side exit and leaned against the outside wall of the assembly hall, enjoying the cool air. It had stopped raining for once, though the clouds felt as thick and heavy as they always did, burying the town in a permanently damp vapour. The grass was slick with rain, and drops on the trees shone in the moonlight like glass beads.

I was interrupted by a cough, from further along the wall, and the flicking of a lighter. My companion was cloaked in darkness, besides the glow from his cigarette, but I could smell him, and see the outline of his head against the night sky. Mr Ivers.

'I'm glad I caught you alone,' he said. 'I've been wanting to talk to you.'

The end of the cigarette zipped back and forth like a firefly. His hands were shaking.

'Oh?' I replied.

Surely he couldn't be planning to proposition me. I took another look at him, now that my eyes were beginning to adjust to his presence in the dark. I'd probably get used to the cigarette smell, and it had been a while since I had been with Dominik. There was little time for romance, with all the moving from one city to another, and by the time the shows ended, I was exhausted, ready to drop into bed.

I'd considered just paying for it, hiring an escort, but the Internet had proven little help in that regard, full of women who offered the same services but very few ads for men that looked legit. I had been so worried about the embarrassment or risk that might ensue if I got it wrong and had given up.

Maybe it would be interesting to go with Mr Ivers again, for old times' sake. We could probably even go back to the scene of the crime.

I spread a flirtatious smile over my face and moved a little closer to him.

'You know, I'm sure we could find a way to get into the changing rooms again, after the show. You probably even have a key.'

'Are you fucking crazy?' he hissed, visibly shocked by my suggestion.

'But I thought you—'

'God, no. I'm getting married in a month. I only wanted to speak to you to say that I was sorry and check that you . . . you hadn't talked about it. I don't have much money, but if it would help you to . . . move on, I can pay. I have savings, not much, but—'

'You think I want money?' I interrupted.

'Look, I know it won't make it better, and you're a bit of a hotshot now, aren't you, so you probably don't even need my money,' he sneered.

'I don't want your money, and I'm not going to tell anyone.'

'Thank God. Thank you.'

His shoulders relaxed and he took a heavy drag on his cigarette. 'You were pretty good, by the way. On the violin, I mean,' he added, smiling as he dropped his stub on the grass and ground it down with the vigour normally reserved for crushing particularly revolting insects.

He turned and walked back into the assembly hall, just as

a bell rang to signal that everyone should return to their seats.

I sank down onto my haunches, watching the last red embers on his cigarette butt, still burning despite the pressure from the flat of his shoe, flicker and die.

I wanted Dominik at that moment more than I had ever wanted him before.

# 10

## *Under the Boardwalk*

'I thought I'd call,' Lauralynn said.

Dominik had been working on his novel for a few weeks now. There was little else for him to do. He had life down to a routine. The compulsory few hours in his office at the library, or calling on some of the other fellows' similar cubicles to discuss all sorts of literary gossip, and then the subway down to SoHo. He didn't even eat out now, relying on the diverse delivery services: sushi one day, Mexican another, Italian or organic health food from the place off Greenwich Avenue, or just bagels.

It had proven tough going at first. The cursor on the white screen of his laptop endlessly blinking on and off, ideas careening in all directions inside his head, most often too fleeting to catch in flight before another emerged, only to fade away in the cold light of rational thought. Writing about facts was so much easier, he realised, after the initial surge of enthusiasm for the new project. You just stuck to the elements you had researched, presented them as cleanly and cogently as you could and then gave them an opinionated spin. This fiction business was another thing altogether.

He knew the story he was trying to tell, almost down to the last detail. The things his characters would do, the ways they would react, the dance of death and pleasure they would find themselves involved in, but still he could not focus on them properly in his mind. Get under their skin. Fully perceive what made them tick, as if they were not even creatures of his own creation.

He'd then set aside all the books and printouts of old magazine and newspaper articles he had accumulated about Paris in the immediate post-war period – about the black jazz musicians, Existentialism and the French bohemian crowds who filled the streets and cafés of Saint-Germain-des-Prés – and had spent a slew of evenings rereading some of his favourite novels in an attempt to analyse how the writers had gone about bringing things to life, seeking out the technique beneath the skill. It had only made the whole prospect of writing a novel even more problematic. He didn't feel up to the task. Maybe this was a talent he just didn't possess?

Summer was now in Australia. The tour was going well, though the return to her roots was summoning many mixed emotions. She would send him an email every few days in an attempt to describe how she felt, and he tried to imagine the places where she was, the damp streets, the faces of the people and how she might appear to them, the particular way she dressed, walked, that very specific mix of innocence and unwitting provocation she carried in her wake wherever she went.

He hadn't seen Summer for over a month. He closed his eyes and tried to remember her face, the colour of her eyes, the shape her lips made when she pursed them in the throes of pleasure.

Her pride, her unpredictability.

In front of his eyes, the cursor continued to flick in and out of existence.

On the run from an unhappy first love affair, his young heroine had fled the ordinariness of East Texas and a place called Nacogdoches where she had grown up and landed in Paris, where she would meet an English journalist and their story would unfold against the uncommon but fascinating historical period he wanted to write about. The male character was naturally based on himself, on what he might have been in another life, but Elena's character was still proving elusive and all his attempts so far to make her credible had, in his opinion, failed abysmally. He didn't even know what she looked like.

His thoughts were mercifully interrupted by a phone call. It was Lauralynn.

'Hi, Lauralynn. How's life?'

'I've come to ask you a favour.'

'Tell me.'

'I have a week off. I want to come to the city. The atmosphere is quite stultifying here. So fucking provincial, even though it's a university town. I might turn into a Stepford wife if left to my own devices . . .'

'Surely not?'

'I'm not kidding you. Anyway, any chance of you putting me up?'

'Hmm . . .' Dominik was taken aback by her request.

'Summer's still away, isn't she?' Lauralynn added.

'Yes,' Dominik admitted. 'For at least another couple of weeks. She's Down Under . . . Hadn't you thought of Miranda's maybe?' he asked.

'I'm afraid she's given no signs of life since the party in Brooklyn,' Lauralynn said. 'Maybe it was a step too far for her. Still essentially a vanilla sort of girl, I guess. Now wallowing in shame, no doubt, or too shy to come back and ask for more. Anyway, her place is rather small. Might prove uncomfortable cohabiting for a whole week. I gather you have quite a bit of space.'

'Only one bedroom, though . . .'

'No worries. I'll bring my own sleeping bag along. Wouldn't want to make you feel uncomfortable. You know me, I'm invisible.'

'Oh, yes?'

'Totally.'

Dominik pondered for one moment. 'I suppose . . .'

'Thanks, you're a real pal. You'll see, I won't impose on you. Anyway, when was the last time someone cooked properly for you, eh? Can Summer cook?'

'Just the basics,' Dominik confessed. 'We mostly order in.'

'How lazy,' Lauralynn said. 'Give me your address, then. I should be getting into Grand Central early afternoon. I'll come straight down. Anything you'd want me to bring?'

'Can't think of anything. Might be nice if you could somehow conjure up a certain someone from Australia and beam her up, but I think that's even beyond your extraordinary powers . . . You can leave your paddles, whips and other toys back in New Haven. There will be no need for them. Oh, and no handcuffs either.'

Lauralynn giggled. 'Handcuffs are for wimps,' she said. 'For middle-class couples in search of thrills and naughtiness. The smut folk, I call them. Outside of the vanilla crowd, I've only come across handcuffs used extensively in fiction. It's another world altogether, Dominik. Too many people confuse reality and fiction,' she added. 'Now, restraints, well, that's another matter altogether . . .'

That's when it clicked for him.

What was wrong with Elena, the character in his novel in slow progress.

She was still unreal even to him. A fabrication.

If he lent her Summer's face, her words, her body, then she would feel authentic. Flesh and bone. No longer a parody.

He hurriedly provided Lauralynn with the loft's address in Spring Street, rushed back to his laptop and began frantic revisions on his opening chapter and imagined Summer hailing from the East Texas wilderness and a narrow-minded small-town environment. An hour later, he felt as if the character now had a new dimension, was believable. Summer had never been willing to talk much about her life in New Zealand, her life before him. This might also help him to understand her better, he felt.

Lauralynn proved a perfect houseguest, tidily parking her rolled-up sleeping bag and keeping out of sight during the day in one corner of the loft. She also volunteered to sweep up, dust and clean the living and kitchen spaces, which had been somewhat neglected during the course of Summer's absences on tour, when Dominik could not be bothered to be in the least domesticated. The fact that she preferred to do so wearing only her knickers and a cheerful smile was an undeniable, if pleasing distraction, but he had seen her naked before, during the threesome with Miranda, and when she'd sunbathed topless, so there was nothing unduly provocative about her attitude. Just another manifestation of her unbound mischief, of course, as she knew all too well the effect it had on Dominik. It was high summer and even with the air-conditioning on, the heat seeped in from the outside torpor with surprising ease. He normally walked across the loft barefoot, so this was just taking things a logical, natural step further.

'I used to live close to here,' Lauralynn said. 'I was born in New York.'

'I didn't realise.'

'My parents had a ground-floor apartment on Sixth Avenue close to the corner of Bleecker Street. Our windows overlooked Minetta Lane. There's a small theatre there. Mostly experimental stuff, then and now, but when I was a kid, I always thought it was something of a sleazy dive. Endlessly fascinated me. I already had a strong imagination,' Lauralynn said.

'When did you move away?' Dominik asked.

'I must have been ten or thereabouts.'

'Only child?'

'No, I have a brother, although we've never been close.'

'Where did you end up?'

'Out of the city, Long Island, to be closer to my grandparents. My parents felt it wasn't the right place to grow up. I begged to disagree, of course. Greenwich Village is such a great place to be for a kid. So many small parks and playgrounds the average New Yorker doesn't even know about, and the hustle and bustle of the big city all around you. I loved it.'

'I can imagine.'

'They bribed me – promised me horse-riding lessons out there on Long Island.'

'I can just imagine you riding a horse.'

'Lady Godiva, you mean?'

'No,' Dominik smiled. 'Just that you must look great in riding gear.'

'I am. It's where I got my first crop. One thing led to

another. I began trying it out on my little brother, then later with others. It was in jest, of course, but it gave me a taste for inflicting corporal punishment, however mild and innocent it was at the beginning. A slippery slope. I got the itch to dominate people. Never wanted to figure out why. Just the way I am, I suppose.'

'Where is your brother now? Still on Long island?'

'No. He's a marine. Likely in Afghanistan. We don't have much contact these days. Our parents are both dead now. My mum of cancer, my dad in a car crash shortly after my mother died. We grew apart. He went to live with relatives out of state, and I was already at university. Things happen.'

'I didn't know marines liked to be on the wrong end of a riding crop,' Dominik observed.

'You'd be surprised,' Lauralynn remarked.

'Where did you learn to make your own pesto?' Dominik asked Lauralynn, as they relaxed on the couch after their meal. She had conjured up the flavoursome green sauce full of basil, pine nuts, garlic, olive oil and Parmigiano from individual ingredients she had ordered on the Net and which had been delivered to their door, alongside the homemade pasta, which she had cooked al dente with the lightest of touches.

'I once lived in Genova in Italy,' she said, 'with a local count who had a taste for my kind of punishment. Between scenes, he taught me to cook the Italian way. Ligurian food is very characteristic; they use a lot of garlic. You didn't mind it being so strong?'

'Not at all,' Dominik replied. 'Although it means we might be well advised to steer clear of other human beings for a few hours still. They'd be repulsed – we probably smell of garlic a mile away!' He could still feel the taste on his lips and licked himself clean again.

'Fuck other people,' Lauralynn exclaimed. 'I've always been highly suspicious of anyone who truly dislikes garlic.'

'So first there was horse-riding; then, it seems, came the cello. Or was it the other way round?'

'More or less the same time,' Lauralynn answered, 'once we'd transplanted to Long Island. My parents had always loved music, but had missed their time in life to take up an instrument, although they both sang in the church choir. They had lovely voices. Initially, I was not enthusiastic. I played the piano too, not to a great standard, and tinkered along with a few instruments until I found my very own. There is something wonderfully sensual about the sound of a cello, isn't there?'

'As you know, I'm more of a violin person,' he smiled at her. 'Its sound can be so pure, not dirty like the cello, I find.'

'Dirty is good,' Lauralynn said.

'Trust you to say that.'

'And for a woman, there is that ineffable feeling holding the instrument between your thighs, the wood against your skin, the sounds you're extracting from the instrument bouncing along your flesh, as if your whole body is controlling its resonance.'

Dominik was having difficulty holding his eyes open after the richness of the meal Lauralynn had prepared and as the heat of the afternoon began to drain his energy.

'Shall we put a CD on?' he suggested.

'No,' Lauralynn said. 'This is my week off. I don't wish to hear a single sound.'

'I might doze off otherwise,' he pointed out.

'So let's go for a run,' she offered.

'A run, in this heat?' he protested.

'Why not?'

'I do many things, but I don't run.'

'Oh dear! A walk, then, nice and slow for an old man like you?'

'I could manage that, I suppose.'

Lauralynn beamed at him. 'No, I have a better idea. Why don't we go to the beach?'

'Where?'

'Have you ever been to Atlantic City, seen the boardwalk? There's a beach there too, I think.'

'Never been.'

'Me neither,' she said. 'So let's do it,' Lauralynn said decisively. 'Is it Penn Station or Grand Central, or can we get that far on the subway?'

'I'll find out.' He opened his laptop and logged on.

'It'll be just like going on a date,' she remarked.

'I feel as if I'm in the movies,' Dominik said.

The Atlantic City boardwalk unfurled as far as the eye could see, like a long beige carpet bordered on one side by the sea and on the other by an irregular parade of colourfully painted buildings. It was still mid-afternoon and the neon lights of the outlying tall hotels had not yet been switched on.

'I want an ice cream,' Lauralynn informed him.

'Wouldn't you rather have frozen custard?' Dominik suggested, noticing the array of choices inscribed over the façades of the many cafés and parlours dotting the promenade.

'Absolutely not. That's my idea of hell, and today I want a piece of heaven.' She laughed like a child.

'We could even go to the Steel Pier later,' he suggested. 'Go on the rides?'

'Maybe . . . Let's see.' She walked over to the nearest café and examined the list of flavours on offer.

Crowds of badly dressed weekenders and tourists and a group of visitors with kids in pastel outfits, racing down the boardwalk on diminutive scooters, milled about them.

'Chocolate fudge. That's the one that I want,' Lauralynn exclaimed enthusiastically, pointing at the list with an animated finger. 'What about you?' Her eyes were wide open, and her smile appeared so effortlessly unforced.

Dominik gave a final glance at the choice of flavours and opted for a combination of raspberry and Belgian chocolate.

'Cone or tub?'

Lauralynn looked down at her tight white T-shirt and up at the sun in the deep-blue sky. 'I think a tub would be more advisable.'

'Done deal.' Dominik leaned against the counter, gave the uniformed kid their order and dug into his jeans pocket for a ten-dollar bill.

'Isn't this exciting?' Lauralynn said.

Why had he never thought to bring Summer here, or Coney Island, or another place designed for ordinary fun? They hadn't even been to Central Park to sit in the grass and watch the kites fly in the wind or had a picnic together. The small epiphanies of life. Had they been too much in thrall to their emotions, their cravings?

Maybe there was something wrong about them. Were they even normal?

'A penny for your thoughts?' Lauralynn's voice reached

him through a fog of mental haze as he scraped the bottom of the paper cup for the last, almost liquid, remnants of his ice cream.

'Nothing important,' Dominik replied.

Lauralynn looked at him quizzically. 'Summer?'

'I suppose so,' he agreed.

'She's really got under your skin, hasn't she?'

'I suppose she has.'

'Seems to me you're no longer in charge.'

'I sometimes wonder what the point of the whole thing is.'

'That's just the problem with you, Dominik: you think too much.'

'Easy to say.'

'You should relax more. Take matters as they come. Go with the flow of things.'

'Hmm . . .' he mumbled.

'Tell you what,' she said.

'Yes?'

'Let's go down to the sand.'

He looked out to the narrow beach below the boardwalk. Scattered silhouettes were dotted across it, with a few heads bobbing here and there in the sea.

'No way we can go swimming,' Dominik remarked. 'We haven't brought anything.' They wouldn't even be able to strip to their underwear, as Lauralynn was braless and he had slipped his jeans on with no thought of underpants.

'Just dip our toes in the water,' Lauralynn said, 'under the boardwalk. Just like in the songs and the movies, no?'

They ventured further up the boardwalk until they found a set of stairs that led down to the sand. They descended and took off their shoes. The sand was coarse and still damp, and after loitering briefly in the wave-swept spume on the edge of the beach and enjoying the feel of the water round their ankles, they retreated back and installed themselves in a dry spot of sand under the boardwalk's rafters.

Lauralynn giggled like a child.

'What is it?' Dominik asked her.

'I feel we should be in black and white,' she said, thinking back to countless movies she must have viewed when she was younger.

'And silent?' he added.

'Absolutely,' she smiled. 'Come here.' She gestured. He shuffled across the sand until he was right next to her.

And she kissed him gently.

Above them was the ever-present animated sound of families and passers-by strolling down the boardwalk and kids' scooters in full flight.

Dominik closed his eyes, one hand on Lauralynn's thigh, the other digging into the wet sand with two fingers, tracing arcane hieroglyphics with his mind switched off. He knew there was nothing sexual about Lauralynn's sudden kiss, just an affirmation of the way she felt right then, at peace with herself. Nonetheless, he felt his cock harden and wondered if he asked, whether she would go as far as giving him a blowjob. She had done so when they had been together with Miranda, he remembered, recalling the feel of her mouth wrapping itself round him. He knew, though, it would spoil the moment and he willed his erection to subside.

Later, Lauralynn said, 'Thanks for bringing me here, Dominik. It's been a wonderful day, really.'

'There's no rush to get back to the city,' he said. 'We can stay the evening.'

'I'd like that.' They were now back on the boardwalk, and the sun had faded, though the sky was still blue, duller and not so hot. The crowds had thinned, as had the way they were clothed. The night people were coming out, like vampires from their coffins, a different nocturnal race, beckoned by the neon lights now dotting the boardwalk's horizon.

'A nice meal?' he suggested.

'Are we suitably dressed?' she asked. They both wore jeans, she with her flimsy white T-shirt, the shape of her hard nipples clearly visible beneath the stretch of the material, and flat ballet pumps, while he only had a grey short-sleeve shirt with a button-down collar.

'It's Atlantic City. I'm sure places here are not that formal,' he said. Or would it be like some London clubs he had visited, where he had been loaned a tie or even a jacket by the establishment in order to fit in with the house rules? There were still shops open on the boardwalk, he reckoned, where they could find a summer jacket if need be.

Lauralynn's eyes lit up. 'After our meal, I want to visit a casino,' she said.

'Why not?'

They ended up at the Tropicana. Jackets were not required.

What came as a surprise to Dominik was that Lauralynn turned out to be a reckless and compulsive gambler. He was anything but. He had twice visited the gambling Mecca of Las Vegas in the past for seminars and conventions, and had managed the remarkable feat of not even risking a dime on the ever-present slot machines liberally spread across the city from the airport corridors to the washrooms of hotels and restaurants. He'd never even been tempted to sit at a table.

He had once played poker on a regular basis with friends when he had been at university, but the stakes had been low (and when their grants had been stretched as far as they could manage, they had actually played with matchsticks), but he knew no other card games and lacked even the curiosity to learn their rules.

Lauralynn first attacked one of the roulette tables and quickly trebled her small original stake with a judicious game of playing the red and black almost alternately, her gut instinct dictating the occasional variation. It was either luck or divination. As soon as two bets failed in a row, she abandoned that table and moved to another. At the next table, there were cards involved, but Dominik didn't have a clue what game was being played. Again, her success was surprising, as her pile of chips quickly began to grow. Dominik had no idea how much she had made, ignorant as he was as to the specific value of each coloured chip, but it was evident she was beginning to attract attention to herself, as groups of onlookers were congregating around the table where she was in action, many of them men with a predatory air about them. But women too.

After a time, the size of her winnings settled down and she moved to yet another table and dealer, where things grew quieter for a while. Dominik was getting bored watching her now, even though Lauralynn stood out like a sore thumb among the other gamblers, her cascade of blonde hair falling to her shoulders and lapping against the whiter-than-white collar of her T-shirt, sitting tall and imperious like a thoroughbred.

Finally, she tired of playing, gathered her chips and rose

from the chair as the eyes of all the others round the table followed her.

'I need a drink,' she told Dominik.

'I daresay you can afford one now,' he said.

This time, Dominik forgot to tell the barman to go easy on the ice, and his Coke was tasteless and watered down.

'You're a risk-taker,' he remarked, sipping his drink.

Lauralynn's eyes were still shiny from the excitement of her gambling. 'Life is all about taking risks,' she answered.

'There is a thin line between risk-taking and being reckless,' he added.

'I think that is exactly your problem, Dominik,' Lauralynn said. 'One part of you wants to forge ahead, take risks, but there is another you who wants to weigh things, consider, holding you back. You can't commit fully to things.'

'Is that so?'

'But then I'm just a poor cello player and a girl to boot. I don't have a degree in psychology ,' she grinned.

'Very funny.'

'I'm buzzing,' Lauralynn said. There was no escaping the spectacle of her nipples as they stretched the thin cotton of her T-shirt. 'Sex would be nice right now,' she added, looking around at the other customers at the bar, all couples or single men. None appeared of interest to her.

'But not with a man? Or me?'

'I don't fuck my friends,' she said.

'You just kiss them or suck them off, if the circumstances are right,' Dominik remarked.

'Oh, that . . .' she said. 'Just riding the wave, part of the dynamics of that particular situation. With Miranda. A pity about that. I wonder if Victor put her off somehow,' Lauralynn added. 'Or if she just chickened out. She didn't use her safe word, though, and she could have. I thought she'd be up for more.'

'Anyway,' Dominik pointed out, 'don't feel obligated to stay with me. I can make my way back to the city. If you want to go on the pull, find someone . . .'

'No, that wouldn't be fair,' Lauralynn said.

'As you wish.'

'Tell you what,' Lauralynn said. 'I've made almost a thousand bucks tonight. We'll get ourselves a cab home. Can't be bothered with trains. It'll be faster at this time of night anyway. My treat.'

'Very generous of you.'

During the lengthy taxi ride into Manhattan, she mostly dozed, her head against his shoulder, her breath slowing, the heat from her body a warm blanket of softness.

Back at the loft, she gave him a peck on the cheek, turned her back to him and, oblivious to his attention, stripped off her T-shirt and jeans, and casually inserted herself inside her sleeping bag in the semi-darkness of the loft, her long body disappearing quickly into its folds, unavailable, now switched off. Dominik slid the partition that separated his bedroom from the principal living space, undressed and lay down on the bed.

He quickly fell asleep.

An hour or so later, he was awakened by a series of soft sounds coming from the direction of Lauralynn's corner. He heard her moan and realised, with a jolt of arousal, that she must be touching herself. What thoughts or images, whose face or body was she evoking as she did so? Dominik wondered, and brought his hand down to his cock and began to masturbate, albeit more quietly.

They both climaxed within seconds of each other.

*

'One day, she'll feel distant. Then the next day, she sounds needy, demanding, angry even.' Dominik was telling Lauralynn about Summer and the sparse emails she had been sending him at random times since she had arrived back in New Zealand. 'I end up not knowing what she really wants from our relationship. Or what I want . . .'

'Sounds a right case of "can't live together, can't live apart" to me,' Lauralynn said.

'Maybe.'

'The problem is the same,' she added, 'whether you're just an ordinary couple or folk with dominant and submissive elements, as I see it. It's how to deal with the happy ever after.'

'She likes to play with fire,' he said. 'That's what attracts me to her, makes me take things to extremes sometimes. On the other hand, it also scares me, as I don't know what she will want to do or have done to her next. It's as if she expects too much of me, but also rebels against it. I don't want us to end up one day like Clarissa and Edward, old-school libertines, a parody of ourselves.'

'Ed and Clarissa are good fun when you get to know them. They were just playing a part, Victor's theatrical hosts. Besides, I'm sure it doesn't have to be that way.'

'Me too, but I'm struggling to see things clearly. What happens when her tour is over? I'll be running out of time with the fellowship by then. I'll have to make a decision as to whether I should remain in New York or go back to London. I could ask her to come there with me. As a solo performer, surely she can be based anywhere, no?'

'I suppose so.'

'I could order her, of course, insist she come with me,

return to London, but I'm scared shitless she might say no and that would be the end of everything that binds us together.'

'Why don't you?' Lauralynn said.

'I would if I could. I just feel I don't understand her enough yet.'

'Understand?'

'How she feels, what she feels . . .'

Lauralynn was sitting on the edge of the loft's long orange couch. Dominik was at the other end, his laptop on his knees, the Wikipedia page on modern jazz still flickering on his screen like a reminder of his real life. He'd been investigating the black musicians who had played on the Paris Left Bank in the early 1950s for his novel. He was thinking of having his heroine, Elena, sleep with one, but was still concerned that having an interracial scene so early in the book might attract concerns of racism if he wasn't up to the task of evoking it delicately enough.

'Have you ever subbed?' Lauralynn asked.

He was taken short by her question.

'No. Never. It's just not what I am. Surely you should know that well.'

His mind flashed back to Kathryn and how she had intuitively brought out the dominant hidden within him all those years back. The look in her eyes that signified her surrender, not just that sexual thing but the unmistakeable rendition of the soul as well as the body. Of Claudia, who'd encouraged him to expand the limits of his transgressive self and never flinched as he'd unveiled his dark side. Of Summer . . .

'Sometimes,' she remarked, not quite as casually as it sounded, he noted, a gleam of mischief illuminating the pale blue of her eyes, 'you have to experience some things in order to understand them properly.'

'Meaning?'

'You know what it feels like to possess another, to control them, to have to an extent power of life and death over them, no?'

'Yes, though you put it somewhat melodramatically . . .'

'But do you ever really know what it feels like for them to be owned so to speak, used, filled?'

'I'd like to know, sure, but I'm straight. I don't think it's never occurred to me, but the idea of being used by another man just doesn't arouse me somehow. I'm not attracted to the gender. It's not prejudice, I assure you, just taste, like my not consuming alcohol.'

'Don't knock it,' Lauralynn smiled. 'Being filled has its distinct pleasures, a wonderful sensation when accomplished well. I've tried it – maybe I prefer women, but I have a past life, you know . . . I wasn't born this way.'

Dominik remembered how Summer, on that one occasion, out of the blue, had pushed a finger inside him as they fucked wildly and how vivid the experience had been, had pushed him well over the edge and he had orgasmed with unusual intensity. Was it because he had been suddenly penetrated, or was it just a result of the pleasure he had taken from her being so forward and wanton? he wondered.

Watching him, Lauralynn grinned. 'I see I have you thinking, don't I?' she said.

Dominik pondered. 'You have,' he confessed. 'I am pretty sensitive there. Maybe a penis would prove an interesting experience, but then it would have to be somewhat detached from the man wielding it. A faceless man, a disembodied cock, what have you.' He smiled in turn. 'Just to know how it feels,' he struggled to explain himself.

'Oh, I think I can do better than that, but you'd need to trust me. No holds barred, so to speak. It's more fun that way, when there's an element of surprise. "Stop" can be your safe word, if you need one.' Lauralynn wet her lips and gracefully brushed her hair back from her forehead as he'd often seen her do when excited.

Dominik gave her a quizzical look. 'Sounds ominous, but I think I could manage that.'

'Why don't you take the train down to New Haven next weekend?' she said. She was returning there later that day. 'I have a rehearsal on Saturday morning, but if you caught the one-thirty, you'd be there mid-afternoon. Oh, and pack an overnight bag,' she added. 'I'll make it interesting.'

'Is that a promise or a threat?'

She picked him up at the station. Barely more than half a dozen people had alighted from the train. It felt like a ghost town. They walked straight from the platform into the car park, where a solitary cab held vigil in the hope of a customer. Lauralynn led him past a row of pick-ups, Jeeps and SUVs in all sizes and colours to where a gleaming ivory-black Kawasaki motorbike was parked. She handed him a spare helmet.

'Is that yours?' Dominik asked.

'My pride and joy,' she replied, holding up her long hair and stuffing it into the helmet so that its wild strands would not be caught blowing in the wind. She wore black denim jeans, a blue leather riding jacket and what appeared to be cowboy boots; she looked like a warrior queen in the suburban desert of New Haven Station.

She was certainly full of surprises, although Dominik felt nervous about the next particular surprise she held in store. For him.

They first stopped for a snack in a small café by the river. Lauralynn had a ferocious appetite and ate twice as much as Dominik could manage, leaving as he did most of his gargantuan BLT sandwich, barely hungry enough to dust off the substantial side salad.

They returned to the powerful Kawasaki, Dominik holding tight to Lauralynn's waist. It was a ten-minute noisy drive out of the sleepy town into the woods where Lauralynn took a sudden left turn into a leafy driveway and the bike soon screeched to a halt. The isolated house was an architect-designed, rambling faux-colonial mansion built alongside a quiet brook.

'I only rent the artist's studio at the back of the house,' Lauralynn pointed out as they struggled out of their helmets. 'It has its own entrance. Anyway, the owners are away in India right now, so I have the run of the place.'

'Looks idyllic,' Dominik remarked. 'Very private.'

'That it is.'

She unlocked the door to the studio and they stepped in.

The circular interior was vast, with a high-ceilinged bay of skylights through which the light above poured in. Dominik could imagine how pleasant this would be for a painter or whatever type of artist worked here, but wondered what the acoustics might be for a musician. In one corner of the improvised room Lauralynn had carved herself a space: a couple of chairs, a futon, a long metal rail on which she hung her clothes, her cello case on the wooden parquet floor, a couple of suitcases open in disarray. She visibly lived, as he expected, in a permanent state of flux, ready to move on at a moment's notice.

She walked up behind him, tapped his shoulder and whispered seductively in his ear, 'Now's the time, Dominik. Close your eyes.' He obeyed.

He waited a moment while he heard her shuffling around him, up to God knew what.

Then he felt an elasticated blindfold being slipped past his hair, its pressure being adjusted above his ears until it covered his eyes. He opened them. He was in pitch darkness now.

He smiled, remembering the blindfolds he had instructed the group of accompanying musicians in the crypt to wear. So was Lauralynn taking her revenge upon him? Giving him some of his own medicine?

'Undress.'

Again he followed her instructions. She had already seen him in the buff, that evening with Miranda, so it was nothing she hadn't seen before, though it didn't stop him holding in his stomach one moment. Instinct.

'Get on your knees.'

Again the sound of her now bootless feet shuffling by his side.

Sharp nails grazed his flank, journeyed across his bare butt, then roughly gripped his inevitably dangling ball sack.

Dominik flinched. The mistress was checking out her merchandise. He felt himself growing hard. Nothing he could do about it. Not that he was ever going to call Lauralynn 'mistress'. Never in the world.

'Hands. Above your shoulders.'

He raised his arms in response and felt her tie his wrists together. Probably a scarf: the material felt silky. Every time

Lauralynn approached him, he could feel the heat from the sheer closeness of her body, her smell, a blend of unknown spices and sweat. His throat twitched.

She retreated and all of a sudden Dominik felt cold, without her immediate presence. He could hear the chirrup of birds in the woods beyond the house, the soft purr of water running down the brook, more shuffling noises, almost coming from two separate directions at the same time. Was she not on her own? Had someone else entered the room? He had not heard the heavy wooden door to the studio open or close, but maybe there was another way in through the main house.

Again a hand patting his rump.

Then the thwack of something sharp and biting on his arse cheek. The tremor of initial pain raced through his body. Oh, come on, he thought, this is all too ridiculous. Does she think being spanked is going to turn me on? He could feel his testicles retreating inside him in reaction. A bead of sweat formed between his nose and lips in anticipation of the next blow, but it didn't come.

'So you want to understand how it feels?'

He nodded.

Then he felt something being stuffed deep into his ears, cotton. Buds of some kind? The silence became abominable and he was floating in a bubble of solitude. Naked. Alone. Two of his senses eliminated, sight and hearing. He didn't think she would gag him and block his speech, his sounds; surely that would be counterproductive, as she would be intent on enjoying his moans, his sighs, his likely protests. All part of the game.

He waited.

Sensed a shadow looming over him, behind him, likely obscuring the blue of the day peering through the skylights.

He felt hot breath down the back of his neck as she leaned over and a finger, cold and greasy, probed his sphincter, wetting it, testing his elasticity, liberally applying some form of lubricant to his opening. Dominik held his breath, now sensing what was to follow.

A blunt instrument, an ersatz cock, he guessed, pushed its way in, breaching him with surprising ease, stretching his arse lips until he could accommodate its tip. This was followed by a violent thrust inwards and he was invaded totally, felt as if he was being split apart. He bit his lips. The pain was intense. The entire periphery of his arsehole was open and forced, literally on fire, as if the wrong sort of cream had been applied, and that instead of soothing him, it was setting him ablaze down there. He tried to control the sensation, refusing to allow any sound to pass his lips.

He attempted to clench his muscles to prevent the object from reaching deeper into him, but he'd lost control, and following a few feeble thrusts, she was entirely inside him.

I am being fucked, he thought. I know what it feels like for a woman to be filled, invested in depth.

Inside the blindfold, his eyes were now closed, although it made no difference to the situation.

Clarity of thought returned to his brain and this was the moment for Lauralynn to begin a series of metronomic movements inside him: a quick partial withdrawal, followed by another deep attack, a short respite, the feeling of being vacated and empty, and then filled again and again and again. At first involuntarily and then consciously, he began to align himself with the rhythm of his fucking, riding it, flowing with it as the initial pain quickly began to fade. It was not replaced by pleasure, as he had hoped, but by a stampede of uncommon physical sensations he was registering and mentally filing away with every successive minute that ticked by, ever the observer, the academic. His body began cooperating and facilitating the flow and outflow of the artificial cock now ploughing into him.

He quickly lost sense of time, isolated in a cocoon of sightless silence.

At one stage – he had no clue how long for – she withdrew from him. Why? Instead his arse was caressed by the flow of the air coursing through the studio space, avid to be filled again, begging to be used, abandoned.

Then she was riding him again, and this time her thrusts were softer, the organic nature of the dildo connected to her strap-on harness (he knew she was not manipulating the dildo manually from both the natural sway of her body behind and the contact of her warm hips against his spread buttocks every time she advanced onto him) now more pliant, less rigid, almost as if it was a real flesh and blood penis now digging its way into him. Again he suspected there was a man there who had taken Lauralynn's place and was now buggering him. Surely not? And then he thought, Damn, who cares? There was little he could do about redressing matters now. Put it down to experience. She had said no holds barred and had been true to her word. He could no longer get totally hard, although he had been perilously close at one stage, when a hand had cupped his balls and taken hold of his cock and travelled up and down it as he was being fucked from behind, checking on his state, teasing him, playing with him.

Finally, Lauralynn (or whoever was impersonating her, if there actually was a third, male participant in the studio) began tiring and the force of the thrusts inside him began to diminish. After one rather violent final push that almost brought him down flat on his stomach with its ferocity, she (or he) withdrew from him. Again that characteristic feeling of emptiness, feeling the air caress his bruised opening – a soft, ambient breeze flowing across his hole and a wave of premature post-coital sadness.

His hearing was restored. The shuffle of feet. The sound from the brook outside and the manic chirping of small birds in the distance.

Dominik waited for the blindfold to be removed. Shuffled from his knees to sit on his somewhat tender backside. Relaxed.

She delicately pulled on the blindfold's elastic and raised it slowly across his forehead and then his hair, taking care not to ruffle it. She was now fully dressed. Or had she even undressed to fuck him? It was as if nothing had happened. A faint smile was painted across her pale lips, her blonde hair catching the rays of the sun filtering through the glass ceiling.

'Now you know,' she said.

Lauralynn had baked some potatoes and served them with a bowlful of sour cream, alongside a selection of cold charcuterie cuts.

They were sitting on the lawn across from the house, the patio floodlight on, watching the waters of the brook flow downhill.

'Victor tells me you've agreed to attend his going-away party,' Lauralynn said.

'I have, although I don't know much about what's supposed to happen,' Dominik admitted.

'Neither do I,' Lauralynn said. 'He's being unusually secretive, the canny old bastard. Very unforthcoming.'

'Has he invited you?'

'We've a gig in Boston that weekend anyway, but no, he hasn't asked me. Sort of makes me suspicious.'

'It's just a party.'

'I know. But beware of Victor. He's more dangerous than he appears.' She dug her spoon into the steaming potato left on her plastic plate.

In his pocket, Dominik heard his phone vibrate. Just a message.

He knew only one person who sent him text messages.

He pulled the phone out, excused himself to Lauralynn and took a few steps to the edge of the water.

'I want you so much.'

Summer.

It must be very early morning in New Zealand, or Australia, or wherever she now was.

Why did she have this knack for contacting him at the wrong time?

# II

## *A Visit*

Predictably, as so often seems the way with long-haul flights, I was seated next to an unattractive and annoying businessman all the way to San Francisco. At least it was better than a screaming child. When not asking me an endless stream of questions, he tried to win me over with a detailed and unwanted lesson in the art of digital media streaming, a subject I still knew little about even after the many hours spent listening to him with my brain switched off as the long flight from Sydney made its way through the skies.

He wore red braces, sported a side parting in his hair and had short, chubby fingers, a perfect combination designed to turn me off from the onset of our conversation.

I tried to sleep, but knowing I was less than a day away from Dominik kept me soundly awake and neither could I concentrate on the in-flight movies.

Susan had been talking about the prospect of a European tour, to follow up on the success of the one that had now come to an end, but had warned me it could be at least another six months before she could pull it off. That was all right with me. I felt bone-tired and dreaded the idea of walking onto a stage ever again.

When he discovered that I had six hours to kill in transit at San Francisco, the blank-faced businessman bluntly suggested we take a room in one of the airport hotels and 'enjoy a quickie', as he put it, although he warned me that his connection to Omaha was due long before mine to La Guardia, and that he would only be able to devote a couple of hours to me.

He appeared genuinely surprised when I declined his offer, and I was grateful when the signs on arrival diverted him to a different immigration queue for US nationals. Hopefully, his luggage would arrive before mine and I'd seen the back of him.

It was an American writer, I think, who'd said that 'you can't go home again' or something of the sort. I'd read about it in a magazine left hanging around in Dominik's loft once, though I hadn't given it much thought. Until lately. The trip back home had me realise that America was my home now and that New Zealand, however much I romanticised it, would never be the same again.

I had made my choices.

I checked my watch, an old multi-coloured Swatch I used to wear in my teens and that I had found buried at the back of my childhood bedside drawer. It would be quite late in New York, so he would probably be home had he gone out for the evening. I dialled Dominik's number.

'Hello.' Yes, his voice was sleepy, but warm, deep, familiar.

'It's me.'

He cleared his throat. 'It's good to hear from you.'

'Did I wake you up?'

'Of course, but it doesn't matter. You know me, I'm an early riser.'

'I'm in San Francisco. At the airport, in the transit

lounge. I'm taking the red-eye, so should be in New York early morning.'

'I'm in London . . .'

'London?' A sharp stab pierced my heart. Had he returned to England?

'Just for a few days. Had some business to settle. Family stuff, things to do. I'm returning to Spring Street after the weekend.'

A wave of relief flowed through me.

The text message I had sent him a few days previously to warn him I was on my way back, with the concert tour finally over, had somehow not reached him.

We both agreed it was unimportant and wouldn't have made a difference. He'd already made arrangements for the London trip anyway, so wouldn't have been able to pick me up from the airport. It was the middle of night where he was and I felt a bit guilty for waking him up, but his voice was as soothing as honey, and sitting there in the lounge, lullabied by the sparse night-time announcements and sipping a tepid beer, I wanted to keep him on the line for as long as possible.

There were a lot of things I wanted to say to Dominik, but the geographical distance that separated us, the time difference and my tiredness conspired to keep the words stuck at the back of my throat and all I could come up with was small talk.

We parted with the vague promise that we were both looking forward to seeing each other soon.

As I stumbled my way out of the arrival hall at La Guardia the following morning, violin case under one arm and pulling the heavy suitcase behind me, its squeaking wheels burdened with all the gifts from family and friends in New Zealand, bleary-eyed and only halfway conscious, I was surprised to hear my name called out.

'Summer!'

It was Simón. I attempted a smile, looked down at his feet. The flamboyant pointy boots. The wild curls of his hair. The perpetually enthusiastic smile.

'How did you know I was arriving now?'

He pecked me on both cheeks, the fragrance of his aftershave fresh and dizzying, and gallantly seized the suitcase handles from me.

'We have friends in common, remember? Susan told me you were returning. She also happens to be my agent, or didn't you know?'

'Of course.'

'You look good.'

'Thanks.'

'I gather the tour went really well. You're the talk of the town, or at any rate the Gramercy Symphonia . . . Everyone is so pleased for you. Excited. The whole gang.'

'Thanks, Simón.'

'Welcome home.'

There was a limousine waiting for us, with a proper chauffeur, uniformed and everything. Simón had decided to court me with all guns blazing, it seemed.

The drive into town was slow going, as we got caught up in bumper-to-bumper rush-hour traffic full of commuters making their way to work in the city. I had no energy for conversation, but Simón had enough for the two of us, bombarding me with questions about the places I'd played and how the repertoire he had been instrumental in selecting had been received. He was careful not to tread on personal waters, just asking where I wanted to be dropped off and avoiding any queries about Dominik and my future plans.

By the time we reached SoHo, the sun was already high in the summer sky. After New Zealand and Australia, it felt like a whole new world. My world.

As the driver carried my well-travelled luggage from the boot of the car and set it down by the steps of our building, Simón asked, 'Your boyfriend couldn't be bothered to greet you at the airport?'

'He's in London,' I said.

I had another four days until Dominik's return. On the first day, I slept. Like a log. Barely moving from the bed, tiptoeing to the toilet when I could hold on no longer or shuffling my way to the kitchen area to pick at old pieces of cheese in the fridge and sip straight from a milk carton that hadn't yet reached its expiry date.

It was blissful to be lazy, with no plans or commitments. The loft was as I remembered it, spacious, familiar, homely in its sleek and pared-down vastness. I hadn't unpacked properly and didn't plan to for at least another day. I wandered naked, dancing along the polished wooden floor, watched a gaggle of pigeons through the windows as they settled in a shadowy corner of a nearby roof. I even ventured shyly into the built-in wardrobe and caressed some of Dominik's hanging clothes, my bare skin rubbing against the cashmere of his sweaters, my fingers gliding across the exquisite fabric of his suits.

I surrendered to the peaceful ordinariness of expectancy.

Simón rang twice, but I didn't return his calls. I then switched my mobile phone off altogether. Even if Dominik did call and missed me, he would be here in a few days and there were words I would rather exchange with him present than over the phone.

By the second day, I was going stir crazy and, having finally showered, made my way out onto the Manhattan streets. Within a block or two I felt famished and treated myself to a wonderfully fat burger and chunky chips from a busy diner on the corner of La Guardia Place and Houston. I bit into it with health-defying relish. My trainers would be waiting for me at home, but they could keep for another day.

In Washington Square Park, a flock of foreign nannies congregated by the childrens' enclosure with their push-chairs and charges, while the dog walkers criss-crossed the alleys with determined strides as they pulled the animals along, or sometimes it was the other way round. The squirrels leaped from tree to tree, whizzing along the sparse grass borders. At the north-west corner, a bunch of ill-dressed chess players sat at the games tables, seeking partners or challenges. There were no musicians today. I sat and spied on the crowds, focusing on the small children, wild thoughts careening in all directions through my mind as I tried to concentrate on what normality with Dominik might possibly entail. Or if normality with the two of us together was even possible.

I'd left my phone back at the loft, but remembered a public one at the corner of University Place, fed it a few quarters and called Cherry. We'd left on strained terms and I felt I owed her an apology. The number was no longer in service. Maybe tonight I'd go to the bars and clubs I knew she frequented.

Finally, I made my way back downtown.

I took another shower; my body was still re-accustoming

itself to the heat of a Manhattan summer and I was roasting after my short winter in New Zealand. Then I did some yoga exercises. The sun-salutation and downward-dog poses always helped clear my mind. In a corner of the loft by the orange sofa, my violin case still sat where I had left it on arrival two days before, lonely and calling to me, begging me to come and open it. I realised with a shock that I had not touched or played the Bailly for three whole days, what with the long flights and my last couple of inactive New York days. Never had such a long period gone by without me at least practising or going through the scales. But I hadn't missed playing, hadn't even noticed.

At first, the thought was frightening, but then I took comfort in the fact that it meant I could change. Nothing was permanent. Even my love for my music.

I deliberately blanked the violin case and stepped over to the small desk where Dominik often used to work with his laptop when he was at home. He'd taken the computer with him to London, and there were just a few pencils and pens scattered there, a couple of abandoned memory sticks, a sleek black stapler and a handful of thin folders lying across its almost empty surface.

I negligently opened one of them. It contained a bunch of pages he must have printed out back at his office at the library, as we had no printer here.

I picked up the top page.

Read the opening lines.

I had half expected something about Paris, the period I knew Dominik was researching – dates, facts, quotes – but not this.

It was a story.

Set in East Texas in a small town I'd never heard of. About a young woman with flame-red hair.

Intrigued, I grabbed hold of the rest of what appeared to be a first chapter and sat down on the sofa, pulling my legs up under me, my favourite position for reading, something I realised I'd done little of for months now.

The familiar minutiae of small-town life, a curious similarity to some of the few things I remembered telling Dominik, about where I had grown up in New Zealand, but now more fantastical, subtle variations on the true story and as a result more interesting and somewhat alien at the same time, as if it was seen through the eyes of an outsider who couldn't quite grasp its reality.

Surely not?

Dominik was writing a novel.

I quickly skimmed through the chapter, which appeared to be unfinished, and rushed to the other folders. Only one appeared to have further excerpts from Dominik's novel. Just four pages, with large blanks between some of the sections. Elena, the character, was now in Paris, in the early 1950s, the period I was aware Dominik had been avidly researching. Was his choice of Elena for the heroine's name a coincidence?

Before I could read any further, I was interrupted by the buzzer. Someone was downstairs. I walked over to the intercom. I wasn't expecting anyone. Maybe it was Simón hoping to find me in. I debated whether to answer, unsure if I was quite ready to confront him and let him know once and for all that I had decided it was best if we remained platonic friends.

Just in case it was someone else or something important, a delivery for Dominik maybe, I pressed the button.

'Hello?'

'Let me in, Summer.'

A voice that chilled me, that I recognised without a shadow of a doubt.

Victor.

I let him in.

'How did you know where I lived?'

'Come on, don't underestimate me, my dear.'

'We have nothing to say to each other, Victor.'

His thin smile was, as ever, unreadable. He was formally dressed in a grey suit, shirt and tie, as if he was arranging a business deal rather than visiting an ex-lover. His black shoes were polished to within an inch of shiny perfection.

'Oh, but I think we do . . .'

He put a foot forward and entered the loft, closing the door behind him as if he owned the place. I retreated towards the shelter of the sofa and he followed me, deliberate, silent. His thin beard was cut in its usual pattern, trimmed with razor-blade precision.

'We have unfinished business,' Victor said, soft-voiced.

'I walked out. I changed my mind. It's a road I no longer wish to take,' I protested.

'Quite the little star now, aren't you? Travelling the world with your fiddle and all that . . .'

'It's not a fiddle, it's a violin,' I protested, aware I was taking his bait.

'Whatever.'

His gaze swept over me and I realised that I was only wearing one of Dominik's shirts, half buttoned up at the front and covering me no further than mid-thigh. I had casually slipped it on after I'd dried myself from the shower and then had become totally absorbed by my reading. When Victor had buzzed at the door, it had put me in a state of shock and I hadn't even thought of changing into something less revealing. I pulled on the shirt, not that it made much difference.

'Once a slut, always a slut,' he remarked.

I looked down. Sitting on the edge of the orange sofa with my legs drawn up, I was fully exposed. Damn.

'I prefer you shaved.'

'It's none of your fucking business any longer. Can't you understand?'

'Understand? Look who's talking.'

'What do you mean?'

'A woman who's lying to herself. Who refuses to accept what she is, Summer. You're fighting against your own nature. Tell me, are you happy? Right now?'

His question took me by surprise.

Of course I wasn't happy, by a long way. I was confused, torn, but it was about Dominik and how he and I could coexist, find the right balance in our lives; it had nothing to do with Victor and his absurd parties.

'Won't you even offer me a drink? No need to make coffee – just some water will do.'

'No.'

I wouldn't do anything for this man, not even get him a glass of water.

'So be it.'

He was standing on the edge of the kitchen area. I shouldn't have sat down, as he now towered over me, though he wasn't especially tall. He took a step forward and I hissed, 'If you come any nearer, try and touch me, I'll scream, I swear.'

'Don't be absurd. Firstly, no one around will hear you. These older buildings have such thick walls, and your windows are closed and, anyway, only overlook roofs.' He pointed in the direction of the back of the loft. 'Secondly, do you think I have any ambition to fuck you again? No way. I found you too passive, you know.'

I blushed. It was the first time a man had ever said such a thing to me. I knew it was me being ridiculous, because the man was an arsehole, but nevertheless it hurt.

'So what do you want?' I finally said.

'To continue where we left off. Complete your training. Transform you, my dear pet. You have so much potential; it's a shame to waste it.'

'I don't want to be owned.'

'I realise that. I was wrong to assume it was your goal, but there are other ways, you know . . .' He smiled, a rictus so full of insincerity that I felt like slapping him in the face for his condescension.

'Are there?'

'Indeed.'

'And if I keep on saying no?'

'As I said, there are ways.'

For a brief moment, I was encouraged, as if by confronting him with a brick wall and refusing to play along with his intrigue, he might fade away or give up on his evil plans.

'I still say no, Victor. I'm no longer interested. What I decide to do in the bedroom is none of your damn business, but I can assure you that your involvement in that part of my life is something I will never desire. Anyway, I'm now with Dominik for good, and he should be back any minute, so maybe it would be best if you left,' I lied.

'Dominik is in London,' he calmly stated.

He now stood right in front of me. I nervously buttoned up the top of the shirt, concealing my cleavage from view.

Victor casually slipped a hand into the left-hand pocket of his grey suit jacket and dug out a BlackBerry. His fingers quickly played along its miniature keyboard and he handed it over to me.

'You will say yes,' he said as I nervously took it from him.

'Why?'

'Just press play.'

I looked down at the small screen and the frozen image displayed on it.

It was me.

Standing naked in a room full of strangers, wearing a dog collar.

Taken at the auction Victor had organised the previous year.

I froze. Memories flooding back, and together with them a buzz of excitement I was unable to repress.

My finger hovered over the BlackBerry's keypad.

'Enjoy,' Victor said.

Just a touch, no lighter than the breeze, and the picture grew animated and a whole gallery of photos unfolded.

There must have been another camera hidden in the room where the balding man with the glasses had taken me after he had won an hour with me at the auction. I hadn't noticed, had been in too much of a daze no doubt. It wasn't a video but rather a slideshow. Someone had set the camera to an automatic timer and taken photographs of the room spaced at regular intervals.

I watched the pictures on the screen flash by with terrible

fascination, as if I was watching a horror film and could neither bear to keep my eyes open nor look away. This was the first time I had seen myself as others might see me. I had on occasion, when a teenager, taken a few nude pics of myself in front of the bathroom mirror, which I had quickly disposed of later, terrified my parents or brother and sister might come across them by accident, but this was so much more real.

I felt as though I was observing someone else on screen, a porno. I'd tried as hard as I could to forget everything that had happened with Victor. The pictures were even more shocking than my memory of the night. The man with his belt mid-air about to slap down on me and my face buried in the blankets. At the time, the pain had been a helpful way for me to lose myself in sensation, so I didn't have to think about what was happening, but in pictorial form it looked much worse than the vision that had remained in my head.

I hadn't even been able to summon up a memory of the man afterwards; he could have been anyone. I couldn't have described his face or the length or girth of his cock. I watched him on screen now, his mouth angry and his body shifting position as each picture flashed by. Had Victor even asked me at the time if I was OK with it? I couldn't recall if I had the option of giving my permission. The thought horrified me, even more so the idea that I hadn't tried to stop him.

The phone felt as threatening as a grenade in my hand, but I couldn't bring myself to look away or hurl it out of the window. The rhythm of the still images was insistent, and all of the pictures were rough, violent. The sheer obscenity of watching this man drilling in and out of me, and the way

I moved to accommodate him was truly shocking, as were the continuing expressions on my face, beautiful and ugly in turns, frozen in time.

Finally, the gallery of images came to an end.

*But it's not like that!* I wanted to scream. This is what people would see if Victor published the pictures, which was no doubt what he had in mind. The times that I had with Dominik, the rope lessons with Cherry, the scenes I'd witnessed at the clubs that I had been to, none of them were like this. Those things had all been loving, fun, insanely sexy and pleasurable, but that's not how the world would view it if they saw Victor's awful slideshow, me wearing a collar, my face at times suffused with sadness and the man behind with his belt bearing down on me evidently full of rage. Those nights had been something else altogether, a nightmare that I had been manipulated into and had managed to almost forget until now. I wanted to choke Victor with the mobile phone, but that would only get me into more trouble.

'Edifying, no?' I heard Victor's voice, a long way away.

Consumed by horror, I realised that I was wet, under the minimal curtain of Dominik's shirt obscuring my uncovered genitals. The intention was all wrong and Victor's motivations criminal, but the images themselves, the memory of the fucking, turned me on.

I remained silent, aware that whatever I could say in response, he would know how to turn it against me.

'You pull some delightful faces when you're being fucked, Summer, don't you? You'd make a great hard-core silver-screen star, no? Pity we couldn't produce a talkie, all moving and singing! Both welcoming the pleasure you're being granted and fighting it with every sinew in your body.

Mind against matter, eh?' He quietly laughed at his dubious wit.

'You bastard!'

He walked over to the kitchen counter, took hold of a glass and poured himself some water. I was frozen to the spot.

Part of me wanted to throw the BlackBerry against the wall and see it shatter into a million pieces; the other begged to watch the succession of images over and over again. I guessed, though, that he had downloaded them to somewhere safe as insurance, and I'd just be acting in an overly melodramatic manner.

'I don't think it would win you an Oscar, my dear,' Victor said, 'but if it were leaked, I daresay your life as a classical musician might meet some unwelcome stumbling blocks, no? Sex tapes or variations thereof are for minor starlets or reality-show strumpets, not for serious artists. I'd say. And . . . ohhh . . . what if your wonderful Dominik, the amateur dom, were to see it? Would it make him happy?'

I was about to say yes to his final query, if only to provoke Victor, but he didn't allow me the time to do so.

Standing straight, he set down the now empty glass and said, 'The choice is yours, dear Summer. I will require your services one last time. If you accept, the photographs will be destroyed. You have my word as a gentleman. This is my number in New York.' He set a small rectangular card down on the granite surface of the countertop.

'What . . . ?'

'No questions asked. If you agree to attend the event, you will obey every single instruction and go through with it.

That's all. You will not be hurt, damaged in any physical way. Again, you have my word.'

I remembered the register, opened my mouth.

He anticipated my question. 'No marks. Nothing permanent.'

'But—'

Again Victor interrupted me. 'A day and a time. A place. You present yourself. I don't want you to know anything more. I want you nervous. You look so much more beautiful when you are vulnerable, my dear. So much more.'

I had run out of words.

'Call me within the next forty-eight hours with your answer. I'll see myself out.'

He turned and walked out.

Between Victor's visit and Dominik's return to Manhattan, I fell into a deep depression, tossed around like a grain of sand in a bubbling sea of emotions.

It wasn't fair.

Just when I'd thought that Dominik and I could work things out, build a life together, unusual though it might be, I was faced with another of Victor's schemes, something that could ruin my career just as it was getting started. I could go to the police, but my heart sank at the prospect. What would I say? They would take one look at my lifestyle and laugh me all the way out of the building. Even if they were more open-minded than I imagined, it would be too late if Victor managed to leak even one photograph. I might lose everything. If it went viral, it could reach Te Aroha. If my parents read about it in the paper, I couldn't bear it.

I wanted to talk to someone about it, but Cherry seemed unavailable and there was no way that I could mention it to

Chris, my best friend in London. He thought Dominik was bad news. He'd probably arrange a hit man to sort out Victor, knowing how protective he sometimes was.

Thoughts of Chris made me nostalgic. I missed him terribly. He'd been the only guy in my life besides my old violin teacher, Mr van der Vliet, who had never made a pass at me, and I missed the safety of his company and his conversation, knowing that we would never be more than friends and that his advice was not given with any desire to get me into bed with him. I'd given up on wondering why Chris and I had never physically fancied one another. He was certainly attractive to other women and had a crowd of would-be groupies trailing him after every gig. Maybe it was because we were both musicians, so I wasn't as impressed by him as his fans were.

Chris was sweet and quite old-fashioned at heart. We didn't talk about our sex lives, but the few times that he'd accidentally learned more about mine, he had made it clear that my sexual exploits worried him. He didn't understand the kick that I got out of some of the things I liked to do, and he presumed it dangerous. He didn't see it as something fun and safe in a controlled environment; he just thought that a dom was a control freak who might hurt me. I hoped I'd be able to change his mind about that one day, but for now I planned to take my time and ease him into it. More than anything I didn't want to lose him, so conversations about my problems with Victor would need to be had with a different friend. Not Chris.

I remembered Lauralynn, but didn't even have a number and had not seen or spoken to her in almost a year. She'd always been so full of self-assurance, she would undoubtedly have wise words to say on the matter. I realised how lonely and isolated I had become. Spending that brief time back home with friends and family had made me realise how few friends I had.

Dominik had become my port, my one fixed point, a harbour in the storm, but if I were to reveal the circumstances and what had provoked them, I knew I could lose him for ever.

I was fucked.

That evening, I got drunk, for the first time in as long as I remembered. I deliberately mixed beer and spirits, wandered up to the West Village and sampled half the bars around McDougall and Sullivan. I wasn't sure what I was seeking: solace in alcohol and or just the soft, warm shelter of passing out. I've never been a happy drunk; I usually end up morose and irritable, which is probably why I didn't attract any attention at the bar – a blessing, no doubt, as I was in no state to choose a bed partner wisely. Not that I was seeking anything or anyone in my current condition. Life was complicated enough as it was.

I dragged myself back to the loft just in time to make it to the toilet bowl, where I threw up in spectacular manner. Bone-tired and feeling hollow, I willed myself to crawl to the bedroom, where I collapsed on the bed and quickly passed out.

When I woke up the next morning, the sun hadn't yet risen and a splitting headache gripped my head in a vice. There was nothing in the bathroom cabinet for it: Dominik was not the sort of guy who self-medicated, and the only pills inside were my own birth-control strips. I peered at my face in the mirror: I looked awful, dark lines under my eyes, an unsightly blemish on my right cheek, hair like I'd been pulled through a hedge backwards. I sighed and tiptoed back to the bedroom to try and sleep again. The bed sheets stank of sweat and alcohol. I would have to get them washed and dried before Dominik returned.

I lingered in bed for hours, unable to switch off my mind. Out of the corner of my eye, I could see the violin case at the far side of the living space, beckoning me, abandoned, but I couldn't summon enough energy to get up and practise even a little. Time went by ever so slowly. Every time I glanced at my watch, the progress of the day became slower and slower.

I was halfway to Victor's deadline and my thoughts were a mass of confusion. The dull thud pulsing in my temples wouldn't go away.

I wanted to cry, but couldn't even find the energy to do so.

'It's me.'

'I was expecting your call.' I could almost see the smirk spreading across his handsome face.

'How clever of you.'

'Well?'

'Well . . .' My throat tightened as I attempted to take control of my feelings, not allow him further satisfaction from hearing the strangled sounds I was trying to force out.

'Get to the point, Summer,' Victor said. 'It's an easy choice: is it yes, or is it no? Come on.'

'The photos will be deleted, no copies made?'

'Yes. You have my word.'

'That's just it. Can I really trust you?'

'You'll just have to, won't you?'

'I suppose so.'

'So that means yes, does it?'

I sighed. 'And . . . once it's over, you'll never bother me again. You will leave me alone. No longer be a part of my life?'

'If that's what you want.'

'It is. Absolutely.'

'Fine.'

I still couldn't get myself to say the fatal word and kept on trying to draw things out. 'And no cameras this time, no phones or anything?'

'Of course.'

Did I have a choice? This or throwing away my musical career and no doubt Dominik in the process.

'Anyway,' Victor said, 'I plan to have you masked for the occasion.'

'How tacky.'

'Not at all, my dear. Don't we all like rituals? You will look splendid. Black, of course, unless you have other colour preferences.'

I had a sudden vision of the woman in the cage back in New Orleans. I wasn't even sure whether she had in fact been wearing a mask, but Victor's throwaway mention of ritual conjured the memory and I felt a familiar twinge in my stomach.

'Whatever,' I blurted out.

'So we have an agreement?' Victor asked.

'We do.' My heart fell.

'Perfect.'

It would be the one night, one of the many thousands I would now be totally free to enjoy on my own terms, I told myself. One night. And it would just be my body, not my mind or my heart. I would lock those away for the few hours it would take, away from Victor's evil thoughts and the gaze of strangers, keep them pure. Sadly, I knew all too well that the body quickly heals and shame leaves no traces, on the outside at least. Just the one, final adventure and then I would be free and in control of my life again. Surely not too much of a price to pay. Or would it be?

'When?' I asked.

He laughed. 'Are you in such a hurry?'

'No. Just want to get it over with,' I replied.

'In that case, you will have to moderate your enthusiasm for a little. I will let you know.'

'Oh . . .'

I'd hoped that it could all take place before Dominik's return. That it would be a thing of the past, as so many other things I had concealed from him, by the time we were together again.

'I will be in touch, Summer,' Victor declared.

'Please—'

'Oh, don't worry, I will be the absolute soul of discretion,' he added, then hung up.

All I could do now was wait.

Dominik set his luggage down and walked towards me. I'd been sitting waiting on the couch, wearing one of his shirts, the charcoal-blue Ralph Lauren one he liked me to sleep in whenever it had been too cold to sleep naked. I also had on a pair of white cotton knickers I'd bought the day before at Gap. Demure, almost innocent.

'You're back,' he said, the kindest of smiles transforming the ambient sadness of his face.

'Yes, the tour is over. Nothing on the horizon for months now,' I said.

'Wonderful.'

I rose to kiss him.

His lips were soft but dry. I licked them, immersing myself again in the feeling of his physical presence, his heat, his smell.

His eyes X-rayed me, full of unformulated questions I had no wish to answer right now.

'Welcome back,' I said.

'You too.'

His hand drifted to my shoulder, pulled me firmly against him. I opened my mouth, but his fingers flew towards his own, intimating I should not speak a word further.

'Shhhh.'

That familiar sensation raced through my stomach. Memories of all the silences we had shared. The silence that always followed the music. An unforced ritual that had become specifically ours. The Dominik I knew was back, and he didn't want to know anything about the past. All that mattered was the 'now', us together in this room, the rest of the world shut out.

Holding me tight against him, our hearts beating in unison and just a few inches apart, his other hand moved upwards and firmly grabbed my hair in his fist. Pulled. My head moved back, following the angle of his movement, baring my throat. He approached his mouth and, with his lips, pinched the taut skin and pulled on it. I shuddered. Then his lips let go and his teeth delicately bit into the skin, not quite piercing it, testing its pliancy. At the back of my mind, I wondered if this was how a cannibal would rip out my throat, or whether the vampire Dominik might have metamorphosed into while I had been travelling would feed on my blood. My legs wobbled.

I knew his teeth would leave marks on my neck. His mark.

He lingered there, as if hesitant about biting me fully, cutting sharply into the skin and drawing blood, or just eating me in one swift, violent movement, feasting on me.

He finally released his hold on my hair and, with one swift action, tore the shirt off my chest, sending some of the buttons flying across the loft's wooden floor.

Standing there, facing him, almost naked, I had a sudden impulse to fall down to my knees, unzip his black trousers, pull out his hard cock and impale my throat on it until I felt like gagging, play the slut I always wanted to be for him. Instead, I waited, eager to see what he would do next.

Dominik circled me and, with another pat on my shoulder, indicated for me to spin on my heels until I faced the back of the orange sofa. Then he bent me over and deliberately pulled my knickers down, leaving them bunched round my ankles. A finger tested me. In both holes. He moved my legs apart and suddenly entered me raw, his path made easier by my copious wetness. I welcomed the way his cock filled me, fitted me like a hard glove.

Right now, there was no need for ropes, restraints, ball gags, toys, though I hoped he'd have some of that in store for another occasion. All I wanted was the steadfast movement of his cock inside me, the sound of his breath as his pleasure mounted, and the feel of his balls against my buttocks every time he reached my depths.

It was New York and autumn was now approaching and

Dominik was inside me and the music of his movements punctuated the rough way his fingers toyed with my arse cheeks. At that moment, I was happy. No thoughts of tomorrow. Or yesterday.

Would that time could stand still and this never change.

# 12

## *Joining the Waltz*

Summer would hate this, Dominik thought, as he entered the building that Victor had arranged for the event and surveyed its interior.

The surroundings were sumptuous, and garishly so. It would likely have cost a fortune, even for one night, though perhaps it belonged to a wealthy member of his circle of acquaintances.

The building was an imposing mansion overlooking the Hudson in an area of Manhattan he had seldom ventured into, a millionaires' row known only to the few, carpeted entirely in red in a manner that imitated royalty but only managed to be macabre, like a building in some old horror film in which all of the floors had been splashed with blood.

Ornate gold-framed mirrors lined either side of the hallway, creating an illusion of width. Dominik could see himself reflected from every angle, an unwelcome vision that made him hurry to get out of the corridor as quickly as possible.

He walked up the flight of steps at the end of the hall, which veered off in two different directions at the top with no sign notifying the guests which way they should turn. Dominik chose the left-hand path.

The door opened before he had a chance to raise his hand to the old-fashioned knocker. A young woman stood on the threshold and beckoned him inside with a graceful sweep of her hand.

She was dressed in a blood-red lingerie set, the same colour as the carpet. Rather than covering her breasts and genitals, the small pieces of fabric merely framed them, the G-string open at the crotch and the bra just a triangle with her small breasts poking through. Her brown hair was pinned up, and resting on top of her chignon was a tall red feather, which had the effect of elongating her so she looked like a very feminine giraffe. She carried a silver tray, which looked too heavy for her slight arm to hold. On top of the tray rested several rows of shot glasses.

She held the tray out to Dominik.

'No, thank you,' he said politely. 'I don't drink.'

'Oh, no,' replied the woman. 'It's not alcohol; it's chocolate. The ancient Aztecs believed chocolate to be one of the strongest aphrodisiacs, you know.'

'Well, if you put it like that, it would be rude not to.'

He was surprised to find that the sweet liquid was also warm, as if taken from a pot of chocolate that had been melted on the stove. There was a slight bite to it, a little chilli and nutmeg, he thought.

'Delicious, thank you.'

She inclined her head in a slight nod in response.

The house was palatial, Dominik noted, looking around at the vast expanse of the area in which he now found himself.

He was pleased to see that the carpet did not run the full length of the room, but just the outside, creating a border round the central dance floor. There was in fact a couple dancing the waltz on the wooden floor, though no music was playing.

Dominik recognised them as Edward and Clarissa, the couple who had hosted the event involving Miranda. Clarissa was also dressed to match the carpet, in a floor-length red gown with a white lace ruff like a Victorian queen. He began to suspect that Victor had given out some wardrobe instructions to the other guests that he had not provided to Dominik.

Edward was dressed in full wartime regalia and looked like a military hero, or a despot, depending on your point of view.

Dominik headed for the long table at the end of the room, which was set up with champagne in buckets, rows and rows of champagne flutes, large bunches of grapes and mango cut into pieces resting on wooden platters, and even an ice sculpture, a plump cupid aiming an arrow directly into the room. Not the god of romance as many people thought, Dominik mused, but rather the god of erotic love, filling the victims of his arrows with uncontrollable desire.

He had to stifle a laugh when he noticed the chocolate fountain, probably a past gift from a well-meaning aunt who had no idea that it would end up a centrepiece at this sort of party. So that was how they kept the chocolate warm. He'd been beginning to think that Victor was some sort of magician.

'Having a good evening?'

Dominik turned to see a Japanese woman wearing a white corset delicately patterned with tiny red flowers. In any other circumstance, he would have found the pattern appealing, but in these surroundings it made him imagine that the woman had been recently shot in the side.

'Yes, thank you. So far at least – I've just arrived.'

'Have you been to Victor's parties before?'

'Just the once, but it was a more informal occasion. Nothing like this.'

She picked up a glass and leaned over the table to find a bottle, exposing part of her breast and a pale-brown nipple as she did so.

'Allow me.'

Dominik took the bottle from her and tilted it, pouring the fizzy liquid into her glass slowly so that it wouldn't bubble over.

'Thank you. Won't you have a toast with me?'

'Not unless I can find a soft drink. I don't normally drink.'

He resolved to stop explaining himself. Why did people seem so perplexed by his choice to avoid alcohol? As if a person couldn't have any fun at all if they weren't leathered.

'Probably wise in these sorts of situations.'

Dominik frowned, hunting with his eyes for an alternative. Not a party of teetotallers, judging from the beverages on offer. By the time he turned back, his companion had been swept away into the crowd by a man wearing a pair of black and gold rubber shorts and a wrestler's mask. Dominik watched the man's muscled back ripple as he walked and felt a brief pang of envy. Perhaps he ought to take up running, as Lauralynn had suggested, or at least make some sort of return to the athleticism of his university days.

Not that Summer seemed in the slightest interested when he gained or lost a pound. He doubted that she even noticed.

Edward interrupted his flow of thought. 'I think we've met before, but I'm not sure that we were formally introduced. You were at Victor's last little soirée, I believe?'

'Yes, Clarissa and Edward, isn't it? I'm Dominik.'

'Call me Ed, please. Only Victor calls me Edward, and Clarissa when she wants to wind me up. As you can see, Victor enjoys maintaining a certain theatricality.'

Ed plucked a grape from one of the platters, dipped it into the chocolate fountain and then popped it in his mouth with a satisfied smile.

Clarissa continued the conversation. 'He always pulls out all the stops. Apparently, he has some sort of surprise planned for us later. God knows what that will be. Do you know him well?'

'No, not especially. We're acquaintances, that's all.'

'Good. I didn't want to cause offence if you were a friend. I don't think he's well liked, to be honest. People come to his parties for the spectacle, and the champagne is always good.'

'Is this it, then? Seems a bit tame for Victor. I had expected more.'

'I think most of the action will be taking place in the dungeon, and the playroom, once everyone has arrived and warmed up.' She pointed to two archways in the opposite wall, both covered by thick red velvet curtains. 'I believe they open at midnight.'

'A dungeon and a playroom?'

'Yes. Victor has catered for all sorts tonight. There's a room for BDSM play with all the usual equipment, and another room for the swingers in our midst.'

'Or the libertines, for those of us who don't like to be called swingers,' interrupted Ed. He had chocolate stuck to the bottom of his thin moustache.

'Yes, dear,' replied Clarissa, rolling her eyes. 'So you're new to the scene, then?'

'I suppose you could say that.'

Dominik had never been a fan of organised swinging or BDSM parties, preferring to act out his fantasies in the privacy of either his own mind or his own home. The episodes in London when he had joined other men in evenings of excess had, in retrospect, been somewhat lacking in eroticism, just episodes of lust unbound. He'd never attended a fetish club, and had seldom watched any public fetish play besides the vision of Victor topping Miranda. At least, he had hoped that Victor was topping her, and not assaulting her. From what he knew of Victor, the reality might have been either way.

'You're lucky that you have all this available. When we started out, we thought we were the only two kinky people in the world.'

'You're not new to this, then? How did you discover it?'

Dominik's curiosity was piqued. Perhaps it was possible to sustain a relationship in these sorts of circumstances.

'No, old hands, both of us. We met in high school. Been married for thirty years. Started getting dull after a while, so we tried experimenting to spice things up and one thing led to another and here we are. It was harder when the kids were still living at home. Little did they know that their parents were sneaking off to the hottest underground clubs in the New York area when we booked babysitters and told them we were off to the movies. Now we have the house to ourselves and can do whatever we like.'

'And your children . . .' Dominik began, then swallowed his sentence back, rooting around in his mind for a polite way steer the conversation away from this uncomfortably intimate topic.

'Did they turn out OK, you mean? Yes, they're both

lovely, though dull as dishwater. One of them ended up working as a divorce lawyer, of all things, and moved to Wisconsin. He's back in New York now, playing trombone with an orchestra. Our daughter married the local minister's son. God knows how that happened. They disapprove of us dreadfully, though we're careful to keep the cat in the bag, so to speak, in case our daughter decides we're a bad influence on the grandchildren. People are so silly, you know.'

'Yes, I suppose they are.'

'Oh, here he comes, the lord of the manor. Looks a bit ridiculous, don't you think? Latex should really only be worn by the young and slender.'

Edward scowled at her. 'Rubbish. The young and slender don't have a monopoly on glamour. We're proof of that, surely?' he added with a satisfied smile.

'Yes, quite.'

Victor was wearing a rubber ringmaster's outfit in red, black and gold. His face had been painted like a clown's, with smeared red lipstick around his mouth in a parody of a smile. He carried a whip in one hand and had a top hat balanced on his head at a jaunty angle, which he removed when he arrived in front of them and took a low bow.

'I'm so glad you could make it,' he said to Dominik with a snakelike smile of satisfaction.

'Thank you for the invitation.'

'I'm sure you will be delighted with the show I have arranged.'

'You won't even give us a clue what's in store?'

'And ruin the surprise? Never. Now, if you'll excuse me, I must greet the other guests. It's not easy playing host, but someone's got to do it.'

Clarissa waited until he was out of earshot before resuming their conversation. 'He's just absurd. Quite mad. I'm going to find out what it is he's cooking up.'

'Are you sure that's wise?' Ed asked.

'Well, someone has to check on him. There's a difference between kinky and psychopathic, you know. We can't have the newbies thinking we're all insane if he's going to unleash some mad trick on an unwitting audience.'

She turned on her heel swiftly and disappeared through the entrance to the dungeon.

Summer had received the call from Victor four days earlier, just enough time for her to get a Brazilian-style bikini wax and have the resulting redness fade.

His timing was probably not a coincidence, she thought, as the beautician smeared the hot, thick liquid, waited a few seconds for it to dry and then tore off a strip, quickly placing her hand down on Summer's flesh to ease the sting.

She'd heard it said that there were different types of pain. Just because a person enjoys the thwack of a flogger on their bare bottom doesn't mean that they will be lining up to visit the dentist or take delight in the stubbing of a toe.

Summer was certainly not a masochist, sure, but nevertheless she found a visit to the bikini waxer one of life's little pleasures. Perhaps it was the act of peeling her knickers down for a stranger, or the light touch of the girl's soft fingers separating her lips so that she could ensure the wax went onto the right bits and didn't tear off anything important, or perhaps it was the fact that she was really very attractive, and smelled like shampoo.

Whatever the reason, Summer found the process arousing, and that night she had lain awake while Dominik slept and pleasured herself to orgasm. For reasons that she couldn't explain, even to herself, the thought of him lying there unaware while she masturbated gave her a thrill. It was the idea that she was doing something wrong, that she might be caught out that had turned her thoughts to sex. That and the feeling of her skin, which was now extra smooth to touch following the ministrations of the beautician.

Dominik hadn't noticed her hairlessness yet, but he would of course. She would tell him that she had fancied a change. Since that occasion at Charlotte's party when he had shaved her smooth with the razor in front of all of the party guests, he had given no indication that he preferred her to groom herself in one way or another.

He seemed to enjoy observing the way that she elected to play out her moods in her dress and hair, but he didn't suggest that she change herself one way or another to please him. Summer liked that about him. It was one freedom that she would have found difficult to relinquish.

She had told Dominik that she was meeting Cherry tonight to make things up with her, so he shouldn't be surprised if she was home late, or not home at all.

Dominik had muttered in response that he had an engagement of his own, though he hadn't elaborated. He seemed distracted and withdrawn. Maybe spending their first Saturday night together separately was a bad idea, but there was nothing to be done about it.

Summer couldn't confide Victor's plans to Dominik: it had been part of the deal that she never reveal any of it in exchange for Victor's silence. Besides, she was terrified that Dominik would despise her if he discovered the things that Summer had done. He knew her nature, to an extent, but she didn't think he was aware how far she had gone, what lines she had crossed without him.

Fortunately, he'd left the loft earlier that afternoon to work at the library, giving her time to finish her preparations and organise a car to the address Victor provided.

Simón called just as she was leaving.

'How is our star? Recovered from the long journey home yet? Ready for an impromptu rehearsal tonight?'

'Actually, I'm still not well. Can I have another day or two?'

'Is there something that you're not telling me? Has that Englishman of yours upset you? It's not like you to turn down a rehearsal. I'm worried.'

'No, I'm just tired. Truly.'

He didn't sound convinced.

Victor was waiting for her when the car pulled into the underground garage of the mansion that he had procured for the event.

A hideous-looking place, she thought, as the metal gates at the entrance clanged open. It had nothing of the art deco artistry of the place in New Orleans that Dominik had taken them to. This was like something that a footballer would dream up, the sort of home that was just a vehicle to display wealth ostentatiously with no thought to how it fit into its surroundings. Probably brimming with velvet and faux-gold trimmings she thought, though she wouldn't have the opportunity to check, as Victor whisked her straight indoors through a long, dark passageway and into a room fitted with dungeon equipment.

She found the paraphernalia comforting now, rather than intriguing or frightening. The presence of the padded St Andrew's Cross, a couple of spanking benches, a cage, a metal frame that looked a bit like a horse and the array of crops, whips and paddles on display made an unfamiliar place familiar.

In the centre of the room was a red velvet curtain, hanging on a round rail to form a tent, a bit like a miniature big top in a circus.

Victor swept the curtain aside to reveal a ceremonial dais decorated with fabric and flowers, a little like a sacrificial altar. Above the stage was a spotlight.

'I've gone to a lot of trouble for you, my dear, as you can see. I hope you approve.'

'I'm no stranger to the spotlight. I'm sure I'll manage.'

'It would be my guess that you're rather looking forward to it,' he said smugly.

Summer did not reply, but his words cut her like a knife.

Was she looking forward to it?

She supposed she was. In her heart she knew that Victor was vile. But there was a part of her that responded to his commands, a darkness at her core that Victor seemed to recognise and be able to draw out and skilfully manipulate. She knew he was bad news and not a safe person to explore her sexual quirks with, but like a moth to a flame, Summer felt her resistance to Victor crumble under the strength of her desire.

She wouldn't give Victor the satisfaction of knowing that were true, though.

'Come here,' he said.

She stood in front of him, pleased that she had worn her highest heels and was a few inches taller than him.

'Strip.'

She had anticipated this too and had dressed in a strapless, long, black stretch-cotton dress, which she was able to easily slip in and out of in one move. Summer found few things more humiliating than struggling to get out of her clothes in front of an audience, particularly when that audience was Victor.

Then he produced a length of rope.

Dammit, had Victor been spying on her? He always seemed to know exactly what her trigger points were.

The rope was thick, well used and softened from frequent washes. She would likely be able to sustain the constriction for a long period of time without excessive pain, discomfort or nerve damage.

'Kneel down.'

He motioned to the altar, which she noticed was quite comfortably padded, lined with a mattress rather than the hard stone her imagination had somehow conjured up in response to the situation. It was short, and there were steps at either end, roughly the right height for a man or woman to stand on and have easy access to the person who lay on top. Her.

Summer shuddered as she felt the length of rope gently running across her skin.

Victor chuckled in response to her involuntary sign of pleasure and she resisted the urge to kick him. That wouldn't help anything.

He bound her gently, so delicately that she began to relax despite her best intentions to the contrary.

Fuck it, she thought. After this, I will never see him again. What difference does it make?

The bindings were firm but not particularly tight, and she observed that Victor had adhered to all the rules of safer bondage, not putting pressure on any of her nerve centres and leaving a finger space between her flesh and the rope for circulation. He had evidently done this before, and was so far behaving true to his word that she would not sustain any permanent marks or come to any harm.

Then she tried to move her head. She wriggled, testing the sensation again, working out what he had done to her.

'Finally,' he said softly, in a voice that brimmed with glee, 'I've managed to get you to do something other than just lie there.'

He had tied her lower body in a harness and had fixed a knot in the rope that ran between her legs, which he had then attached to her hair, so that each time she pulled her head forward, the rope pulled tight and rubbed against her clitoris. With a little well-timed wriggling, she would be able to bring herself to climax without the aid of a helping hand, either hers or anyone else's.

'Cat got your tongue?'

Summer tried to stay as still as possible, inwardly cursing her body for betraying her as she felt the rope between her legs begin to dampen, wet with her own juices.

Victor gave it a few hard tugs. 'Like that, do you?' he said, as Summer tried and failed to stifle a moan. 'Good. Now, as I promised, I'm going to slip a mask over that pretty face of yours, just to make sure that none of our guests recognises you. Keep the famous violin player anonymous, eh? You won't be able to see, I'm afraid, but knowing you as I do, I'm sure that will add to your enjoyment.'

She bowed her head to allow Victor to slip the covering over her, obscuring the top half of her face. She noted immediately that her mouth had been left unencumbered. Of course, Victor would not miss an opportunity to have one of her orifices available for use.

Satisfied with her face covering, Victor ran his hands

over her body, in the manner that one might pet a cat. He reached for her breasts, tweaking each nipple playfully. She ignored him.

'You really are no fun at all. I honestly don't know what that man sees in you. Now, I really must get back to my other guests. It won't be long now.'

Summer did not look up as he left, though she felt a sweep of air across her naked body as he pulled the curtain round the rail, separating her from the rest of the room.

A few minutes later, she heard the deep clanging of a gong.

Victor clapped his hands together like a delighted child as the crowd in the main room gathered to hear his address.

'About time,' Ed whispered into Dominik's ear. 'I was beginning to worry that the Viagra might wear off before he lets us loose on each other.'

Dominik frowned. He hadn't even considered taking a chemical aid, though he guessed that many of the other men in attendance probably had. He wasn't that bothered about the sex. He wasn't really sure why he had come at all. Or not mentioned it to Summer. Curiosity's sake, he supposed.

A suspicion began to gnaw at him as he thought of Summer. She had been behaving strangely since her return from the last tour. An air of sadness lingered over her, and he felt as though she had been hiding something from him.

Could Victor somehow have involved her in all this? He certainly wouldn't put it past the man; he looked smug enough tonight, and he had seemed to hint that something would happen this evening that Dominik would find particularly interesting.

Edward wasn't the only member of the throng growing impatient. All around him, couples and groups of people were embracing, kissing, stroking. A man standing in front of them had idly hitched up the skirt of the woman he was with and was running his hand over her arse. He was using his other hand to hold up her skirt, apparently aware that Ed and Dominik were watching, and choosing to give them a better view.

'Mind if I join you?' Ed said to the man pleasantly, as politely as if he had asked to join two strangers at a dinner table.

The man looked at his partner, who nodded her approval.

'Shall we?'

The three of them moved towards the playroom.

Edward turned back to Dominik. 'Come along, then,' he said. 'You might as well see what it's all about.'

Only a few minutes had passed since Victor's announcement that all of the rooms were available for use, but during that time, it seemed that at least half of those in attendance had made a run for it and were already fornicating on the benches and cushions by the time they got inside.

Dominik had never seen so many people having sex at once.

He stood still for a moment, looking around him and feeling foolish. The mass of flesh that he saw – breasts swinging and cocks either flaccid and dangling down or pointing stiffly to attention, legs idly opening and labia on display – did not turn him on, though he found it interesting to view, in an objective sort of way, the way that he felt about modern-art displays in trendy galleries or museums.

The woman they had been watching earlier caught his

eye. She came over and laid her hand on his belt buckle, questioning. He nodded. She deftly unbuckled him and pulled his trousers down, then began to tease the end of his cock with her tongue, willing it to life.

Oddly, in the sea of sex all around, Dominik found that he could muster an erection only if he blocked out the other bodies and just concentrated on the woman in front of him.

She was about the same age as he was, he reckoned, though it was close to impossible to tell these days. Her long, brunette hair covered each of her nipples like two curtains, but could not cover her rather large breasts. From the back she was heavily set, with the muscled thighs of a person who engaged in manual labour or sport, and a large, soft backside, the sort that a man could knead as he thrust into her from behind.

The thought made his cock suddenly spring erect. Despite his initial misgivings, Dominik suddenly felt that he would like to feel this woman's legs wrapped round him, but that end of her was busy. The movements of her mouth round his cock had become more frantic and hurried, and he flinched from the occasional grazing of her teeth as her face was knocked around by the friction of the rest of her body as her partner fucked her.

Dominik was about to withdraw, to save the possible damage to his penis and take his attentions elsewhere when he realised that the woman was close to orgasm. It would be ungentlemanly of him to distract her by moving now.

Edward had covered his hand with a latex glove and was probing her arsehole. He looked a little like a mad scientist, but the extra stimulation certainly seemed to be giving her a great deal of pleasure. She seesawed between Dominik and the men behind her like a piston, pumping herself harder and harder against whichever cock or digit happened to be inside her until her body began to shudder and she let out a long sigh and then collapsed happily into a heap in front of them.

'Thank you,' she whispered, to no one in particular, eyes closed and lips spread in a wide smile.

Dominik leaned down and stroked her hair, feeling a burst of affection as she nestled against his hand.

Perhaps this wouldn't be so bad after all.

Summer had just begun to wonder whether Victor had broken one of the major kink commandments and left her bound and alone when she felt a subtle change in the energy of the room and caught a slight whiff of a sharp perfume, a fragrance with a hint of lemon.

Unwilling to advertise her presence to an unknown arrival who might not have good intentions, she held her breath and her body perfectly still. The curtain opened just the same. Whoever it was had found her, though she guessed that Victor had no doubt advertised some sort of show to his guests, and with the presence of a stage and a stage curtain, it was fairly obvious that something interesting might lie behind it.

She kept her head bowed, hoping that if she didn't move, the person might leave her alone.

'Hmm . . . So you're the star of the show.'

Summer recognised her voice. She cast her mind back, mentally rifling through sounds and images to identify this person from her past.

That was it. Mistress Clarissa, the woman whose request for a drink had given her an opportunity to access the cupboard where Victor had locked her phone and clothes, so that she could send a text message to Dominik and later make her escape.

'I suppose I am,' Summer sighed. She had got used to the sensation of the rope knot brushing her clitoris now, and without any mental stimulation to go with it (surely it had not been Victor's presence that had turned her on?), she had just become bored and tired and was looking forward to going home and falling into bed.

There was a long pause.

'I recognise that accent and the colour of your hair. And, I confess, your figure. Though I am sure that there must be other redheaded kinky New Zealanders in New York. You were at another of Victor's parties, weren't you? I believe you ran out before the main event. I hope he hasn't tied you up to avoid that eventuality this time.'

'Yes, that was me, but no, I haven't been tied to prevent my fleeing. I'm here of my own free will. Victor and I had a falling-out . . . and I didn't want to be tattooed.'

'He's not your master, then, or your dominant?'

'No. I have someone else.'

'And does your someone else know that you're here?'

'No.'

'Do you think that's wise?'

Her tone was quizzical rather than officious, but nonetheless Summer was irritated. Why didn't people mind their own damn business? If she had chosen to be strung up as a party centrepiece, then surely that was her affair.

'Maybe unwise, but necessary.'

'And you're aware of what you're letting yourself in for, what Victor has planned for you this time?'

'Quite a lot of sex, I guess. I'm rather looking forward to it, as it happens,' Summer said defiantly.

'Well, so long as you're certain, then so am I, and the rest of the guests, I'm sure. I hope you don't mind my intrusion. I wanted to make sure that everything Victor had planned was . . . legit. Now if you don't mind, I had better make my escape before the show gets started.'

Dominik left the room to find some refreshment feeling rather buoyant. His experience with Ed and the other couple, and his conversation with Clarissa had given him hope. If other people could work it out, then so could he and Summer. They might need to sit down and talk about it, work out what they both wanted, but at least he knew it was not impossible.

Clarissa caught his hand as he went in search of the woman with the chocolate shots. That someone in such scanty lingerie and a plume on her head as long as her legs could maintain any degree of camouflage was an indicator of the astonishing costumes that pervaded the crowd.

'All kosher,' she said, 'and something of a treat.'

'Oh, really? What has the ringmaster arranged, then?'

'He has a girl in store as a party piece, someone I have encountered before actually, though it didn't go so well last time. I'm rather surprised to see her again, but I spoke to her and she affirms she's actually looking forward to it.'

'Oh? Well, that's a relief.'

'A redhead. Edward will be pleased – he has a soft spot for redheads, as all men seem to these days. Whoever said that gentlemen prefer blondes?'

A heavy dread fell down on Dominik's shoulders, as if all the air in the room had turned to lead.

He made his excuses to Clarissa and hurried to the dungeon.

Glanced around. The other players were fully engaged in their partners, and the sound of various implements landing on exposed buttocks and backs drowned out his movements.

He moved to the middle of the room, lifted the curtain and peered through.

As he had feared, it was Summer. She was lying bound and naked on a raised platform, moaning softly.

His first instinct was to free her, to loosen her binds, to cradle her in his arms, but the expression on her face, her obvious arousal, stopped him.

He closed his eyes and imagined what it must be like to be her, senses obscured but for the sound and smell of the activity taking place all around, floggers beating down on bare skin, the moans and cries of a room full of aroused people, the scent of sweat and perfume, her pressure points alert and expectant, waiting to be interrupted by a stranger's touch.

He felt himself getting hard.

Then his eyes snapped open.

She had lied to him, told him that she was meeting a friend.

He remembered what Clarissa had said. Summer had allegedly told her that she was looking forward to it, that she had volunteered for this.

Why, Summer? He wanted to shake her. If he had known that Victor had invited her here, then they could have come as a couple, enjoyed all of this together. Did she think so little of him that she thought she had to go behind his back?

He retreated into the antechamber. Victor stood there, with a cruel smile on his lips.

'Lovely, isn't she? Though I have to say I really do find her rather dull. I'm sorry you had to find her before I started the show. Curious, eh?'

Victor smelled of rubber, talcum powder and whatever spray it was he used to shine his latex, which gleamed like polished glass in the light.

'What the hell are you playing at? Did you tell her I'd be attending?'

'Oh, no, she doesn't know that you're here. I bet she didn't tell you what her plans for the evening were, though, did she?'

They were both whispering to avoid disturbing the other occupants of the room, but the fury in Dominik's voice turned his whisper to a hiss.

'No, she didn't, but there must be some explanation. If you've coerced Summer here against her will, then I swear to God I'll kill you, Victor.'

'There was no need to. You don't know her very well, do you? Hasn't she told you about our liaisons? It's not the first time that your Summer has enjoyed a party like this. She's rather popular with my acquaintances, in fact.'

Dominik's heart sank. Summer had always been unusually quiet when Victor's name was mentioned. If she had wanted to date the man or attend his parties, that was one thing, but doing it behind his back was another. Keeping him informed was the only thing that he had asked of her.

He sank down into one of the benches that Victor had set up for the audience.

The gong clanged again.

Victor waited for the players to finish their scenes and then proclaimed the beginning of the show.

One by one the partygoers filled the room, laughing and giggling, most of them in various states of undress, many of them drunk. A woman sat down on his right-hand side wearing what appeared to be a pair of patterned tights, pulled all the way up to the underneath of her breasts like a jumpsuit. A thick spiked collar encased her neck.

Edward sat down on the other side. His face was smeared with three different shades of lipstick. 'This had better be good,' he said, 'as I was having a wonderful time in the other room.'

Dominik grunted in approval. He was no longer in any mood to talk.

The lights dimmed. He heard the sound of metal scraping against metal as the curtain was drawn back.

Then a spotlight shot down from the ceiling, irradiating Summer in a beam of light. She had now been untied – Victor must have ducked under the curtain and released her – and she was resting on her knees and elbows, as if waiting to be used from both the front and the back.

Victor stepped into the stagelight in front of her and clapped his hands together.

'Ladies and gentlemen,' he said, 'for this evening's entertainment, I have a beautiful volunteer. She has asked me to arrange for her deepest fantasies to be fulfilled, to be used and abused by strangers until she can take no more. Naturally, I was happy to oblige. I present a true slut, for your pleasure.'

To demonstrate her readiness, Victor plunged a finger between Summer's thighs and she moaned, shifting backwards, as if inviting him to enter her again.

'As you can see, my dears,' Victor added dryly, 'she is ready for you.'

He leaned forward and gently scooped some of the hair back from Summer's masked face.

'But I'm sure they would like to hear it from you. Tell them what you are.'

'I'm a slut,' she said, in a clear, methodical voice.

Each word was like a knife in Dominik's side, but he was rooted to the spot, transfixed by the sight of her.

'And what do you want?'

She paused, licked her lips. 'I want to be fucked.'

Victor looked at Dominik and his face spread into a maniacal smile. 'That's an invitation if ever I heard one. Now, of course, let's keep it safe, sane and consensual. The safe word is "Vivaldi", which she will use if she wishes to stop the proceedings at any time. You will find condoms, lubricant and other accessories right next to the bed. Please, enjoy.' He gave a low bow and stepped to the side.

Edward elbowed Dominik in the ribs. 'Best to be first in these sorts of situations, don't you think?'

'Please, go ahead. I would rather watch for a few minutes.'

He was up on his feet before Dominik had completed his sentence.

She had even used their music as her safe word, with Victor, of all people. He felt foolish, like a jilted teenager.

The other guests had begun to circle. Ed was running his hands through Summer's hair, pulling it.

She tilted her neck back, baring her throat, a hard smile spreading across her lips. It was an expression that Dominik had seen many times before during their own lovemaking, the look she gave when she was most aroused.

At least it was Edward's cock that would be first and not Victor's; Dominik was not sure if he could have accepted that. Perhaps the stupid man couldn't wriggle out of his latex easily enough to join in.

Another man, one whom Dominik had not seen before, was heading for Summer's mouth, his cock bouncing up and down as he approached her with his prominent erection.

Dominik held his breath for a moment, hoping that perhaps she might use her safe word if a cock was thrust into her mouth unaware, but instead she opened her mouth wide and leaned forward instinctively to invite him in.

Beads of sweat appeared on her skin like teardrops and Dominik followed the path of each droplet that rolled down her body. Her breasts swung back and forth like pendulums, the soft slapping of her flesh drowned out by the louder groans of her companions.

A woman with hair cropped like a pixie and an androgynous figure, bones as delicate as a bird's, slid under her body from the side and began to suck Summer's nipples.

The man who had been standing at Summer's mouth dutifully moved away, kneeled down in front of the tiny woman and separated her labia with his lips. Another man had taken his place at Summer's head in less time than it took Dominik to take a breath. He was masturbating with the aid of handfuls of her red hair.

Dominik's view was obscured now as the small stage was surrounded by men and women who were waiting to touch her or to fill her in some way.

Occasionally, one of the participants would step back to mop their brow or change a condom, and for a moment or two before another person stepped in, Dominik would catch a glimpse of Summer's pale skin, now slick with sweat, her body in a perpetual state of motion, back and forth in response to the pressure of a cock inside her or flinching in response to a caress.

If he closed his eyes, then he could pick out the familiar sound of her panting, imagine how her heart was racing, imagine how it had felt to have her wrapped round his shaft, the way that she seemed so present in her body when they made love, reacting to his slightest touch. He began to get hard again, in spite of himself. He watched as she wrapped her mouth round another man's cock.

Surely she must be beginning to tire, he thought, but she showed no signs of slowing or of sated desire. It was as if she was trying to wipe out all the unsatisfactory sex she had ever had with this one night of endless fucking.

Perhaps it was anger that prompted him to move, or his own desire.

When the man with his cock in Summer's mouth moved away, Dominik was there to replace him.

He looked down at her face, the curve of her mouth, her forehead furrowed in concentration, senses alert to the change in position. He ran his hands over her neck and shoulders, felt her relax against the pressure of his touch. He took her hair into his hands and pulled her head back, then bent down and kissed her.

For a moment, she responded as she always did, opening her mouth and humming a gentle and satisfied sigh.

Then she pulled away and lifted her mask. She'd recognised his touch.

'Stop, please,' she said, moving herself into a sitting position.

The crowd that had gathered around her stepped back immediately.

She shifted forward and looked around for something

to cover herself with, a towel or her dress, but there was nothing. She wrapped her arms round her chest to hide her breasts.

'What are you doing here?'

'Victor invited me. Evidently he invited you too.'

'What did he tell you?' she asked in a whisper.

'He told me about all the other times, if that's what you mean. Why didn't you tell me?'

'Why didn't you tell me? Is this your first time to one of his parties?'

'Well, no, but . . . I didn't think you cared, and I couldn't seem to find the right time. You're always out. Rehearsing. With Simón.'

'Right. So you can fuck whoever you like, whenever you like, and I can't?'

'That's not what I meant.'

'But it's what you said. And it's what you do. Go to hell, Dominik.'

She swung her legs over the stage, stood up and strode across the room to the exit, her shoulders back and her chin held high.

The room fell into an embarrassed hush. Just the sound of a single man clapping rang in Dominik's ears.

Victor.

# 13

## *The Landscape After the Battle*

Simón was waiting for me when the yellow taxi pulled up outside the SoHo apartment. He was sitting on the front step, his legs out in front of him, feet crossed at the ankles encased in his familiar snakeskin ankle boots.

'I knew you'd have to come home eventually.'

'What the hell are you doing here? It's three in the morning.'

'You didn't answer any of my calls. I was worried about you.'

I pulled my phone out of my bag and flicked through my messages and missed-call list. Simón had called almost every hour since I'd spoken to him about skipping rehearsal.

'Sorry. I must have had it on silent.'

I tried to get my key in the door, but my fingers were shaking like leaves in the wind.

Simón stared at me, then jumped to his feet and took my hands in his. He looked me up and down. I hadn't so much as glanced in any of the mirrors that lined the hallway that led to the front doors at Victor's mansion. I had no idea how I must look, but I knew that I was sweaty and shaky, and my hair was a mess. I hoped that no one had given me any love bites at least.

'What happened? Did Dominik hurt you? I'll make him regret it if he has.'

'No, nothing like that. We were at a party and we had a row. He'll probably be back here any minute.'

'Come and stay with me. You can have some time to think things over. A safe place.'

'I can't just disappear. He'll think I've left him.'

'He'll probably appreciate the space, and you're not going to be able to have any reasonable conversation with each other when you're both in this sort of state.'

I didn't have the energy to argue. Besides, I wasn't looking forward to the conversation I'd have to have with Dominik. Perhaps a day or two apart would do us good.

'OK. I'll get my things.'

'Leave it. You can come back when he's out. I have everything you need.'

'My violin . . .'

'You can use one of mine.'

He took my hand in his and guided me along to West Broadway to hail a taxi, the best place to find one at this time of night. The first two had their off-duty sign on, but the third stopped at Simón's signal.

My heart beat faster and faster with each car that passed us, imagining that one of them would contain Dominik, hot on my heels with an apology. I would tell him everything that had happened between Victor and me; we would make it up to each other. Start fresh with a new slate.

But he didn't come.

Simón pulled me against him inside the cab. I rested my head on his chest and he laid his arm round my shoulder. He began to run his hands through my knotted hair and I relaxed against him, allowing his kindness to sweep my worries away, at least for tonight.

'You smell different,' he said sleepily as he shook me

awake when we pulled into his street. 'Have you changed your perfume?'

That's the scent of ten men and a couple of women, I thought, but didn't say aloud.

'The party was crowded. I need a shower.'

'I'm happy to accommodate anything you need.'

'Really?'

'Of course.'

I looked up into his dark-brown eyes, filled with warmth, and in that moment I wanted him, if for no other reason than to drive the feeling of other people away. I leaned forward and kissed his lips.

He hadn't shaved and his chin felt rough against mine. I ran my cheek over his stubble, enjoying the scraping sensation.

His hands were shaking as much as mine had when he entered the code to buzz us into his apartment building.

'I thought you said this wasn't a good idea.'

'I don't care about good ideas any more.'

'Well, I'm not going to argue with you.'

He pulled me into the lift and wrapped his arms around me, pressing his lips against mine like a man possessed.

By the time the bell for his floor dinged, I had his shirt unbuttoned and was working at his belt buckle, eager to get our consummation over with before either of us changed our minds. I'd done enough that night that I might be ashamed of in the morning, so sex with one more man seemed almost unavoidable, like finishing off the last cookie in the box.

We kissed with the abandon of two people who think this might be their last night together as he led me into the bedroom and pushed me down onto the bed. He ran his hands under my dress and began to shimmy the fabric up round my waist, his movements aggressive, his eyes glittering with unconcealed desire. When he kneeled down between my thighs, I grabbed a handful of his thick hair in each hand and pulled him up to my face.

'No, please, I just want to be fucked.'

Simón seemed happy to oblige. I wasn't in any mood for foreplay, and I didn't want him to taste the flavours that must still permeate my skin: the various scents of other people, the lubricants, the sharp chemical tang that condoms always left behind. He was heavier than Dominik. The feeling of his body over me was pleasantly crushing, and his hair fell across his face. I breathed him in, my hands sinking into his mass of dark curls. I wrapped my legs round his waist and clung on to him as he buried himself inside me, hoping that with every thrust he would drive away the sensation of other men. More than anything I wanted to rid myself of the memory of Victor. He had barely touched me, but the cloying smell of his cologne was trapped in my nostrils, threatening to turn my stomach with every inward breath.

It was over in minutes. Simón was tired and he had been waiting for me a long time. At least he didn't apologise. I suppose he thought that there would be other times, and maybe he was right about that.

'Will you ever tell me what's wrong?' he asked, as we lay side by side, his arm resting over my torso, drawing me against him as if he wanted to hold me there for ever.

The weight of my pause filled the room like a drum roll, as if the silence had a sound of its own.

'Maybe, but not tonight.'

'I'll be here for you, whenever you're ready.'

I waited until he fell asleep before getting up and having a shower. I didn't want him to think that it was being with him that had made me feel dirty. He deserved better than that.

I'd spent enough time at his apartment now that it felt like a second home anyway. I knew where he kept the fresh towels and that he had a full-length mirror in the bathroom that I could check myself out in.

There was barely a mark on me. Somehow I thought that my skin would be stained with the weight of my sins. I didn't know what I expected to see. A scarlet letter burned onto my heart? But there was nothing. The reflection that stared back at me was as pure as the driven snow, though I knew that my genitals would be red and swollen, and would probably take several days to recover.

People say that it's the eyes that are windows to the soul. I think we'd learn more about each other if we directed our attention to parts lower down.

I turned the water on and stepped underneath, then turned and fiddled with the tap. The temperature was up as hot as it could go, but it still wasn't hot enough.

There wasn't a shower in the world that could wash this feeling away.

Dominik knew that what had happened had altered everything between him and Summer for ever.

It was not a question of blame. They all had to accept a heavy share of responsibility for the unfortunate course of events: Victor, Summer and him in equal proportions.

Words could no longer repair what had so brutally come apart at the seams.

Victor had engineered it all, a devious master of ceremonies, intent on using both of them, manipulating Summer and Dominik to this point of no return. Out of mere cruelty? For gratification? Or maybe just mischief, like a child who sees a pile of bricks in perfect alignment and can't help but kick them down and scatter the pieces all over the carpet, bringing chaos out of order.

When given a choice, Dominik had somehow come up with the wrong words, not found the kindness in his heart to forgive or understand, involuntarily becoming the villain in his mad desire to play with Summer until the ties that bound them were stretched to breaking point. Yes, it was his fault, from the moment he had caught that glimpse of her playing the violin in the London Underground and imagined how he could lure her into his spider's web, his bed, his life on terms he couldn't even now fully understand.

And what about her? How much had she ever known about the forces manipulating her sexuality? Had her heart ever opened up to him, or had she just been prey to her inner desires and selfishly indulged them all along?

If only he could see her now, look deep into her eyes; maybe there would be an answer lying there, a clue to this terrible jigsaw puzzle where feelings and cravings waltzed in mad abandon and made him feel so helpless.

It had been forty-eight hours and Summer still hadn't returned to the loft.

Maybe she was staying with a friend. Cherry possibly, Susan, her agent, or, more likely, her conductor friend Simón, whose rehearsal space had always been suspiciously available to her at all times.

Her clothes still hung in the shared wardrobe alongside his, in now uncomfortable proximity, and he would on a regular basis thread his fingers between the softness of the fabrics with a deep pain gripping his heart, dragging the smell of her body from the depths of the varied materials. Like an old pervert, he realised. At least he wasn't manically rifling through her underwear. Not that the thought hadn't occurred to him.

He couldn't help notice the Bailly, snug in its now battered case, sitting in the far corner of the loft's living space. He was surprised she had left it here, not returned to retrieve it. As if leaving the violin to its own fate was a final indication that she had no intention of seeing him again, a poignant reminder of what had brought them together.

No, it wasn't his fault, Dominik decided. And neither was it hers. They had just been pawns, victims of their lust and the contradictions of desire.

Whereas Victor was another matter altogether. He'd known all along what he was doing. He had to bear the bulk of the responsibility for the sad, sordid even, events that had unrolled.

'Hi, Lauralynn.'

'Hello, Dominik. How are you?'

'To be honest, bloody angry . . . How did Boston go?'

'Piece of cake,' Lauralynn replied. 'What are you angry about?'

'Your friend Victor.'

'Oh dear, up to his old tricks again, is he?'

'I don't really want to talk about it. Do you know where I can reach him? I've mislaid the piece of paper I'd written his address on. I need to discuss something with him.'

'Really?'

'Please, Lauralynn . . .'

'Don't do anything you'll come to regret, Dominik,' Lauralynn said, but then gave him the address, which he had, of course, never even had in the first place. Something she seemed well aware of.

'Dominik?' But he'd already disconnected.

It did not go well.

Ambushed at his apartment, Victor would not allow Dominik in and insisted they take the conversation outside. Both men were reluctant to face up to each other in a bar or somewhere overly public. The building where Victor lived happened to be a few blocks away from Central Park, close to the Dakota, and they ended up by the pond, not far from the Hallett Sanctuary. Night was nearing and passers-by and tourists were growing scarcer.

Victor's initial reaction was flippant when Dominik brought up the subject of the party and the way he had manipulated Summer into participating.

'But you had an opportunity to stop the proceedings, didn't you? You just stood back didn't you? Allowed her to go through with it. I was merely an observer by then,' he pleaded, his customary superior smirk painted across his face, like a red rag to a bull.

Dominik felt bile rising up his throat, every single word of Victor's like a stab to his heart, reminding him of his infamy and what now clearly appeared to be the biggest mistake of his life.

'It just took me by complete surprise,' he protested. 'I still have no idea why she agreed to get involved with you in the first place and be at the centre of that grotesque orgy. I'm sure you planned it that way all along.'

'Well, I do concede I might have been a bit mischievous,' Victor said, dragging his step along the darkening path, hands in his pockets.

'You set it all up, Victor. Now, I'm not saying you openly lied to either Summer or me, but you sinned by omission, clearly. How could you?'

'Neither of you was innocent, Dominik. Anyway, what's a little sin between friends, eh? Sin makes the world go round,' he laughed gently.

'You fucking creep.' Dominik's patience was at boiling point, increasingly stirred by Victor's nonchalance, the man's seeming indifference to the situation he had slyly provoked. The man actually looked smug, as if Dominik's anger made it all so much more amusing.

Victor stopped, turned to Dominik and put a hand on his shoulder. 'Look,' he said, 'she's just a girl. She's disposable. You shouldn't get on your high horse. Anyway, she wasn't even a great fuck, was she?'

Dominik brushed Victor's hand away from him.

He was simmering inside, and out of nowhere, the thin line between anger and fury snapped. He bunched his fist and punched Victor in the jaw. The other man stumbled back, falling to the ground as much as from the impact of Dominik's hand as by the element of total surprise. He raised a hand, an instinctive signal for his aggressor to stop, and opened his mouth.

'You're crazy,' Victor shouted out.

It took a few seconds for the pain in his bruised knuckles to register, at which point Dominik flinched. He'd never been a violent person – he couldn't even remember the last fight he'd participated in – but hearing Victor speak of Summer as if she were an object, with no respect for her mind or her body, had filled him with an uncontrollable rage. He had never fought for a woman's honour before, but in that moment he realised he would go to any lengths to defend Summer, to protect her from predators like Victor, who saw her weaknesses and her naivety as an opportunity to exploit.

He swore under his breath and looked over at Victor's face, contorted in a rictus of both pain and shock, his mouth pursed, lips trembling.

'You bloody well asked for it,' Dominik cried out. Victor now looked so small, but he still had the deep-seated feeling that the man was mocking him. With a final glare, Dominik turned to leave.

'That's right, go back to your worthless whore.' The words were muttered under Victor's breath but loud enough for Dominik to hear. He paused, turned and, with a kick more violent than he'd intended, sent Victor sprawling.

Reality returned in a rush and Dominik reeled back in disgust at what he had just done. Victor lay groaning on the ground. Dominik glanced around him. No one nearby. His assault had in all likelihood gone unnoticed. What should he do? Stay around until Victor recovered?

In a nearby tree, a bird tweeted cheerfully and the weight of what he had done dawned on Dominik. He'd fought a man, a man who was smaller and a good decade older than himself. And all over a woman. It was worse than a cliché; it was pathetic. He turned and walked away.

*

The few days without Dominik had been the final nail in the coffin.

I asked Simón to wait for me outside as I collected my few belongings. I'd tried telling him that I didn't have much stuff and that having lived in three continents already, I was perfectly capable of packing the contents of one suitcase on my own, but he insisted on following me around, as if he were afraid that he might lose me if I was out of his sight for more than an hour.

I let him come in the end, but I wouldn't allow him in the actual loft. That would have been the final blow – if Dominik had come home and found him there, or if he could somehow sense that another man had been in the bedroom that we had shared together.

The apartment felt empty even before I folded my few clothes into my case and gathered up my shoes and toiletries. With the tour, I supposed I'd been gone months before I'd actually left for good.

'Wow,' said Simón, when I carried the case down the stairs, 'you really don't have much stuff. I presumed you were exaggerating.'

I'd tried to sit down and write Dominik a note before I left the flat – telling him that I was sorry, providing him with some kind of closure – but the words just wouldn't come. He was the writer, not me.

In the end, I just took my stuff and went, hoping that he'd somehow understand all the things that I couldn't say to him.

Moving in with Simón happened without any conscious thought. At first, it seemed the obvious place for me to go. He easily had the space for an extra person, particularly since I'd started sharing his bed. Plus he had a dedicated rehearsal room, which saved me the trouble of finding a space to play that wouldn't upset any neighbours. Going to a hotel would have been silly. I could have taken refuge at Baldo and Marija's. Cherry probably would have offered her couch if I had tracked her down and explained the situation, but I was too proud to admit that she'd been right. I'd been too proud about almost everything.

He was quick to make room in his wardrobe for my clothes. An empty drawer appeared overnight in his bathroom cabinet. My things gradually began to find a home in his apartment. We went out on dates together and to dinner parties, and his friends presumed that we were an item before I had a chance to say that the arrangement was temporary.

Before I knew it, I was in another relationship.

Simón was passionate and had a libido higher than any man I had ever dated. Higher even than Dominik. We had sex morning and night, and often during the middle of the afternoon as well. Our lovemaking was frequent and furious, and though I knew I ought to spend some time on my own before diving headlong into another life with yet another man, I didn't think that I could manage without it. His body over mine blanked out all the uncomfortable thoughts that chased me in the middle of the night.

My mind often turned to Dominik. I wondered whether we could have ever made it work. If I'd been honest with him. If he hadn't been so jealous. If I hadn't gone on tour. So many hypothetical situations.

I missed the hardness of his touch. Everything about Simón was soft and warm, from the heat of his body to the golden colour of his skin, his easy laugh and the vigour with which he approached everything from sex to food to music. He had an enormous appetite in every respect and a cheerful optimism that Dominik had lacked but which sometimes got on my nerves. He had a spring in his step that matched the spring in his hair, and the bounce threatened never to leave either.

It was like living with a ray of sunshine. Eventually, I began to long for rain.

One night, we went out to the cinema. Simón spent most of the film running his hand under my skirt, while I tried desperately not to respond to avoid upsetting the people sitting next to us. It was a superhero film, the sort that attracted kids as well as adults, and we were surrounded by families. Simón was the very opposite of Dominik in this respect as he was in most others. Besides being appropriately attired, which was crucial to him, he cared very little about the way that he appeared in public.

He had wanted to walk instead of catching a taxi home. He'd noticed his trousers getting tighter since we moved in together and had suddenly taken a greater interest in getting his daily exercise. Or perhaps it was part of a plan that he had hatched earlier, and the sex shop that we happened to walk past on Sixth past 18th Street was by design and not by accident.

'I thought we might try something new,' he whispered into my ear, his voice full of mischief.

'Oh?'

I didn't know whether to be offended. I had thought the sex we were having was pretty good. We certainly had enough of it, and the thought that he might not be satisfied troubled me.

He walked straight to the section with the restraints on

display, everything from satin bed ties to spreader bars and thick leather cuffs.

'What do you think?' he asked.

I picked up a pair of flimsy-looking pink fluffy handcuffs, the sort that wouldn't look out of place at a hen party. The leather cuffs were much more my style, but I didn't want to scare him by demonstrating that I already had quite a bit of experience with this sort of thing.

'Oh, God,' he said, 'I'd feel like an idiot wearing those.'

'*You'd* feel like an idiot?'

His face turned red. It was the first time I'd seen him blush. 'Never mind. It was a stupid idea.'

The sales assistant was looking at us curiously.

'No, it's not a stupid idea. I just presumed that you meant for me.'

'Remember that night we first kissed?'

'Yes, of course.'

'You had a piece of rope in your bag. I thought . . . You seem like the kind of girl who might enjoy being in charge. I've always wanted to try it. Not being in charge, that is.'

My heart sank. I knew perfectly well that it was completely hypocritical, but I had never been able to get used to the vision of submissive men either in clubs or in the few private scenes that I had witnessed. The thought of Simón on his knees in front of me made my skin crawl. Somehow I had never expected this of him. Another black mark against my powers of observation, or further evidence of how self-centred I was. He seemed so naturally authoritative, particularly when he led the orchestra. After all that I had been through, though, I could hardly deny him the opportunity to try it. Maybe it would be different with someone to whom I was attracted.

We left the shop with a set of black satin scarves and some novelty lingerie Simón had taken a fancy to.

As the saleswoman packed our purchases into a discreet bag, I could almost hear the sound of Dominik's mocking laughter ringing in my ears.

That night, I tied Simón's wrists and ankles to the bedposts. His eyes glazed over and he purred as though all of his Christmases had come at once. I stared at the wall over the headboard as I rode him and wondered for the millionth time what it was that I truly wanted. I closed my eyes and played with myself, drumming up a flood of images in my head. Dominik appeared in all of them, but despite that, I didn't orgasm.

Simón fell asleep with the restraints still on him minutes after he came. I untied him gently and moved his limbs together so that I could slide into bed alongside him.

Sleep evaded me like a thief in the night.

I got up quietly and pulled my case out of the hallway wardrobe. I had left the length of rope in one of the zip pockets, the only place I could think of that Simón wouldn't come across it by accident. I put the case back and then went into the bathroom with the rope and a bottle of lubricant.

Simón was a heavy sleeper, but I turned the water on anyway to drown out the soft sound of my masturbating. I could see myself in the mirror as I did so, the rope pressed firmly against my throat.

I was not suicidal in the slightest, nor seeking self-harm. I never pulled it so tight that it might do any damage, even temporarily, but that gentle restriction of my breathing heightened my arousal enough to make me orgasm within minutes.

How I wished it were Dominik's hand that did it instead of a noose round my neck.

Dominik took the subway back to Spring Street. The moment he opened the door to the loft, he knew Summer had been there in his brief absence. The smell of her perfume hung faintly in the air, and her row of shoes no longer crowded the minimalist line of the corridor wall that led into the apartment's main living space.

The violin had gone, and she had, no doubt in a rush, also taken all her clothes. She'd forgotten her toothbrush, some make-up, an assortment of cream and shampoo bottles and tubes, and the old strip of probably out-of-date birth-control pills that had been lingering in the bathroom while she had been touring Australia and New Zealand, like a bequest to him, something to remember her by.

Not even a note.

Even though this didn't come as a surprise, Dominik's heart dropped.

It brought a sense of closure to their relationship.

For the following two days he stayed in, neglecting his minor duties at the library, unable to concentrate on much, let alone researching or writing. He was fearful that any time the door buzzer went off it would be Victor, or the police. Even if Victor didn't bring charges, there was a chance a passer-by had witnessed his attack. He knew that the assault would have looked overly violent, and if someone saw it and told the police, they might choose to arrest him.

* * *

By Saturday morning, he'd reached a decision. He packed his stuff, sent a series of apologetic emails, resigning from his fellowship and offering to reimburse any monies he had already been paid to the real-estate company who owned the loft. He took a yellow cab to JFK, knowing that hiring his customary limo service would leave a record of his movements. Here, he booked himself on the first available overnight flight to London.

Hampstead was still asleep in the early hours of Sunday as he alighted from the taxi, searched for his house keys at the bottom of his carry-on bag and opened the door to his house. The heath, in the distance, was greener than ever, a particular shade of green that somehow only belonged to English climes. Now holding his luggage in both hands, he gave the door a gentle kick and the dry odour of his books reached him like a wave of welcome.

He was home.

Two months went by. Time for Dominik to regroup. He agreed with the university to extend his sabbatical for a further two terms and gradually fell into a steady writing routine. He woke, as he always did, early every morning before first light, hammered out a required amount of words on the novel and then allowed himself to relax in the afternoon, reading, catching up on DVDs or walking the heath if the English weather didn't conspire against him.

Of course, Summer was still on his mind and not a day would go by without painful memories as well as joyful ones piercing the mask of his enforced emotional silence. As he trod the damp grass of the heath, he couldn't help recalling the sight of Summer making her way across it, towards the bandstand where she had played for him privately for the first time. It now felt like a lifetime ago. He knew it was inevitable and there was no point in fighting it. He just had to accept these bittersweet feelings and survive them as best he could. Maybe time would bring a measure of solace, but he wasn't betting on it.

Having manoeuvred himself one late-winter day into something of a corner with a particular character in the book not behaving as he had expected, which required him to tear up a whole chapter and rejig an important section so that the diverse protagonists' psychological motivations made better sense, he was feeling both drained and aimless when the doorbell rang.

He was wearing his dressing gown and hadn't shaved for four days. He buckled the belt tight round his middle and made his way downstairs. Probably the postman with a late delivery, he reckoned.

It was beginning to rain quite hard outside, he noted, as he passed the landing window, and the bell rang again, more insistent this time. The house's porch afforded no protection from the elements.

He took the latch off, slid the key in the top lock and unlocked the front door.

'Hey!'

'Oh . . .'

Lauralynn stood there, holding a newspaper above her blonde hair in a vain attempt to keep herself out of the rain. She was soaked, her thin T-shirt clinging to her generous curves.

She was anything but her customary seductive self, all bedraggled from having travelled through the pelting showers, but her aura of sexiness was unavoidable. How could it not be?

'Won't you invite a wet girl in?' she asked, a faint smile on her full lips.

'Of course.' Dominik opened the door wide and ushered her in. 'This is a surprise, but it's great to see you. Excuse my dishevelled appearance. I wasn't expecting anyone.'

Lauralynn shook her head, a thin cascade of water drops flying in every direction. 'I don't think I'm looking much better,' she remarked. 'Pouring rain can do that to you. It began pelting down the moment I left the Tube station. You took a hell of a long time to open the door. Didn't you hear me? There were lights on, so I knew you were in.'

'I was in the upstairs study. Probably didn't hear the bell first time.'

She wore a pair of skin-tight black jeans and her usual black leather jacket over a white T-shirt.

Dominik guided her to the kitchen. 'Need something to warm you up?' he suggested.

'Absolutely. Some piping-hot beverage of your choice if you can manage it, to be followed in rapid succession by something stronger. I know you don't drink, but I know you're sophisticated enough to have a bottle or two stored away somewhere, no?'

'You know me well.' He switched the electric kettle on and searched one of the cabinets for a jar of instant coffee.

'Instant?' Lauralynn remarked. 'I would have expected a sleek and shiny espresso machine at the very least.'

'Sorry to disappoint.'

She'd been back in London for ten days already, she explained. The Yale maternity-cover contract had come to an end and she had been offered a further six-month extension, but being stuck in the suburbs didn't suit her. She was too much of a big-city animal. Had it been New York, she would have gladly remained in America, but she had been growing tired of having to watch the clock and rush for the last train to New Haven from Grand Central whenever she'd gone roaming in Manhattan.

'You left in a hell of a hurry,' she later said as they sat down sipping their coffees.

'I know.'

They exchanged knowing glances.

'Victor is all right,' she said. 'Not that you asked,' she added.

'I didn't.'

'You broke his nose.'

'Cheap at the price.'

'Didn't think you had it in you, Dominik.'

'You'd be surprised.'

'He's also left New York by now. I heard he took up a position at the university in Kiev. The green, green grass of home and all that . . .'

'I'll know to avoid Ukraine in the future.'

'I believe that would be wise,' Lauralynn concluded.

'So what are your London plans, then?' he asked her.

'Nothing much. I've a bit of money saved. In no rush to do much really.'

'Where are you staying?'

'I'm crashing on some friends' sofa in Camden Town. I'll soon have outstayed my welcome, though.'

'Still have your sleeping bag all rolled up and ready to go?'

'Of course. Have sleeping bag, will travel.'

'This is a big house. There is still some space between all the books, I guess, corners where a sleeping bag could fit in.'

'Is that an invitation?'

'The nearest I'll get to one,' Dominik said.

'In that case, I accept, Professor.'

'It'll be nice to have some company. There was a time when I was comfortable on my own, but things have changed. It was good with Summer while it lasted, but I messed it up.'

'I think the problem was that you never knew what exactly you wanted, Dominik.'

'You can say that again.'

'I think what you need is a teacher.'

'Do I? That would be an interesting reversal of roles, no?'

'Want me?'

What did Lauralynn mean?

She noted his puzzlement. 'You might know a lot about books and other arcane stuff, but there are many other things I could teach you, Dominik, about women, lust, control, what makes people tick.'

'Is that an invitation?' Dominik smiled.

'And the lessons come free. With bonuses along the way.'

Dominik remembered the threesome with Miranda and knew exactly what the canny Lauralynn had in mind.

'Where do I enrol?' he asked.

'Right now,' she said. 'So where do you hide your booze?'

Life went on, as it always does.

Eighteen months or so went by in a flash, time swept

away in the peaceful flow of life with Simón and my music career.

I'd been out of town for a couple of weeks, playing gigs in Memphis and Charleston. Being on the road is like travelling in a cocoon, and I liked it that way, mistress of my own universe. It made a nice change from having to explain myself to Simón every time I wanted to do anything without him, even if it was just a walk to the corner store. I never even switched the TV on in my hotel rooms – just read trashy novels or listened to music, sometimes simply sat in silence and stared at a blank wall. The apocalypse could have come and gone and I never would have known about it. I didn't give a damn about the daily news.

I ran every day when I was on tour. It was my way of making friends with a new city, taking in the sights and smells, ignoring the tourist trails and exploring the depths of suburbia instead. People were much more interesting than museums, anyway.

When I was back in Manhattan for just a few days, I took advantage of my familiarity with the shopping scene to buy a new pair of running shoes. I'd blown the toes out of mine, a fact that gave me no small thrill of satisfaction. I prefer my shoes worn in – they just don't look right brand new – but I'd run all the cushion out of them and had no wish to turn an ankle, so I took the subway to Union Square, with a view to visiting the cluster of shoe shops on Broadway, both north and south of Astor Place.

The spring crowds were out in force, darting in and out of stores as if shopping was about to go out of fashion. After the relative seclusion of lonely hotel rooms, the pushing and shoving and queues for the service assistants to fetch the other half of the display pairs quickly got on my nerves.

Maybe I would get more peace south of Houston, where the shops were decidedly more upmarket and the crowds thinner and less frantic. It wasn't as if I didn't have the money to splash out a bit extra, and as a bonus, I'd pass one of my favourite ice-cream parlours on the way. I hadn't had pistachio ice cream since I was in Europe and I suddenly had a craving for it.

I crossed the street at the first set of traffic lights.

The window of Shakespeare & Co. greeted me as I reached the opposite pavement. It was one of the last remaining independent bookstores in the city and somewhere that Dominik had always liked to visit. He spent his time there while I went shopping at the nearby clothes stores and never seemed to mind how long I spent trying on dresses or shoes. He would have happily stayed and browsed the shelves all night if the staff had let him.

The window was its usual busy mess of volumes in all sizes and colours. I had wondered if Dominik had liked the place so much because it reminded him of the shelves in his own house, no order of any sort.

I was about to continue my trek down Broadway when the image of a violin on the cover of a book at the far end of the window caught my eye. I slowed down and peered through the glass.

I stopped in my tracks, frozen in shock, shoppers jostling me from both sides. A strapline across the cover stated it had been a bestseller in the UK, but all I could focus on was Dominik's name emblazoned on the cover like a brand and a photo-like illustration of a violin. He had finished his manuscript, then, and managed to find a publisher.

I walked in and found a pile of his books on the new-fiction table at the front of the shop. I picked up a copy in the way that I might approach a hot plate on the stove. Tentatively.

I opened it, turned past the title page. There was a dedication:

*To S.*
*Yours, always.*

## *Acknowledgements*

Thanks as always to our agent Sarah Such of Sarah Such Literary Agency and our editors Jemima Forrester and Jon Wood, as well as Tina Pohlman at Open Road Integrated Media in New York, and our foreign publishers in Germany, Italy, Sweden and Brazil, for believing in us, and of course Rosemarie Buckman at the Buckman Agency and Carrie Kania at Conville & Walsh for sterling work.